Murder at an Irish Bakery

Books by Carlene O'Connor

Irish Village Mysteries

MURDER IN AN IRISH VILLAGE

MURDER AT AN IRISH WEDDING

MURDER IN AN IRISH CHURCHYARD

MURDER IN AN IRISH PUB

MURDER IN AN IRISH COTTAGE

MURDER AT AN IRISH CHRISTMAS

MURDER IN AN IRISH BOOKSHOP

MURDER ON AN IRISH FARM

MURDER AT AN IRISH BAKERY

CHRISTMAS COCOA MURDER
(with Maddie Day and Alex Erickson)

CHRISTMAS SCARF MURDER
(with Maddie Day and Peggy Ehrhart)

A Home to Ireland Mystery

MURDER IN GALWAY

MURDER IN CONNEMARA

A County Kerry Mystery

NO STRANGERS HERE

Published by Kensington Publishing Corp.

CARLENE O'CONNOR

Murder at an Irish Bakery

 AN IRISH VILLAGE MYSTERY

Kensington Publishing Corp.

www.kensingtonbooks.com

KENSINGTON BOOKS are published by

Kensington Publishing Corp.
119 West 40th Street
New York, NY 10018

All Kensington titles, imprints, and distributed lines are available at special quantity discounts for bulk purchases for sales promotion, premiums, fund-raising, educational, or institutional use. Special book excerpts or customized printings can also be created to fit specific needs. For details, write or phone the office of the Kensington Special Sales Manager: Attn. Special Sales Department. Kensington Publishing Corp., 119 West 40th Street, New York, NY 10018. Phone: 1-800-221-2647.

K and the Teapot logo is a trademark of Kensington Publishing Corp.

Library of Congress Control Number: 2022947427

ISBN: 978-1-4967-3081-7
First Kensington Hardcover Edition: March 2023

ISBN: 978-1-4967-3087-9 (e-book)

10 8 7 6 5 4 3 2 1

Printed in the United States of America

Murder at an
Irish Bakery

Chapter 1

"Stop the show. Sugar kills! Stop the show! Sugar kills!" The thirty-something outraged lad paced in front of Pie Pie Love, Kilbane's best bakery housed in a historic flour mill. He was tall and handsome, if you ignored the vitriol pouring out of his gob. In addition to the passion he was bringing to the task, he seemed dressed for the part of a protester: denims, a T-shirt with the word SUGAR overlaid with a skull and crossbones, and a flannel shirt to protect against a mercurial spring. The limestone mill was set back in a vibrant field next to the Kilbane River. Unfortunately, no matter how loud the river babbled, the magnificent nine-meter cast-iron waterwheel mounted to the side of the building remained immobile, and the water simply meandered around it instead of powering it up. The mill was built between 1850 and 1870 and Garda Siobhán O'Sullivan had read somewhere that the original wheel had been wooden. Despite the switch to cast iron, it hadn't churned for as long as Siobhán had been alive, nearly thirty years, and the bakery sourced its flour elsewhere.

Siobhán didn't know the cost of repairing such a structure, but she knew—the waterwheel notwithstanding—

that the family-owned mill was in dire need of basic repairs. The O'Farrells had operated this flour mill, and now bakery, for several generations. Fia O'Farrell was the last living member, and given she was single and past middle age, many wondered what she envisioned for its future. The back room, which used to house events, and the ground, middle, and top floors of the mill, which used to be open for tours, had all been closed to the public for over a decade. But it was still a gorgeous structure, and the bakery, which was housed in the very front portion of the building, was as cheerful inside as it was out. Siobhán took in the outdoor tables with colorful umbrellas, flowers beaming from planters along the front of the building, and the banner above the wooden doors that read: WELCOME IRISH BAKERS!

It was going to be a good day for Pie Pie Love, not to mention all of Kilbane, and Siobhán for one was ready for the festivities to begin.

"Join the health revolution. Sugar is not your friend!" the lad bellowed.

Neither is noise-pollution before coffee, Siobhán thought, but she kept her piehole shut. She needed to remain calm, which was why she was actively ignoring him while studying the gorgeous stone mill. Perhaps he would grow tired of screaming into the abyss. Why hadn't he waited until the crowd was allowed in, or was he simply rehearsing for that very moment?

Garda Aretta Dabiri sidled up next to Siobhán, throwing a worried glance at the protester. "What are you staring at?" she asked. Aretta was the most recent addition to the Kilbane Gardaí. She was a petite woman with gorgeous dark skin, a calm presence, and a strong drive to excel. Her family was originally from Nigeria. She was the first female garda of African descent and a fantastic addition to the team. Siobhán's brother Eoin had a little crush on her, and although Siobhán got the feeling it was mutual, the pair had yet to do anything other than wear out their smiles around each other. "You seem fascinated with the wheel," Aretta remarked.

"This was always my favorite place to come as a young one," Siobhán said. "Each time I asked my da if he could make the wheel turn."

"Was he able to make it take a spin for ya?" The glint in Aretta's eye showed she was only messing.

Siobhán laughed. "He would pretend to blow on it, and meself and James would try to blow on it, and then Da would scratch his head as if he were puzzled and say, 'I thought for sure the pair of ye were filled with hot air.'" She laughed at the memory then shook her head. "It's been stuck for ages."

"Nice memories, but it's a pity the wheel is stuck," Aretta said.

Siobhán nodded. "Perhaps the proceeds from the baking show will change all of that." Historic structures came with historic maintenance, which came with historic price tags. Siobhán often thought if she ever owned a gorgeous flour mill, the first thing she would do was get the wheel churning again. Siobhán turned to Aretta and grinned. "Because this week is not about wheels, this week is all about the *meals*."

Aretta smiled. She had copped on. "The end of the meal, to be exact?"

"Bang on," Siobhán said. "Dessert. The part that everyone *savors* for last." Siobhán rubbed her hands together in anticipation. Aretta laughed and shook her head. Having a sugar addiction was not something that Garda Aretta

Dabiri suffered from. Siobhán on the other hand was already drooling. *Pies, biscuits, trifles, tarts, puddings, cookies, cakes, and breads. Oh my!* This was shaping up to be the best work assignment of Siobhán's life. And she and her giant sweet tooth intended on enjoying every minute of it. The top Irish bakers in all of Ireland would soon gather here for one week to show off their massive baking skills. Even the famous Aoife McBride had somehow been coaxed to compete. Siobhán's late mam had owned every single cookbook written by Aoife McBride, starting with *Aoife McBride Takes the Cake* and she went on from there, also including: *Pies, Tarts, Cookies, Puddings, and Breads*. There were at least a dozen books in her baking empire. Aoife McBride had been a one-woman enterprise, going full steam. But a few months ago, after a freak-out during a Fan Club Appreciation Day, she'd gone quiet, and rumors swirled about her mental health. Given she lived all the way up in Donegal, the northernmost county in the west of Ireland, Siobhán was cautious to believe anything she'd heard. Gossip distorted as it traveled, everyone knew that.

Even so, the story was that Aoife McBride had unraveled when a fan group of look-alikes descended on Donegal a few months ago to pay her tribute. They dressed in her signature colorful aprons and wigs with thick black hair striped with white, padded their figures, and donned pink-rimmed eyeglasses. Instead of being flattered at the attention, it was said that Aoife McBride was driven mad. Apparently she'd accused one of them of stalking her, and for ages afterward no one had seen or heard from her. Her fans breathed a sigh of relief when this baking show enticed her back into the public eye. Siobhán was very much looking forward to meeting her, and if it wasn't too much trouble, asking her to sign at least one of her mam's books. Apparently, she was here to reveal her new memoir, *Bake Me!* as well as compete in the baking show.

Siobhán had no time to bake, apart from her famous brown bread. Perhaps this week would inspire her to do more. The bakery needed this, and the town needed this, and she needed this. Only Macdara Flannery, aka her *husband*, (husband!), would have enjoyed it more, but alas, work meetings had taken him to Dublin. It was impossible to believe that next month would be their one-year wedding anniversary.

"Stop the show. Sugar kills!"

The booming voice showed no signs of strain. "The lungs on him," Siobhán said.

"He certainly can project his voice," Aretta agreed.

The man brandished a stalk of celery like a weapon and stared at one spot on the building as if he was speaking to an invisible camera. Somewhere there was a cameraman around as well as a director, but Siobhán had yet to meet them.

The door to the bakery opened and Fia O'Farrell emerged without so much as a donut in hand. She was a petite woman with gorgeous silver hair wound up in a tight bun. She wore a cheerful pink top and a cream-colored apron that read: ALL YOU NEED IS LOVE. *Love* was crossed out and above it read: DOUGH.

She put her hands on her hips and glared at the protester. "You're not supposed to be here. If you don't leave, the guards are going to arrest you." She pointed to Siobhán and Aretta as if their blue suits and navy-blue caps with the gold shield had not sufficiently identified them as members of An Garda Síochaná. The Guardians of the Peace. There was little peace to be found at the moment. Siobhán would have preferred the assignment in plain-clothes, but it was eejits like the one in front of them that made that request impossible.

"Do take a rest," Siobhán said to the man. "You'll wear your voice out before your audience arrives."

The comment gave him pause. Perhaps he was capable of listening to reason.

"A rest?" Fia hissed. "Are you joking me?" She planted her hands on her slim hips. "I want him off me property."

"Where is the director and cameraman?" Siobhán asked. It was a two-person crew which seemed awfully small for a week-long production, but the baking show was being independently financed by an anonymous benefactor and perhaps a larger crew wasn't in the budget.

"Unloading their equipment," Fia said with a nod to the car park in the back of the building. It would soon be jammers, and attendants would be on hand to direct cars to park in the field. The venue could hold a hundred persons in the front section of the bakery, with another hundred outside. The show would be streamed onto screens on the side of the building as well as the interior, and heat lamps had been set up outdoors for those stuck outside when the sun went down. And of course, workers would circulate amongst both crowds with pastries available for purchase, not to mention samples from the guest bakers.

Samples! Siobhán, who had been looking forward to this sweet, sweet assignment for ages, literally hearing eggs crack in her sleep, and dreaming of flour sifting through her hands, was put on her back foot by the protester. She heard a mechanical squeak and whirled around to see him holding a bullhorn. "Sugar kills," he blasted out.

Brutal. Siobhán approached. "Enough. You are disturbing the peace."

"There's no peace in diabetes, now is there?" he replied.

"Everything in moderation," Siobhán said. "Including your temper tantrum."

His eyes narrowed into slits as he dropped the bullhorn to his side. "It's my right to protest."

"Then quietly carry a sign, will ya? Whisper your message to the world."

He frowned as if trying to suss out whether or not she was messing with him. "I don't have a sign."

"Now. There's your trouble. You can't pull off a good protest without a sign, now can you? That would be like me coming to work without me handcuffs, pepper spray, and baton." Siobhán smiled, patted the large stick attached to her side, and touched her cuffs and spray on the other side. He took a step back. "Perhaps you should go make one."

He frowned, still staring at her hips. "A stick?"

"A sign."

"Right, so."

She jingled her handcuffs. "That'll show us you mean business."

He crossed his arms and looked away. "You're just trying to chuck me out."

"If you think you can compete with the smells and sounds of a bakery *without* a colorful sign . . ." Siobhán stopped talking and shook her head. "*Amateur*."

His mouth dropped open and he began looking around, as if contemplating his next move. To Siobhán's great shock, he began to stride away, taking his bullhorn with him. Before she could completely relax, he lifted it to his mouth once more. "I'll be back with me sign."

Not if she could do anything about it. As she watched him skulk away Siobhán waited for the tension in her body to ease, but she remained on high alert. "Thank heavens," Fia said. "Brilliant, Garda. C'mere to me. Whatever you did there, I applaud you."

"I don't think we've seen the last of him," Siobhán admitted. She needed caffeine and sugar, stat. She'd forgone her morning brekkie, convinced there would be coffee and delectables provided as soon as she arrived. Her husband (husband!) liked to joke that no one should ever let Siobhán O'Sullivan get hangry. "That's why your initials are SOS," Macdara often said. "When Siobhán O'Sullivan needs to eat it's an SOS!" Technically, they were Siobhán and Macdara O'Sullivan-Flannery now, but not at work. At work she would continue to go by O'Sullivan. And amongst her family and friends. No use getting them all confused when she'd been O'Sullivan for thirty years, now was there? And didn't Siobhán O'Sullivan sound so much nicer than Siobhán Flannery? And despite being on the fence about the name, at least she loved the husband. Thinking about Macdara made her wish he was here; he would have been just as eager for pastries as she was.

Siobhán leaned closer to Aretta. "She's going to offer us pastries soon, isn't she?"

"Sugar kills," Aretta said deadpan.

"Then kill me," Siobhán said. "Kill me right now." It was true that she was a bit bullish without brekkie. Or lunch. Or supper. Snacks and dessert were always helpful for the mood as well. But with Macdara out of town, and without his gentle nudging, she'd decided to skip it this morning and save room for dessert. At five-nine and a somewhat-regular jogger, so far Siobhán had managed to keep her temptations from taking over her figure. And when she was embroiled in a case, she ran around enough during the day to fight the bulge. If anything, watching Macdara's bottomless appetite gave her pause. He somehow managed to stay fit despite eating a lot more than she did. *Typical.*

"How is married life?" Aretta asked. Either she was trying to be polite or distract Siobhán from her cravings. Either way, Siobhán was grateful to get her mind on something other than out-of-reach caramel-coated brownies and strong coffee.

"Brilliant," Siobhán said with a grin. Shortly after they were married, everyone warned them that matrimony would change everything. Every morning Siobhán woke early just to prop herself up on a pillow and stare at her gently snoring husband, wondering if today would be the day that everything would change, resisting the urge to lean over and pinch his cheek, or wind a strand of his wavy hair around her finger. Once assured that he looked like the same man she'd always known—her tall, messy-haired, blue-eyed love—she would rise and dress for her morning run, eager to get back to her new home and make herself a cappuccino.

Her prized cappuccino machine was one of the remnants she'd brought from their former bistro to her farmhouse. Although it took up precious counter space in the kitchen, she wouldn't dream of letting it go. The whirring sounds it made gave her comfort, and the cappuccinos were divine. Macdara more often than not drank tea in the morning, but he seemed to enjoy her love affair with the machine. Sometimes she took her steaming mug in hand and climbed the hill behind their house to watch the sunrise through the trees.

Macdara, not what you would call a morning person, joined her up there for sunsets. They were undeniably still in the honeymoon phase, and the first year had not been as troublesome as they'd been warned. Granted, sometimes she did shriek when his ice-cold toes tried to touch hers in the morning, and he was a mad one for leaving wet towels in a heap on the floor, but they were nothing a good scolding couldn't sort out. Siobhán did not know how long a honeymoon phase lasted, but she intended on enjoying every second of it. She didn't dare wear her gorgeous emerald-and-diamond engagement ring, but she did find herself staring at her gold wedding band several times a day and marveling that she was a married woman.

"How did our protester get past the locked gate?" Aretta said, bringing Siobhán back to the present.

And how had he disappeared so quickly? She'd lost track of him across the field, and now he was gone. For a stranger he seemed to know his way in and out. "Where there's a will there's a way," Siobhán replied, scanning the grounds. The property was surrounded by a limestone wall, and the entrance and back exit were currently secured with gates. She supposed he could have climbed over the wall along the far perimeter and traipsed across the field. That meant he came on foot, or parked his car somewhere illegally, for the bakery was in no-man's-land between Kilbane and Charlesville. Both towns liked to claim it as their own, although technically it was within Kilbane's borders.

"A point could be made that sugar kills," Aretta said. "Diabetes, weight gain, heart health—"

"Please," Siobhán groaned. "It's way too early to debase pastries." Perhaps it was due to her rebellious nature, but the more anyone railed against sugar, the more she wanted it. Given Aretta was a very healthy eater, Siobhán knew to tread lightly. And despite the accusations the lad was screaming across the field, it wasn't as if the bakery was forcing sweets down anyone's gob; on the contrary, folks had to drive a ways out of town to even get to it. And most folks agreed that the drive, and even the long lines, were well worth it.

"Poison here, get your poison here!" Siobhán jumped at the sound of the familiar voice amplified by the bullhorn. The protester was back. He had changed into a white shirt. The word POISON was splashed across it in red paint with an arrow pointing off to the left.

"How's this for a sign?" he said, jabbing at his shirt when he caught Siobhán's eye.

"That is something," she said. Would it rile him up even more if she pointed out that the arrow was pointing to the left but the bakery was on his right?

"You let him come back?" Fia said, sneaking up from behind. "How could you let him come back?"

What exactly did Fia expect them to do? Wrestle him to the ground? Force an eclair into him as punishment? Yes, he was technically disturbing the peace, but all of Kilbane had been invited to the filming. Siobhán could hardly throw him out and allow the others to remain. And given his heightened state of agitation, she certainly didn't think hauling him off by his ear would help anyone. It would be a much better outcome if they helped him calm down and escorted him off the property.

"Sir," Siobhán said, stepping up and raising her voice. "We have not opened the gates to the public yet, and once again you are disturbing the peace."

"Me?" he said, jabbing himself in the chest with his finger. "I'm disturbing the peace? How many people have I killed?"

"I have no idea," Siobhán said. "But if you're confessing to a murder, I'd be happy to escort you to the Kilbane Garda Station."

"Sugar. Kills," he said.

"Technically, nearly everything can kill," Aretta said, stepping forward. "Even water." She glanced back at Siobhán and Fia, both openmouthed, then shrugged as she turned back to the man. "Everything in moderation."

"Ever heard of celery killing anyone?" the man shouted as he removed another stalk from the pockets of his trousers and wagged it at them.

"If anyone needs a cupcake, it's him," Fia said with a sigh.

"I've got one," the man shouted. They whipped their heads back to him, and sure enough he produced a giant cupcake with purple frosting. He drew his hand back as if he intended on lobbing it directly at Siobhán. Part of her wondered if he could get it directly in her mouth.

"If you throw that at me, I can arrest you for assault," Siobhán said. "If I were you, I would stop and think very carefully about what you're going to do next."

Chapter 2

As if drawn out by the drama, the cameraman and director materialized. The cameraman filmed while a woman dressed all in black stood nearby, grasping a clipboard and watching the scene unfold. She had intense eyes accentuated by black-rimmed glasses. Given the attire and props, Siobhán assumed she must be the director. She had short spiky magenta hair streaked with green, a bold move for a woman in her sixties. Siobhán could not yet see the cameraman's face; it was hidden behind his bulky recorder.

"Stop filming, Charlie," Fia said. "You're giving him the attention he craves." Charlie did not stop filming.

The protester crushed the cupcake in his fist with a wounded cry. Siobhán resisted the urge to rescue it from him. Surely, there were more where that came from.

Siobhán approached the man slowly, holding her hand up to the camera. "Give us a minute," she said. Charlie lowered his equipment, revealing a handsome face topped by thick brown curls, and a poor attempt at a beard. The lad was somewhere in his thirties.

"Keep filming," the director said, waving her arms

wildly. She swiveled to Fia. "We were told we could film everything."

Fia sighed, then shrugged and walked off. Siobhán resisted the urge to fight the director on this point, because much like Siobhán, she was only doing her job. Drama might be bad for the guards but it was good for telly.

"I'm Garda O'Sullivan," Siobhán said, stepping as close to the protester as she dared. "What's your name?"

The man's jaw was clenched tightly. He barely glanced at her. "Are you going to shut this nonsense down?" he said. "Or are you going to allow them to peddle poison?" His eyes darted to and fro, as if expecting an ambush from either side at any moment.

"Your voice has been heard," Siobhán said. In the distance, a pair of cows had stopped chewing their cud to stop and listen. "But if you keep at it, you're going to lose your authority and your audience."

He shifted his weight and glanced around. "What do you mean?" He jabbed his thumb at his shirt. "I made a sign just like you said."

"You're raving like a madman. If your goal is to encourage everyone to eat healthy, you're not accomplishing it."

He opened his hand, revealing the crushed cupcake, then flipped his palm down, allowing icing and crumbs to rain onto the ground. *Lucky birds*, Siobhán thought, resisting the urge to dive-bomb the ground. Why hadn't he just peacefully surrendered the cupcake to her? "Look at this mess," he said. He took a bite of the celery and continued to talk. "Sugar is poison. It's pure poison." He pointed his finger at the mill. "And bakers are drug pushers," he said. "Plain and simple, they're drug dealers. And they deserve what they're going to get." A grin spread across his face, and a gleam came into his eyes, and all the little hairs on the back of Siobhán's neck stood at attention.

"What does that mean?" Siobhán said, straightening her spine. "What are they going to get?" She had one hand on her baton and the other ready to grab her pepper spray. When she woke up this morning she never imagined needing backup at the bakery. Aretta stepped up by her side, placing her hand on her baton in solidarity. "Where you from yourself?" Siobhán once more attempted to appeal to him on a personal level.

It was obvious he heard her but he didn't answer. From his accent she would guess he was from a northern county. Had he followed Aoife here from Donegal? Like the cameraman he was a thirty-something lad, well-dressed, and when he wasn't shouting, even handsome, but clearly unhinged. "What is your name?" she asked again.

"I'll talk if you stop this production." He crossed his arms and smirked.

Siobhán shook her head. "I don't have the power to do that."

"Money," he said. "Greed."

She wanted to point out that they were beyond fortunate to have the best bakers in all of Ireland right here, competing, creating delectables right in front of their faces, not to mention saving a local business and donating part of the proceeds to Irish charities. "It's not just desserts they will make," Siobhán said. "I'm sure there'll be some breads as well."

"Carbs!" He clenched his fists. "Carbs break down into sugar and sugar is evil."

"Celery is a carb," Aretta pointed out.

"It's a *good* carb. It helps keep one lean." He ran a shaking hand down his flat stomach. He glanced at Aretta. "She looks like she knows what I mean." His eyes flicked back to Siobhán. "I bet you enjoy a bit of poison, am I right?"

Siobhán clenched her fists. *He was so right.* He was also

working Siobhán's last nerve. But with Macdara in Dublin and her in charge, it wouldn't be a good look if she punched a protester in the face. Would it? Perhaps a pie to the face would be tolerated, but the baking had yet to begin. "Your choice is to continue disrupting this production, or be hauled off by the gardaí." He was acting like a child, but in this case bribing him with a sweet would not be an option.

"I'm staging a protest." He wagged the celery at her, then chomped on it.

"How did you get past the gate?" Besides the cameraman and the director, an ambulance was parked in the car lot; it would be here for the entirety of the production as a precaution. Had the man snuck in with the paramedics?

"I have my ways." His eyes flicked around nervously and sweat dribbled down the side of his face.

"You're on private property and the owner has asked you nicely to leave."

"She's a mass-murderer. Shoving sugar down everyone's throat."

"Murderer!" Fia O'Farrell cried, as she came around from the front of the bakery. "Did he just call me a murderer?"

"That's because you are," he said. "If it were up to me, you'd spend the rest of your life behind bars."

"Stop filming," Fia said. "He's not well in the head!"

"Exactly," the director said. "Keep rolling."

Siobhán gritted her teeth. Neither of them were helping to de-escalate the matter. She tried using her calming voice with the man. Once again she tried diplomacy. "Where are you from?"

"Doesn't matter." He finished the celery stick and reached for the bag at his feet. He rummaged around in it and brought out another stalk. Perhaps his name was Jack and by the end of the day he would plant his stalk and it would grow to the sky. "I'm not alone," he said. "I have an entire army of people behind me." Was he telling the truth? Would a gang of vegetable-wielding eejits soon descend on the property? Should Siobhán call in the backup? "We will not be stopped."

The enormous doors to the old mill groaned open and all heads swiveled as Aoife McBride herself stepped out. Siobhán would know her anywhere. A bright pink apron, thick black hair with white stripes, and those pink-rimmed glasses. She held what appeared to be a makeup brush in one hand and a small compact in the other. The camera, and all heads, swiveled toward her.

"Ms. McBride!" Fia O'Farrell said. "You're early."

"I was inside watching him on the large screen," Aoife said. "His nose has a terrible shine." She waved the make-up brush like it was a fairy wand. "I've got just the thing for him."

"Are the others here as well?" Fia said. "The filming won't begin for hours."

"That lot? And they claim to be bakers," Aoife said with a disgusted shake of her head. "I wake promptly at half three every morning." *Half three?* Siobhán felt the beginnings of a headache. Aoife McBride strode toward the protester, who'd suddenly gone openmouthed. "If we're going to get this on camera, he needs a little powder." She crossed over to him holding the makeup brush aloft like a cross, as if he was in need of an exorcism and she was the only priest fit to do it.

He stepped back and threw his hands up in front of his face. "Get away from me with that."

"Come now," Aoife said. "I need to make sure I don't shine like that on telly and you're going to be my little guinea piggy."

"I will not." He folded his arms like a petulant child.

Aoife put her hands on her hips. "I thought you wanted

the world to hear your message?" Her voice was low and somewhat threatening. The protester cocked his head and then, to everyone's shock, he dropped his arms with a nod as Aoife advanced on him with her powder and brush. She made several swirls around his face, dabbed his nose for a finish, then turned around just as quickly and slipped back into the bakery.

"Well?" the protester shouted in the direction of the bakery. "Am I still shining?" He smiled and tilted his head, then shoved the last bit of celery into his mouth. For the next twenty minutes they tried in vain to convince the man to leave, but he refused. And then, everything changed. The muscles in his face drooped and a gurgling sound erupted as he clutched his throat. His cheeks flashed red.

Siobhán hurried over. "Are you choking?" She moved in to do the Heimlich maneuver, but he thrust his hands out to stop her, as he violently shook his head. "Not choking," Siobhán said. Was this some kind of allergic reaction? He stumbled forward, his face and throat swelling. "Paramedics!" Siobhán yelled. "Hurry!"

There was no need to scream, Aretta was already running for the ambulance, wildly waving them down. Siobhán stepped forward to ease the distressed man to the ground. But before she could reach him, he fell, face forward. Siobhán rushed to his side and knelt. She was out of her depth. Should she roll him onto his side? Was he breathing? By the time she gently rolled him over, the paramedics had reached them. The cameraman moved in closer as Siobhán stepped out of the way of the medical help.

"Have some decency," she said, holding her hand up to the camera. Charlie stopped filming and lowered his equipment.

"What are you doing?" the director shouted. "I didn't tell you to stop filming."

"Ruth," Charlie said. "Leave it." He didn't sound Irish, perhaps American, but Siobhán didn't have time to suss it out.

Ruth clamped her lips and crossed her arms.

Additional paramedics moved in, carrying a stretcher. A paramedic close to him shouted for an EpiPen. "Does he have any allergies?"

"He's a total stranger," Siobhán said. "He was eating celery." Perhaps it was a good thing she rarely ate celery.

"His airways are clear," the paramedic said. "This is our only recourse." He injected the protester in the thigh with the syringe. The poor man continued to convulse and drool pooled around his lips. The paramedic scooped up the bag of celery. "This is what he was eating?"

"Yes. He brought it with him."

He gave it a sniff. "I don't smell anything unusual but we'll bring it with us just in case." They hoisted him onto the stretcher and carried him toward the ambulance. It wasn't lost on Siobhán that all of this occurred right after Aoife McBride had powdered his face. Could he be reacting to that? If so, they needed that powder and brush so they could be tested. Perhaps it contained an ingredient which brought on the sudden attack. Although she doubted the powder contained peanuts or anything of the sort, one never knew for sure. Siobhán didn't want to indulge in her darkest thought. Perhaps Aoife McBride, the Queen baker of Ireland, had just poisoned a total stranger.

Chapter 3

"We need to find Aoife McBride," Siobhán said to Aretta as she hurried toward the entrance of Pie Pie Love.

Siobhán and Aretta burst into the building to find Aoife McBride planted near a case of pastries, cooing over each one like they were her children. This front section of the mill was filled with pastry cases built with lovely cherrywood and protected by sparkling glass. The white granite counter showcased a gilded antique cash register. Behind the counter an open pastry kitchen was visible, and in front of it was a large space that was normally a public seating area. The tables and chairs were gone and six kitchen stations filled the room instead. Behind them were two large refrigerators. On the far wall a large screen was set up. When the doors officially opened, patrons would be allowed to stand and view the show behind red velvet ropes. All the baking would take place in this room. An arched stone entrance led to another room that was being used as the dressing room, and from Siobhán's previous tours of the mill when she was a young one, she knew that beyond that lay an even larger event space as well as a door leading to the working part of the mill.

"Aren't you a lovely little thing," Aoife said, tapping the glass near a scone. "But I wonder if they did right by you. I would have given you a dusting of sugar to make you sparkle." The smell of heavenly sugar and coffee assaulted Siobhán. If Aoife McBride had deliberately done something to harm the man outside, she certainly wasn't acting like it. She pivoted at the sound of their footsteps, and smiled. She clasped her hands and grinned. "Bakeries are absolute heaven," she said, gesturing to the pastries. "That gentleman outside does not know what he's missing."

"That gentleman is in an ambulance on his way to hospital," Aretta said.

"What's that now?" Aoife placed her hand on her heart as her mouth dropped open. If she was putting on an act, she was well rehearsed.

"Didn't you hear the sirens?" Siobhán said.

"Sirens?" Aoife straightened her spine and cupped her hand behind her ear. She shook her head. "I'm afraid my hearing isn't what it used to be."

"They're gone," Siobhán said. "But as Garda Dabiri just stated, they've just taken the man you recently powdered to hospital."

Aoife cocked her head. "I was afraid of that," she said. "It was obvious he needed more help than a little powder could provide." She leaned in. "*Psychological help.*"

Was she genuinely confused or deliberately acting obtuse? "Where is the makeup brush and powder you used on him?" Siobhán asked. Aoife tilted her head as if she suddenly found herself in a play and she'd forgotten her lines. Slowly she pointed to a nearby table, then headed toward it. "Don't take another step," Siobhán warned.

Aoife froze. "Is something the matter?"

"The man collapsed right after you powdered him," Aretta said. "His face and throat were swelling. It wasn't a mental collapse, it was a physical one."

"A sudden reaction," Siobhán said. "Quite severe."

"And you think there's something in the powder?" Aoife McBride sounded genuinely upset. "That can't be."

Siobhán turned to her partner. "Garda Dabiri, can you get gloves and an evidence bag out of the squad car?"

"On it," Aretta said.

As Aretta headed outside, Siobhán studied Aoife McBride. A trickle of sweat ran down her face. She must be in her eighties, but much like her jams she was well-preserved. "I don't understand how any of this could do with my brush or powder." She turned and pointed to a large screen mounted on the wall. I could see the man on the telly, and his face was bright red from all the yelling. I thought he could use a little help."

"A man is raging and the first thing that occurs to you is to powder him?" Siobhán cringed inwardly that she was speaking this way to Aoife McBride but she was on duty now and it couldn't be helped.

"Sometimes all it takes to calm someone is a little kindness." Aoife lowered her head. "If he's allergic to my powder I'm terribly, terribly sorry. He's going to be alright, isn't he?"

"I hope so," Siobhán said. "He's lucky we had paramedics standing by."

"That is a relief," Aoife said. "I swear to you, I was only trying to help."

"Where did you buy the powder?"

Aretta returned and with gloved hands she dropped the powder and brush into a plastic evidence bag. Aoife McBride eyed it as if she desperately wanted to snatch it back. "I purchased the brush and powder at the chemist in town," she said. "Yesterday afternoon. They were having a two-for-one sale. He's the first to use that compact."

"You purchased two powders?" Siobhán said.

Aoife bit her lip and shook her head. "I purchased one powder. The other one was free."

Siobhán swallowed her frustration. "We are going to need the other one."

Aoife nodded again, then hurried into the greenroom. Moments later she returned with a second compact. Aretta added it to the evidence bag.

"Why would you want to use your brand-new brush on a sweaty stranger?" Siobhán asked.

"Kindness," Aoife said. "As I mentioned, I had two of them, and planned on tossing it into the bin afterward."

"Why were you going to do that?" Aretta asked.

"I never share makeup," Aoife said.

Aretta tilted her head. "Isn't it the brush that would have been contaminated, not the makeup?"

Aoife scrunched her face and nodded. "I have multiple makeup brushes." She pointed at the one in the evidence bag. "That's my spare. I would have washed it this evening."

And yet she hadn't. At least there was that. Siobhán removed a small notebook from her jacket pocket "In which town did you purchase the brush and powder?"

Aoife blinked rapidly. "Whatever do you mean?"

"You said you bought the powder from the chemist in town." Given the bakery was situated between Kilbane and Charlesville, she could have purchased it in either place. She was staying at the Twins' Inn with the rest of the contestants and judges, which made Siobhán think she had purchased it in Kilbane, but she didn't want to jump to any conclusions.

"By 'in town' I am referring to Kilbane," she said. If Aoife McBride blinked any harder her fake eyelashes were going to fall off. She spoke cautiously, as if considering every word before releasing it from her mouth.

Siobhán nodded. "Do you have the receipt?"

Aoife patted herself down. "If I kept it then it's back in me room. I don't remember."

"When did you purchase it?"

"We arrived yesterday. I purchased it in the afternoon."

Given she said it without hesitation, Siobhán was inclined to believe her. Siobhán walked a few feet away as she picked up her mobile phone and dialed.

"Kilbane Garda Station, Helen speaking."

Helen was new to the front desk position, but she was a lovely young woman with a cheerful disposition. Siobhán was thrilled to have her as the first point of contact for distressed callers. "Hiya, Helen, Siobhán here."

"Garda O'Sullivan," Helen said. "I hope you're filling your gullet with delicious pastries."

Siobhán laughed. "I've abstained so far." *Not by choice.*

"If a dozen or so donuts or tarts, even a pie, were to find their way to the garda station, that wouldn't be the worst thing in the world."

Siobhán could hear the grin in her voice. "Noted." If only she had money on her. Siobhán would text her siblings and ask them to bring her handbag. Gráinne, Ann, and Ciarán were all coming to watch the first day of filming. Eoin and James wouldn't be able to join them, they were hard at work at the farm-to-table restaurant they were opening on Siobhán and Macdara's new property.

Pleasantries over with, Siobhán asked Helen to contact the chemists in town. "Let them know they are not to sell or touch any of the face powder. They need to remove all of it from their shelves immediately and store them somewhere until the guards collect them." She filled Helen in on the events of the morning.

"Will do," Helen said. "The poor pet, I hope he'll be alright."

"Fingers and toes crossed," Siobhán said. She hung up,

feeling somewhat relieved. At least until they knew what caused the man's attack, she wouldn't have to worry about the same fate befalling someone else. Hopefully he would be okay, and the doctors would be able to explain what ailed him.

Siobhán turned back to Aoife, who was furiously texting someone on her mobile phone. When she noticed Siobhán staring she let out a startled cry, then shoved the phone into her apron pocket. Aoife began to wring her hands, no doubt wishing she had never stepped in to powder the stranger.

"Did you pay with a credit card?" Siobhán asked.

"Cash." A trickle of sweat ran down her cheek, smearing her makeup. She made no move to wipe it off.

"Did you buy any other makeup at the chemist?"

She shook her head. "I was only out of powder. They had a two-for-one sale. Sure, lookit. I go through a lot." She wasn't lying, the evidence was caked onto her face. "Do you really think there was something nefarious in the powder?"

"I won't know until we hear from the hospital," Siobhán said. "But it wouldn't be the first time an item has been contaminated. I have an obligation to imagine the worst."

Aoife placed her hand over her heart. "You poor dear. Thank heavens I went into baking."

"As long as we're chatting," Siobhán said, "my mam had all your books."

"Lovely." She leaned in. "I assume you bake?"

"I make a mean brown bread if I do say so meself." Siobhán grinned.

Aoife tilted her head and made a face, as if she had just taken a bite of it and found it loathsome. "I see."

"I was wondering if you wouldn't mind signing one of my books?" Siobhán's heart pattered as she waited to hear the answer. After a moment Aoife McBride sighed and held her hand out.

"Right," Siobhán said. "I didn't bring them with me. But I can bring one tomorrow."

"Typical," Aoife said under her breath as she turned and walked away.

Fia O'Farrell paced the stone walkway in front of the bakery. Siobhán emerged, and took a deep breath. It was on the cool side, but otherwise it was a grand, fresh day.

"It is exciting that Aoife McBride is here," Fia said. "I can see how her fans might be driven a bit wild."

"You're referring to the protester?" Siobhán said. "I would hardly call him a fan."

An electronic squeak interrupted them, and they whirled around to see Ruth and Charlie behind them. Ruth held up her mobile phone. "The contestants and judges have arrived and they'll be at the back gate any moment." Charlie put down his camera and gave Ruth a thumbs-up.

Siobhán stepped toward him with her hand outstretched. "I'm Garda O'Sullivan and this is Garda Dabiri. We'll be here during the entire production."

Ruth seemed fixated on something or someone across the room and didn't join in the conversation, but Charlie set his recorder on a nearby cart and stuck out his hand. "I'm Charlie Holiday."

"American," Siobhán blurted out as they shook hands. She hadn't been expecting that.

He grinned. "Guilty. By way of the Sunshine State." He must have noticed the puzzled looks on their faces, for his grin faded. "Florida."

A chorus of *Oh* rippled through Siobhán and Aretta.

"Don't sweat it," Charlie said. "Irish names are what trip me up. It took me ages to realize Aoife was pronounced *Eefuh*."

"Disney World," Garda Dabiri said. "Or is it Disney-land? That's what trips me up about America."

"Disneyland is in California," Siobhán said, not at all convinced. They all looked at Charlie for confirmation.

"I never remember either," he said. "But had I known you were fans I would have brought you mouse ears." He stuck his hands on top of his head as if they were giant ears and wiggled them until they laughed. Then he jerked his thumb at the director. "And you've already met our in-famous director, Ruth Barnes, but you can just call her The Boss." He flicked her a cheeky look. "Isn't that what you asked me to call you?"

Ruth shook her head and strode away from them. "I think we should take this opportunity to get a coffee or tea and a pastry," Siobhán suggested. "Do our part to keep this mill open."

"I'm game," Charlie said, opening the bakery door and waiting for Siobhán and Aretta to go ahead of him.

Sweet smells accosted Siobhán once more: sugar, and caramel, and chocolate, and icing all rolled into one intox-icating balm that wrapped around her like a blanket. Fia appeared and took her place behind the counter. "I can start a tab for you if you'll be ordering all week."

"Not a bother," Siobhán said, once more lamenting that she hadn't brought her handbag or any euro. Frankly, she'd been too convinced there would be samples. "I might try to hold off," Siobhán said. "Just window-shopping for now." She tapped the glass and laughed as Fia frowned. Siobhán turned and feigned a sudden interest in the kitchen sta-tions.

"This place is awesome," Charlie said. "What year was it built?"

"It was built between 1850 and 1870," Fia said, coming out from behind the counter to join them. "That's the clos-est we've been able to come to dating it."

"Speaking of history, there is something fascinating that has caught my eye in the greenroom." This came from Ruth, who had also slipped back into the huddle.

"Oh?" Fia said with an arched eyebrow. "And what might that be?"

"Follow me," Ruth said, beckoning with her finger. "Charlie, bring your camera."

Charlie, who had just been about to bite into a chocolate croissant, sighed, and then stuffed the entire thing into the front pocket of his denims. He turned to the cart and heaved up his camera. Crumbs dripped out of his pocket as they all hurried after Ruth. She strode to the greenroom and came to an abrupt stop in the corner. Everyone found themselves staring at a bespoke wooden sign. It had been carved into a large circle and mounted on top of a barrel. Wooden numbers hung on miniature nails placed on the sign. Next to the barrel was a large glass container of additional wooden numbers. Siobhán had to lean in to read the faded red paint. The sign read: 3,650 DAYS SINCE THE LAST ACCIDENT.

Chapter 4

As they all took in the antique sign, Aretta leaned toward Siobhán. "I guess it's lucky the man who had the allergic reaction did so *outside* the building."

"It's quite a lovely sign," Siobhán said. Even if it was capable of delivering a grim message.

"That's a very old sign," Fia said. "But every business has accidents. Especially when you're working around industrial cookers and all sorts of baking accoutrement." She beamed. "I'm very proud of our accident-free record."

"Didn't you have a guest who once severely burned her hand?" Ruth asked.

Fia gasped. "That's a donkey's age. How did you know?"

"The bakery was sued, wasn't it?" Ruth asked. "Just a wee girl who was hurt, wasn't it? Left a scar in the shape of a quarter moon on the back of her hand?"

"As I said, that was a very long time ago." Fia's mouth was set, her eyes filled with rage.

Ruth tilted her head. "Isn't that one of the reasons this bakery is underwater?"

Fia walked away. "Are you here to film me or the baking show?"

Ruth trailed after her. "You're a part of the show, aren't you?"

"I am definitely not part of the show, I am simply the host." Fia busied herself behind the counter, but Ruth would not be deterred.

"I was told everyone and everything is fair game."

Everything is fair game. It sounded somewhat ominous. "Told by whom?" Siobhán asked.

"Our mysterious backer," Ruth answered, barely glancing at Siobhán. It was becoming apparent she did not appreciate the presence of the gardaí.

"Mysterious backer?" Siobhán's alarm bells were going off.

"The show is being financed by an anonymous benefactor," Fia explained. "A sponsor, I should say. I'm convinced it's Aoife McBride herself."

"I agree," Ruth said. "But in order to fairly compete she wants to remain anonymous."

"Who is handling the logistics, if not this anonymous sponsor?" Siobhán asked.

"A solicitor," Fia said. "By the name of William Bains."

Siobhán was digesting this information while simultaneously trying to remember if she'd ever heard anything about a child burning her hand at the bakery and the family bringing forth a lawsuit. It wouldn't have been the type of news her parents would have shared with them, but Siobhán assumed it hadn't been a local. In small towns, everyone eventually found out everyone else's business. Just then someone's mobile phone rang, making everyone jump. It was Ruth's. She turned away and answered. "Got it," she said. She hung up and addressed the group. "The bakers and judges are waiting at the back gate." She turned to Charlie. "I want shots of their grand entrances."

They returned to the bakery. Siobhán and Aretta stood back while Charlie and Ruth headed outside to shepherd in the players. "Coffee or tea?" Fia asked.

"Coffee," Siobhán said, slightly ashamed at the speed and volume with which she answered. *And pastries? Surely, she was going to offer them their choice of pastries.*

"Tea, please," Aretta replied. "Herbal if you have it."

"Ruth is certainly taking her job seriously, isn't she?" Fia said as she prepared their coffee and tea. "I think they intend to turn this production into a soap opera."

"A soap opera with desserts," Aretta said. "Why do you think that?"

Fia leaned in as if she was about to deliver the goods. "She said to be on the lookout for any conflicts that pop up among the contestants so we can play it up for drama." She looked around. "She wants me to *spy.*"

"Show business," Aretta said with a grimace.

"Isn't it exciting?" Fia exclaimed.

"When did someone sue your bakery?" Siobhán asked.

Fia's excitement faltered. She opened and closed her mouth several times. "We settled that," she said. "It was ages ago." The look on her face conveyed there was something quite unsettling about it, but Siobhán's brain had been hijacked with a desire for a pastry, so she let it drop. If only she hadn't forgotten her handbag. Perhaps she could borrow a few bob from Aretta, because she didn't think she was going to make it much longer, taunted by treats.

Fia handed her a cup of coffee. Siobhán thanked her profusely, then took the opportunity to wander over to the stations that had been set up for the six contestants. In addition to the velvet ropes surrounding the kitchen stations, they were all well stocked. Every piece of equipment they might need was set atop each kitchen counter: rolling pins, mixers, whisks, measuring cups, pans, cooling racks, and bowls in a variety of sizes. Blooms, the local flower shop, had made arrangements for each station. They were gorgeous, light pinks and white, perhaps to look like desserts themselves, but Siobhán had a feeling they would soon be chucked out as they were taking up precious room on the counters.

Ruth entered, holding her clipboard. "Time to open the gate for the townsfolk," she announced. "Is everyone ready?"

"Ready," Fia said. She was lit up with anticipation, no doubt imagining the ding of the antique cash register totaling up all the sales.

"We're ready," Siobhán said.

Ruth gestured to the velvet ropes. "Our viewers must stay behind the barrier. Once they're situated and quiet, we'll bring in our bakers."

"I'm going to need some time first," Fia said. "We must allow for them to buy tea, coffee, and pastries."

"But our bakers are here." Ruth sounded petulant.

"My contract says there will be ample time for the audience to purchase coffee, tea, and pastries before any filming begins," Fia said firmly.

Ruth's eye twitched as she seemed to be holding herself back from a retort. It was part of the deal that the bakery would run as usual during the filming. With this crowd, that could take quite some time.

"We can bring the bakers and judges in through the back and they can wait in the greenroom until we call them," Fia said. "You can film them getting ready."

"Fine," Ruth said, throwing up her hands and sounding like it was anything but. "I guess it's pre-pre-showtime."

* * *

Despite the rocky start to the day, there was a buzz of excitement as townsfolk flooded into the bakery. The coffee machine continuously gurgled and the tea kettle shrieked, but both were drowned out by voices raised in excitement, cups hitting plates, and spoons clinking. Siobhán felt an excited buzz take hold of her and took the opportunity to grab a second coffee, and after much deliberating (not to mention a small loan that came attached with a sizable smirk from Aretta), she chose a brownie with cream-cheese icing. *Melt in your mouth.* A soft, chocolatey, icing-infused moment of bliss. It was a good thing Siobhán had never gone beyond baking her famous brown bread. If she ate like this every day she'd need a much bigger wardrobe. She told herself not to focus on Aretta, who was drinking herbal tea and nibbling on a tiny oatmeal cookie. Had she not known the woman, she would have feared that Aretta had given away all of her money and that's why she was eating so little. In reality, this was how she always ate, at least around Siobhán. She was a petite woman, and eating did not seem to be a passion of hers. Siobhán wondered if it took great pains to eat this way, or if she didn't give it a second thought. It seemed too personal a question for colleagues, so she had held herself back from asking. Her brownie with her cup of coffee delivered a hearty dose of nirvana—that is, until her mind flashed to the man who had been screaming in front of the bakery, just a mere hour ago. *Sugar kills.* She momentarily stopped eating, eyeing the half brownie she had left.

"What's wrong?" Aretta said, sidling up to her. She leaned in. "Is it bad?"

"No," Siobhán said. "It's like I've gone to heaven but

the minute I finish it the angels will chuck me off the cloud and slam me back down to earth."

Aretta laughed. "Is that why you're staring at it like that? Already missing it?"

Siobhán laughed. "Yes. But also . . . I was just thinking of our anti-sugar protester. I do hope he's alright."

"I can call the station and ask them to give us an update," Aretta said.

"You're the best," Siobhán said.

Aretta smiled. "I couldn't let you lose your best friend."

"Best friend?" Siobhán frowned. "I'd never seen him before in me life."

"I was talking about that brownie," Aretta said as she strolled away to make the call.

The first of the esteemed participants to enter Pie Pie Love were the judges, Ronan O'Keefe and Philomena Lemon. The doors were wide enough to allow them to step in simultaneously, although the pair seemed startled when neither fell back to allow the other to bathe in the spotlight. Ronan was a large man dressed in a smart gray suit with a red tie, perhaps to match Philomena's long red dress. He waved at the crowd as if he sat upon a float in a parade. Charlie Holiday, who had a bulky recorder to contend with, had to compete with local reporters to get a shot. The pair grinned as cameras flashed around them. Phil, as she'd often stated she liked to be called, was a stunning woman with shiny black hair cascading down her back. If she regularly ate her famous cakes, it didn't show on her slim body.

She had a unique style of waving. Her hand stayed motionless as her four fingers repeatedly bowed to her palm. Perhaps this was so she could flash her long red fingernails, accented with a white diagonal stripe through the middle. She was a walking version of a red-velvet cake. She was only twenty-eight, and recently a certain Royal in London had tweeted about her specialty tea-cakes, sending her skyrocketing to fame. Apparently, she had hundreds of thousands of TikTok followers, something that had captivated the attention of Siobhán's younger sisters, Gráinne and Ann. Although neither of them had started baking, the pair of them had been TikTok-ing ever since. Admittedly, Siobhán was a bit of a Luddite when it came to all these new-fangled apps. But seeing Philomena in person was enough to convince Siobhán that the woman had a plethora of followers. Maybe even stalkers.

Ronan, a heavyweight baker in his own right, with storefronts in bakeries all over Ireland, was balding and middle-aged but he exuded a boyish charm. They were loving the cameras as they paused in front of the pastry cases, draping themselves over them dramatically. "Look at this," Ronan said. "Eclairs, cookies, pies, cakes, trifles, and puddings, and *tarts*!" On *tarts* he made an exaggerated gesture toward Phil. Instead of taking offense, she grinned.

"I need them all in my mouth right now," Phil said, placing an index finger up to her glistening red lips as if she had been naughty and was asking the audience to keep her secret. She lifted her arched eyebrows and fluttered bedroom eyes for the camera. Siobhán was certain she heard Charlie let out a moan.

"I want to savor one at a time," Ronan said, not-so-subtly shoving her aside with his hip. "I remember the time I served a certain famous musician my chocolate-macadamia scones," he crooned. "I never bake and tell, but here's a little hint, his name rhymes with Aw, no!" He turned to the crowd and clearly mouthed *Bono*.

The crowd laughed and clapped. Phil tilted her pretty

head and frowned. "You too?" she said, then waited for the laughter to rise and subside. She stuck out a hip and twirled a strand of silky dark hair around her finger. "He's one of my many followers on TikTok."

"This is brilliant," Ruth said as she turned to Charlie. "If they keep one-upping each other like this we won't even need to dig for conflict."

Volunteers shuffled around with trays loaded with delectable samples from the pastry cases. Siobhán resisted the urge to tackle one of the servers, and it wasn't until Aretta placed her hand on a passing elbow that the volunteer stopped in front of them with the tray and Aretta motioned to Siobhán to help herself. She nearly cried, nearly hugged her partner, who had done it solely for her. Siobhán helped herself to a lemon tart, a glazed donut, and a chocolate eclair. After all, they were cut into bite-sized pieces. That was the only reason she took two of each. That and the fact that the volunteer didn't know Aretta wasn't partaking. And perhaps Aretta would change her mind. And if they happened to be gone by then, surely more would be passed around.

"I see the guards are taking their duty seriously," Philomena remarked. Siobhán's mouth was full, and she froze as the cameras turned on her.

"She's a tall one, isn't she," Ronan said. "And that hair is on fire!"

And now Siobhán's face and neck were on fire as well, no doubt turning shades brighter than her auburn locks. She was wondering if she was expected to say something when thankfully they moved on.

"What a hungry crowd, wouldn't you say, Ronan?" Phil said, her eyes scanning the locals.

"I'd say so, Phil. Either there's nothing else to do in this town, or we're hot stuff."

"Could be both."

"Indeed."

"Let's introduce our bakers!" they said in unison. All heads swiveled toward the greenroom. Siobhán took the opportunity to search for three of her siblings in the crowd, and soon spotted them. Gráinne and Ann were standing near the greenroom as close to the red velvet rope as possible, and yes, it was thanks to a little nepotism that they had been ushered in early, and Siobhán wasn't even going to feel too guilty about it.

She waved at them and they grinned and waved back. They were all so tall, so grown-up. Gráinne was actually getting clients as a personal stylist, and she was traveling to Limerick, Cork, and even Dublin, to style actresses and influencers. Her sheer confidence and commanding voice gave her an air of authority that clients loved. If she thought something was hideous, no matter how the client felt about it, she had no problem setting them straight. She had wanted to style Siobhán for the baking show until Siobhán broke it to her that she would be in her garda uniform all week. Gráinne caught Siobhán's eye again, and winked as she twirled a strand of her dark hair around her finger. Then she rolled her eyes, presumably at all the fashion, or lack thereof, around her. Siobhán wondered if Gráinne was jealous of Philomena Lemon or dying to be best mates with her. Probably, it was a bit of both.

Ann, with her short blonde bob, looking a bit more spiked today, probably thanks to Gráinne, had her eyes glued on the greenroom, eagerly awaiting the bakers. Given the youngest O'Sullivan girl usually showed more interest in everything outside the kitchen, Siobhán was surprised to see the excitement in her. Perhaps there was more to Ann than Siobhán knew. Life had been so busy lately, getting married, moving into a new house—had she been neglecting Ann and Ciarán?

Nonsense. Ann was in her last few months of secondary school and would soon be getting her Leaving Cert. She had received a partial scholarship to Trinity College Dublin, and Siobhán was over the moon. They would find a way to pay the tuition; Siobhán did not care if she had to beg, borrow, or scrape. She spent most of her free time with her camogie team. She was brilliant at the stick-and-ball game, a great athlete all around, and as she grew, her independent streak had grown with her. Siobhán had also never heard Ann talk about a boy, which made her wonder if there was a girl, and she would be totally fine with that; she wanted Ann to be fully herself, but the conversation had never come up naturally, and the more Siobhán practiced it in her head, the more awkward she sounded, and the more she wanted Ann to be the one to come to her with the news. And so she had decided to wait, and so she was waiting.

Ciarán, looking more man than boy these days, and two inches taller than Siobhán, would be a senior in the fall. One more year, and then every O'Sullivan child would officially be an adult. Siobhán was fiercely proud, but terrified. If she could keep them a little bit longer, she would do it. At least none of them had wandered too far. Ciarán had shown no interest in discussing his plans after secondary school, and sooner rather than later Siobhán was going to have to force the topic. At the moment, the youngest O'Sullivan was happily involved with a giant cinnamon bun, his thick fringe flopping over his eyes. Before her very eyes he was changing from a boy to a man. The shock of it had not worn off—his deep voice, his handsome face, his tall and somewhat gangly body. Her brother. Her little brother. Just seeing them gave Siobhán a shot of joy.

She wished Eoin and James could be here as well, but the farm-to-table restaurant was such a huge undertaking. Their vision was coming together. A large, communal space with a warm community feel, like a pub but with chef-worthy dishes, sourced from local ingredients. And Eoin, in addition to being a fantastic graphic artist, was a very talented chef. Siobhán could see their future so clearly. The whole family would remain close, even after they were all grown up. Their parents, Liam and Naomi O'Sullivan, who had been tragically killed in a motor accident eight years ago, would be so proud. Siobhán must have looked worried, for Gráinne suddenly stuck her tongue at her, which was her signature move whenever she was trying to make someone laugh. It worked. Siobhán laughed, shook her head, and forced herself to concentrate. The first contestant had just been announced, the youngest baker, Ethan Brown. Ronan was giving the introduction.

"Ethan is a graduate of the Parisian Baking School, and has since made headlines with his delectable raspberry, apple, and lemon tarts. Welcome, Ethan." The spotlight swiveled toward the greenroom as Ethan Brown stepped onto the red carpet. "Ethan, you may proceed to station one." Ethan waved as the crowd applauded. He was a devilishly handsome lad with a mound of honey curls on top of his head and bright blue eyes.

"I wonder," Philomena said as Ethan continued his procession toward his station. "Will Aoife McBride confront Ethan about the disparaging comment he made about her to a local newspaper?"

Ethan halted on the carpet, and flashed a stunned look

at Philomena. "No!" he said. "I was only messing." Phil wagged her fingers at him.

"Why don't you read a bit of that article," Ronan said. He whipped a newspaper out from behind his back. "I happen to have a copy right here."

"I love a juicy quote," Phil said, stopping to treat Ethan to a wink.

"Please, don't," Ethan said, his voice full of panic.

"I'm afraid you agreed to the rules in advance, Mr. Brown," Ronan said. "I'd hate to see you eliminated before your first bake." Ronan cleared his throat and held up the newspaper. Ethan bowed his head and hurried to his station. Once there he bent down to examine the cabinets as if he wanted to crawl inside. "Aoife McBride may have made a few good pies in her day, but much like some of her failed breads, she's a dish that no longer rises."

Ronan and Philomena turned to the cameras in perfect synchronization and opened their mouths in mock horror.

"I was only messing," Ethan said loudly, flicking a nervous glance toward the greenroom, where no doubt Aoife McBride was boiling like a tea kettle. "I think Aoife McBride is the bees knees."

"Oh, honey!" Phil sang.

"Let's hope the old bee doesn't try to sting you," Ronan said. "Well, that's the buzz on Ethan Brown." He turned to Phil. "Who do we have next?"

"Next we have Trisha Mayweather, the daughter of the late, great Mary Mayweather, who arguably stirred the pot with Aoife McBride when she lambasted her raspberry cake with buttercream icing."

Ronan put his hand over his mouth. "How did she do that?"

"She said, and I quote, 'Whereas fresh cream may not

travel as far and wide, it will outshine Aoife's preservative-filled icing any day.' "

The judges turned to the spectators in unison and behind them Ruth held up a sign that read: ACT SHOCKED. The audience went "Oooooo." Ruth beamed and gave a thumbs-up.

"Will this be the week that Trisha Mayweather steps out from her mother's shadow and ices out Aoife McBride?" Ronan asked.

The judges high-fived each other over the pun as Trisha Mayweather stumbled onto the red carpet, looking as if she had been shoved out before she was ready. Her blouse was buttoned wrong, her blonde hair was filled with static and looked in dire need of a comb, and she had a smudge of red lipstick on her chin.

"My mother was passionate about baking," she stammered. "She and Aoife McBride started out together." She stopped, turned toward the greenroom. "Remember, Aoife? You and my mother used to be friends. Remember?"

"Darling, we're focusing on you right now," Ronan said. "We'll be introducing Aoife McBride in good time."

"If you insult someone and she's not around to hear it, is it still an insult?" Phil asked Ronan.

Ronan grinned and scanned the crowd. "Given we have plenty of ears with us today, I guess we'll never know!"

"It wasn't an insult!" Trisha said. "The fresh cream is much better." Her face was red with anger. "There's only one reason Aoife McBride didn't use fresh cream, and that's because—" Trisha suddenly stopped speaking and stared at the camera as if transfixed. Siobhán didn't blame her; she would get stage fright too if that big lens was focused on her. "What was the question again?" she finally stammered.

"Moving on!" Ronan said. "Please take your place behind your station before you're eliminated."

Trisha Mayweather clamped her lips shut. It was becoming apparent that the judges had been instructed to play up each contestant's rivalry with Aoife McBride, not to mention threatening them with elimination before the competition had even begun. It was somewhat distasteful for a baking competition, of all things, and Siobhán found herself wishing they'd cut it out. She was here for the baked goods, and given the stringent qualification process, couldn't they all agree that each of these bakers were at the top of their game, and it was anyone's contest to win? Why did ratings always have to come from sensationalism? The fault, she realized, lay with human beings. Whether they were just wired for trouble or whether they were conditioned from shows pulling these petty stunts, was a question to ponder another day.

Trisha Mayweather squared her shoulders as Fia O'Farrell ran out to the carpet and offered her a little mirror. Trisha gasped when she saw her appearance, then glanced back at the curtain to the greenroom as if someone back there had deliberately shoved her out, as if she was just coming out of a bender and trying to figure out how she got here. Soon, other volunteers mobilized with combs and brushes, and within seconds Trisha's appearance was on point. She smiled and waved to the cameras before settling into station two and turning to shake Ethan Brown's hand.

"Let's give a warm welcome to our third contestant, Martin Murphy," Ronan said. A thirty-something, strong-looking African man stepped out, grinning and showing off his biceps in a T-shirt.

Philomena stepped forward. "Martin is known for creating baking structures, combining his considerable construction skills with baking. He refers to himself as a baking sculptor." Behind the kitchen stations, a large screen was scrolling through some of his iconic work—his chocolate Eiffel Tower, his caramel Blarney Castle, and his gumdrop-and-icing London Bridge. The crowd applauded and Martin took a bow.

"His family is Nigerian," Aretta leaned over and said. "Everyone from my father's family will be so jealous I'm meeting him up close and personal."

"Bragging rights," Siobhán said, "are the best."

Ronan O'Keefe raised his voice over the applause. "Do you think Aoife McBride will apologize to Martin Murphy for her remarks that she hoped one day he would 'make a chocolate bridge big enough to jump off'?"

The crowd gasped, but when all heads turned toward Martin Murphy, he threw his head back and laughed. "McBride has a wicked tongue," he said, wagging his finger. "But you gotta love the old harpy." He winked as the crowd gasped again, then strolled to station three and jumped over the counter, showing off his athletic prowess. The crowd cheered and clapped once more.

"Our fourth contestant has a name, but should I even bother using it?" Ronan said.

"According to our contract we must use their names," Phil said. "But I have a feeling no one else will use it." They each reached behind them, then thrust up large sponges. The crowd began chanting: "Sponge, Sponge, Sponge."

"That's right, folks," Ronan said. "Please give a warm welcome to Barry Ryan, aka The Sponge."

Barry Ryan was shaped like a barrel and came rolling down the carpet in denims and a yellow jumper. He too was carrying a sponge, coated in icing, squeezing it and dripping it along the red carpet. "Barry Ryan, otherwise known as The Sponge—not for his sponge cakes, which are also delicious by the way, you should try his orange marmalade—but for his claim that he can replicate any recipe with just one bite," Phil said.

"It's not a claim," Barry said. "It's a fact." He squeezed the sponge once more with his beefy hands.

Ronan pretended to be frightened and held his hands up in surrender before whipping a blindfold out of his pocket and wiggling it around. "Even Aoife McBride's secret recipes? Do you think he can crack those? *Blindfolded?*"

"Can't wait to see if he can," Phil said. "Right in front of her face."

"Blindfolded, hands behind my back—heck, you can shove noise-canceling headphones on me ears if you wish. Piece of cake," Barry said. "One taste and I can replicate it to a tee. *Any* piece of cake, pie, tart, pudding, trifle, biscuit, bread, or cookie. *Anything.*"

"Is it getting hot in here or is it just me?" Philomena said, grabbing a nearby mixing bowl and fanning herself with it.

"It's definitely heating up," Ronan agreed.

Barry Ryan made a beeline to Ethan's station, and shook his rivals' hands one by one before arriving at station four.

"And before we get to our esteemed Baking Queen, Aoife McBride, our fifth contestant is our youngest and most inexperienced baker, who will dare to batter-up with all these pros. She only started baking two years ago as a stress reliever while studying law at Trinity College. Please welcome the lovely Sophia Hughes."

A petite young woman with bouncing red curls and high heels stepped out, carrying a basket. She began tossing little homemade candies to the crowd. They went wild, drowning out the rest of the judges' introductions. She stopped in the middle of the red carpet and placed a dainty hand over her heart. "I am so honored to be here this week. Just being in the company of the top bakers of Ireland is a dream come true."

"Isn't she adorable?" Ronan said.

"Sickeningly sweet," Phil added.

Sophia cocked her head, as if trying to suss out whether or not she'd just been given the kiss or the slap. Phil waved her hand in a sweeping motion, indicating that she needed to move along. Instead of shaking the other contestants' hands, Sophia simply bowed, and tossed them candy before settling into station five.

"And finally, the woman you've all been waiting for, please give it up for Ireland's very own Aoife McBride."

Music cued and to Siobhán's surprise, confetti rained from the ceiling as the woman of the hour stepped out. She wore a silver gown, which made her long black hair streaked with gray stand out. Instead of her usual pink, she sported black glasses with diamonds around the lenses, and she was carrying what looked to be a fairy wand.

She waved the wand to the crowd, greeting her subjects as if she was indeed a Queen. Then she stepped in front of Ethan Brown, pointed her wand at him and waited until the crowd shushed.

"I forgive you," she said. Before he could respond she moved down the line, pointing her wand, and tossing out forgiveness. When she reached Sophia she simply shrugged and said: "I forgive you in advance." The crowd laughed as she took her place behind the final kitchen station, number six. She turned to the camera. "Forgiveness," she said, "is what this life is all about. But do not be mistaken. I will not be dethroned. I am the Queen Baker." The crowd went wild.

"Let the Hunger Games begin," Ronan said.

"Are we allowed to say that?" Phil asked.

"Too late to take it back now," Ronan said. "I'm starstruck, so spare the lightning!" On that cue, a prerecorded sound of thunder rumbled through the room, followed by a flash of light over Ronan O'Keefe to mimic a strike. The crowd shrieked and then cheered as they all waited eagerly for the sweet, sweet games to begin.

Chapter 5

The contestants were all safely ensconced behind their stations, and the crowd was more than ready for the show to begin. Even though she was just a spectator, Siobhán felt the anticipation humming through her bones. Philomena took center stage and faced the camera. "As you know, today is a day for B-roll." The secondary footage would act as filler for the final production.

Ronan snuck up behind her. "B-roll!" Philomena jumped and let out a shriek. Ronan howled with laughter. She gave him a searing look. "And when we say B-roll, we're not talking about Barry Ryan's ample middle section," Ronan continued.

Everyone's gaze shifted to Barry Ryan. He laughed and patted his belly with both hands. "I do a lot of tasting. It's a job hazard."

"Today our esteemed cameraman and director will film the bakers warming up with their signature bakes that they will then share with you lucky ducks." He gestured to the crowd, who cheered.

"Lucky, lucky ducks indeed," Phil said.

"Finally," Siobhán said out loud. "Samples." Unbeknownst to her until it was too late, Ronan O'Keefe had swung his microphone near Siobhán and her comment was broadcast to the entire room, not to mention the local television audience. Laughter rolled out, and a few comments about "Kilbane's finest" and stereotypes about guards loving their pastries. Siobhán's face overheated. She moved clear away from the microphone. "Here I was thinking how jealous Macdara would be," she said. "Now I'm a laughing stock."

"Marriage has made you even more competitive," Aretta said.

"He is just as competitive," Siobhán said. "And he thoroughly enjoys it." Perhaps she was a tad more competitive but that was splitting hairs. Macdara had already texted her three times this morning begging for details, not to mention close-up photos of desserts.

Fia O'Farrell stepped up. "Samples are a long time from now, my gorgeous hungry people! All spectators must stay behind the red velvet rope. No disturbing the bakers. But since our lovely Garda Siobhán O'Sullivan is eager for samples, volunteers will be passing around tastes of what we've baked fresh today, although I warn you—they're going to run out quick! My pastry cases are now open and the coffee and tea are flowing."

Siobhán glanced down at her now empty coffee cup. "Go on," Aretta said, giving her a gentle nudge. "I won't tell."

"May I ask you a personal question?" Siobhán said. It was now or never.

"You may," Aretta said.

"Do you enjoy eating and drinking or do you see food as just fuel for the body?"

Aretta tilted her head and studied Siobhán. "I do not enjoy eating in public. I like cooking my own food, in my own home, setting an atmosphere and taking my time."

"Lovely," Siobhán said. "Are you not tempted by all these treats?"

"I did not grow up with all these sweets," Aretta said. "In my family meals take great preparation and are meant to be savored. Perhaps it is cultural."

Siobhán nodded. She didn't know whether to feel happy or sad that she liked her sweets. And chips. Never forget heavenly curried chips. Maybe Siobhán would take a page out of Aretta's book and only eat after great preparation. Set the atmosphere. Take her time. Just then, a volunteer appeared in front of them with a tray of pastries. "Samples?"

Siobhán's hand reacted before her brain could stop her, and before she knew it she was holding a raspberry tart, a slice of lemon meringue pie, and a butter cookie. Yes. Perhaps one day she would take a page out of Aretta's book, but today she wasn't even going to read over her shoulder.

The day of B-roll went surprisingly well; the room was filled with sweet smells and sounds of determined bakers. With all the cookers heated up, some contestants seemed to be standing in front of the shared commercial refrigerators just to cool down. Trisha Mayweather in particular seemed to linger in front of one.

"Is she going through the change of life?" Ronan boomed into a microphone, sneaking up behind Trisha and making her jump. She dropped a carton of milk and soon liquid was seeping into the cement floors.

"Get stuffed!" Trisha said, tears coming into her eyes as she swiped a towel from her station and tried to mop it up.

"No crying over spilled milk!" Ronan shouted. "Am I right?" There was now a line of people waiting impatiently for the fridge. Siobhán nearly felt sorry for Ronan. She wouldn't want to stand between Barry Ryan and a stick of Irish butter. Ronan looked around, but no one would meet his eyes. "Apologies," Ronan said. "I was trying to insert a little humor into the mix." He finally moved out of the way, allowing Barry access.

Fia O'Farrell either felt for Trisha Mayweather or she was calculating the energy bills in her head, for she finally propped open the main door to let in the fresh air and handed Trisha a handheld fan.

"Thank you, pet," Trisha said. The pair threw an admonishing glance at Ronan O'Keefe.

"Note to self," Ronan said. "Never mention the change of life to a woman of a certain age."

"Make it all women," Martin Murphy said. "Better safe than sorry."

"Don't pay any attention to him," Philomena said. "Ronan O'Keefe has been bitter ever since puberty stood him up." It was Ronan's turn to sport a sour face while others laughed.

"We need a mop over here," Barry said, lifting his feet as he moved away from the fridge. "Sticky."

Fia O'Farrell sighed, then enticed a young lad from the crowd to fetch a mop. Siobhán glanced through the open door as a breeze swept in. Every contestant had fun sharing their practice bakes with the crowd, and Siobhán was poised for her turn at a nibble when Garda Vincent Collins stepped into the room. He was just out of the Garda College in Templemore and the handsome young guard had made it clear he wouldn't be in Kilbane long. He was supposed to be manning the station this week, or at least answering the phones along with their station clerk, Helen. He caught Siobhán's eye and waved her over.

"Garda O'Sullivan," he said, straightening his spine as she approached.

Siobhán noted the serious expression on his face. "What's the story?"

He jerked his head to the outside. They stepped underneath the awning. And then, like a light switch had been flipped, rain poured from the skies and the wind lashed at everything in sight. Siobhán closed the bakery doors as a pink umbrella hurtled past them. Garda Collins lunged for it but missed. They watched as the brellie twisted and bounced across the field until it was a mere pink dot in the distance.

"What's the story?" Siobhán asked, hoping to get an answer before one of *them* blew away.

"Cork University Hospital rang. I'm afraid the man who was taken away in an ambulance from this site died shortly upon arrival."

The protester. Siobhán crossed herself. "That's terrible. Did they know what caused his death?"

"Doctor Jeanie Brady is being called in to do a post-mortem."

"Right." Doctor Jeanie Brady was not just an outstanding state pathologist, she had become a good friend to Siobhán and Macdara. "Did he have identification on him?"

"No. The hospital asked me to check with you. I was going to ring you, but Helen said I should come in person because of the filming situation."

"Right."

He waited, staring at Siobhán as if expecting her to do something. He jerked his head toward the doors. "Are you going to close down the production?"

Siobhán was taken aback. She hadn't even thought of that. *Should she?* What if his death was the result of an allergy or another natural cause? She'd already taken the face powder into evidence out of an abundance of caution, and notified the chemist to remove the remaining product from the shelf. "I'm going to speak with DS Flannery on the matter, but until we know a cause of death, I'm going to let this roll." She prayed she would not live to regret the decision.

"Right. I'll be on my way then." He headed off.

"Wait."

He stopped and turned toward her.

"Let's see if we can get a photo of your man and hire an artist to do a sketch. Helen has a list of the artists approved by the garda station. Let's do some canvassing with the sketch, both in Kilbane and Charlesville. Maybe we'll get lucky and someone will recognize him."

"Right, right."

"If we can't get a local to recognize him, we'll need to set up a tip line. Finding his family is our top priority."

"Absolutely." He glanced around the field. "Do you think he has a vehicle parked here?"

Siobhán shook her head. "He came on foot." She pointed to the east toward a limestone wall. "He left to retrieve a T-shirt and exited in that direction. It didn't take him terribly long to come back. I assume he had been parked somewhere beyond the wall."

"A T-shirt?"

"He made a sign," Siobhán said. "A new shirt for his protest." *Poison.*

"What was he protesting exactly?" Garda Vincent asked. "Cinnamon buns?" It was the first time Siobhán had seen any humor out of the lad, so she laughed.

"He was very passionate about healthy eating, I suppose," she said. "May he rest in peace."

Collins stopped laughing and crossed himself.

"Who else is at the station?"

"Garda Hurley and Helen."

Garda Hurley was near retirement. He was no doubt doing a crossword and watching YouTube videos of lads building fences, on his smart phone with his feet propped on his desk. "Do a quick canvass for any abandoned vehicles. After that we sit tight until we hear the results of the postmortem. I will apprise DS Flannery of our situation and we'll go from there."

"Right." Garda Collins nodded, pulled his jacket in tight, then tucked his head and made a run for his squad car.

Siobhán remained for a moment, thinking of the protester. His poor family. Had he really traveled all the way down to Kilbane just to lecture the town on the dangers of sugar? Siobhán messaged Macdara and brought him up-to-date on the situation and her thoughts on handling it.

He responded right away. **Hopefully Collins will find the vehicle. I agree with both the sketch and the tip-line. Keep me posted, someone has to recognize him. How are the sweets?**

She returned to the bakery and sent him photos of all the goodies in the cases, and he sent a drooling-face emoji back along with a sad face. She laughed. Apparently his meetings were all stuffy and boring and he was hoping to wrap up sooner than later so he could join her for the end of the competition. She told him not to worry, that she was eating enough for two. Three if you counted sneaking some of Aretta's allotment. Technically, all of Aretta's allotment, but who was counting?

The day of B-roll came to a close. Collins messaged that he had canvassed the area but had not found any unidentified vehicles. Had their protester come with someone? At least the day was over and the townsfolk had all cleared out of the bakery. The contestants had just finished cleaning their kitchen stations when a sleek black limousine pulled up in front, the engine purring.

"Is that for us?" Ethan Brown asked. "Are we riding back to the Twins' Inn in style?"

"If that's the case, I'm certainly not paying for it," Ruth was quick to say.

"I'm not either," Fia said. "So who ordered it?"

Everyone gathered near the front windows to have a gawk as a short man dressed in a black tux emerged from the back of the limousine. He was holding a stack of red envelopes in his hand. The driver exited, ran around to the boot, and when he reappeared he was pulling a red trolley that was stacked with gifts wrapped in shiny red paper.

"What in the world is that?" Fia asked.

"I think we're about to find out," Siobhán said. They backed up as the front doors opened and the man entered, balancing the red envelopes in one hand as he pulled the trolley with the other.

"Did you know about this?" Aretta leaned in and asked.

"I don't even know what this is," Siobhán said. She turned to Ruth. "I take it he's not a member of your crew?"

"No," Ruth said. "There's nothing on the schedule and I've never seen him before in me life."

"He's not with me either," Fia volunteered.

Siobhán stepped in front of the stranger. It was growing dark outside and the dim bulb mounted outside the bakery shone on his bald head, making it glisten. He had hazel eyes so pale they were nearly yellow, prominent cheekbones, and a pointy chin. There was something about his eyes. Something familiar. "Hello," she said. "I'm Garda O'Sullivan, and this is Garda Dabiri."

"Hello," he said. His voice was deep and commanding. He gestured for her to move out of his way. "Do you mind?"

Siobhán folded her arms across her chest. "I'm afraid we're closed for today. You're welcome to come back tomorrow, although without authorization I cannot let you in with"—she leaned over and pointed to the shiny wrapped presents—"whatever it is you're trying to roll in here."

"Let me put your mind at ease," the man said in an unsettling tone. "My name is William Bains." He looked at her as if this should mean something to her. "I am a solicitor here on behalf of the sponsor."

Siobhán turned to the group with a raised eyebrow.

Ruth stepped up. "Yes, yes, our anonymous sponsor," she said. "I did mention Mr. Bains to you."

Siobhán nodded and stood back. William Bains gave a slight bow.

"Is there a problem?" Ruth asked.

"No problem," William Bains said quickly. "Just a few announcements and tweaks to the game play." He attempted to pull his trolley full of gifts into the bakery.

"I'll need to see your identification first," Siobhán said.

Mr. Bains sighed as if Siobhán were wasting everyone's time, but reached into his pocket and pulled out his billfold. He brandished his identification, but for a moment kept a grip on it, leaving Siobhán playing an unintended game of tug-of-war. His gaze was intense as if he was trying to stare into her soul. Siobhán wasn't in a position to authenticate his motor license on the spot, but she wanted him to know she was watching him. She snapped a photo of his license with her mobile phone.

"Perhaps you want to fingerprint me as well?" he said under his breath as she handed back his identification.

"I could dip your finger in chocolate icing and press it on wax paper," Siobhán said, without a trace of a smile. He frowned. "I'm only messing."

He gestured ahead of him. "May I?"

The solicitor seemed devoid of humor and Siobhán was starting not to like him, but she moved over to allow him to pass. William Bains dragged the trolley to the center of the room. Siobhán had a strong feeling she should stop whatever this was, but she had no evidence that something was amiss, other than that little feeling, and the fact that Charlie Holiday had unpacked his camera and had it trained on the action. She held a finger up to William as she gathered Fia, Ruth, and Charlie around her. "We can stop this," she said. "Whatever this is."

"This is a baking show," Fia said.

"It's part of the deal," Ruth agreed. "We were informed there would be surprises along the way from the sponsor." She glanced back at the man. "I just didn't realize it would be so soon and that Mr. Bains would arrive in person."

Siobhán didn't like this one bit. "As a member of the gardaí, I must state that we do not like surprises. We are providing security for this event and we must be in the loop," she said.

"I assure you, this is just gamesmanship," William Bains said. "I come in pieces." He flashed a smile that was all teeth.

"Do you mean in *peace*?" Ruth asked. "Should we take that again from the top?"

"No, no," Mr. Bains said, waving his envelopes. "I come in *pieces*. I come bearing private messages and secret weapons."

Chapter 6

"Weapons?" Aretta said. Siobhán was relieved to hear some alarm creep into her partner's voice.

"Gamesmanship," William Bains said, thrusting his index finger in the air. "It might be a baking instrument, a special ingredient, a new piece of equipment, or a coveted recipe." He smiled and tilted his head. He seemed to be peering at something on the far stone wall. Siobhán followed his gaze to the large oil painting of Donal O'Farrell, Fia's stern grandfather, that towered on the wall facing the entrance (perhaps so he would be the first face guests would be forced to look upon). The portrait was that of an older man with electric-blue eyes, and a dark mustache. Siobhán found herself staring at it along with William Bains, and soon everyone was focused on it.

"He looks alive," Ronan said. "Those eyes—I swear they're following me."

It suddenly dawned on Siobhán—that's what had seemed so familiar about the solicitor. His gaze. Not that he and the late Donal O'Farrell looked anything alike, but the intense (one could argue *creepy*) gaze was identical.

"Grandfather is always watching," Fia said wistfully. She crossed herself.

"That's your grandfather?" Phil said. She turned to the camera and mouthed: *Creepy.* Siobhán would have said *Jinx, you owe me a Guinness* had it not been for the glare Fia was directing at Philomena. As Fia stood below her grandfather's portrait with the same scowl, Siobhán could clearly see the family resemblance.

"He ran a tight ship, but he supplied this town with sustenance his entire life," Fia said. "If you don't like looking at him, then look somewhere else."

"His eyes follow me no matter where I look," Philomena continued.

"I suppose you'll have to be on your best behavior then," Fia said.

"I get paid more to be on my worst behavior." Philomena threw her head back and laughed heartily at her own joke.

"What do you think?" Aretta had snuck up behind Siobhán. She jumped and let out a little yelp.

"Looks like we won't be able to count on the redheaded garda for protection," Ronan was quick to say.

"That was my fault," Aretta said. "You're lucky to have Garda O'Sullivan, I'd trust her with my life."

"No one needs to worry about a thing," Siobhán said, putting on a bright smile. The protester's death had made her paranoid. Or maybe she was getting agitated from all the sugar. *Sugar kills.* Indirectly one could argue it had indeed killed the protester. What else had killed him? Allergy or poison? Perhaps he was too worked up and his heart gave out. Was it really just this morning? Death was always disturbing and Siobhán would settle down once the cause had been determined. She wondered how the sketch of the man was coming along. She'd stop into the station first thing in the morning to check on it.

"Well?" William Bains snapped. Everyone was staring at Siobhán as she stood mute. Finally, she gave a curt nod. The solicitor exhaled with relief. "Let's get on with it then, shall we?"

Minutes later, each contestant was holding a red envelope, anticipation stamped on their faces. In the middle of the room, in front of the stations, boxes wrapped in shiny red paper with fat white bows had been unloaded from the large trolley and arranged in one big gleaming pile. "Leave your envelopes unopened at your stations," the judges instructed. Ronan and Philomena asked for a private huddle with William Bains, and once finished they were fully on board with his plan. Siobhán had wanted to listen in, but they assured her the discussion had nothing to do with safety concerns. Ronan turned to instruct the group. "In the morning, when you arrive, the first thing you'll do is open and read the instructions in your envelope." Contestants glanced at each other, then one by one gazes flicked to the tantalizing red envelopes. William Bains picked up the handle to the empty trolley and exited the bakery without so much as a backward glance. Moments later, the limo glided away.

"The message inside is just for you, and cannot be revealed to anyone," Philomena said. "If you whisper—or shout—to anyone about your message, you will be immediately disqualified." Sophia Hughes raised her hand. Philomena frowned. "Yes?"

"What if we *show* someone our message?" Her red curls bounced every time she moved her head.

"*Disqualified*," Philomena said. "You cannot share your message in any way, shape, or form."

"That includes skywriting," Ronan said with a grin.

"Your card will have a number. Number one will be the first to choose their secret weapon." Ronan gestured to the pile of wrapped boxes. "Once you've opened your envelope and received your weapon, the judges will announce the first bake. And then, we're off to the races!"

"Another limo has arrived to take us all back to the Twins' Inn," Phil said. Siobhán looked up to see there was indeed another limo waiting at the door. Philomena turned and spoke to Ruth before she could interrupt. "This limo has been paid for by the sponsor."

"O'Rourke's Pub in town is hosting everyone for supper. I hear there will be a trad band playing in your honor. Eat, drink, and do enjoy," Ronan added. "But we urge you not to stay out too late. Get some rest and we'll see everyone in the morning."

Siobhán was knackered when she came home, and her plan was to call Dara then fall into bed without supper. But Ann and Ciarán were waiting in the kitchen, each with a gleam in their eye.

"We waited for you," Ann said, grabbing her hand. "Come see." They led her to the dairy barn, and Ciarán came up behind her and put his hands over her eyes. She heard the barn doors slide open and they guided her inside. When Ciarán removed his hand, Siobhán found herself standing in what was shaping up to be a proper restaurant. It wasn't set up with equipment or furniture yet, but the walls and flooring and roof were stellar. Given the electricity still had to be sorted out, her siblings had mounted numerous battery-powered lanterns around the space, giving it a romantic glow. The wood-beamed rafters above them were so tall that the large open barn felt even bigger. The wide-plank pine floors were stained the same rich brown. Three giant chandeliers made of old-fashioned milk bottles mounted on wagon wheels hung above them. The stone walls had all been painted a fresh coat of white, and the large barn windows had been replaced with new ones and framed in black iron.

A gorgeous panoramic fireplace encased in glass was a central feature of the space. It was situated between two beams in the center of the room where it could be viewed from all sides. It was a giant open space where communal tables would be set up, but there was a private dining room in the back corner, which could be reserved for a party of up to twenty. A large marble counter had been erected for the hostess stand, and behind it decorative white and black wallpaper adorned with ornate flower patterns had been neatly pressed into the wall with shelves overlaid on top. The kitchen would be partially visible behind a half wall. Black-and-white framed photos covered the walls, many of them local sites: the ruined abbey, the town square, Saint Mary's Cathedral, and of course, Naomi's Bistro. There were also family photos of the O'Sullivans throughout the years and photos of random folks from town going about their days.

"C'mere to me," James said. "You've gone as mute as the stone walls."

Siobhán found tears coming to her eyes. "It's stunning," she said. "Absolutely stunning."

"We do have one more surprise," Eoin said. He looked happier than she'd ever seen her brother, bursting with pride. "We've decided on a name."

"Close your eyes again," Gráinne said. Ciarán was happy to put his hands over her eyes once more. Was there any chance at all he had washed them recently?

"We hired an electrician to do the wall behind the counter just so you could see our new sign," Eoin said.

"I helped design it," Gráinne said.

"Your designs are clear, love the wallpaper, pet," Siobhán said.

"On three," Ann said. Her siblings counted to three. Siobhán heard a faint whirr and when Ciarán removed his hands she found herself staring at the name of the restaurant written in gorgeous cursive handwriting in neon hot-pink glasswork: *O'Sullivan Six*. There were no words, it was perfect.

"We didn't forget Mam and Da," Gráinne said. Below their new sign was the old sign for Naomi's Bistro in robin's-egg blue, and below that a framed photo of her parents.

More tears came to Siobhán's eyes. "Group hug!" Ann said. Her siblings moved in, the lads grumbling but, as Siobhán expected, loving it just as much. They parted and Eoin continued the tour.

The electricians for the rest of the space were coming sometime this week, and after that the kitchen equipment and tables and chairs could arrive. "I'm starving," James said. He plopped on the floor. "Let's eat here." The O'Sullivan Six ordered from the chipper, and Siobhán volunteered to pick it up. She hadn't ridden on her scooter in ages, and it was delightful riding through town with the wind through her hair, the vibration of her pink Vespa humming through her body. When she returned they ate on the floor of the restaurant and Eoin cracked open a bottle of champagne to toast. Then her siblings wanted to know all about the baking competition and they talked about all the gossip until Siobhán was nodding off on the floor of the O'Sullivan Six. Her siblings all mothered her, helping her up and tucking her into bed.

The next morning, Siobhán awoke early enough to go for a jog. It was a misty morning and her walled town was topped by a thin layer of fog. She ran hard, circling her beloved abbey, willing herself to burn as many extra calo-

ries as possible. By the time she showered, dressed, and returned to the bakery, Fia, Aretta, Ruth, and Charlie were
already there and setting up for the day. As soon as the
bakers filed in, it was apparent that not every contestant
had followed the sage advice to get a good night's sleep.
Ethan stumbled out first, his hair sticking up, his eyes
rimmed in red. "That was some craic last night," he said
as he winked at Fia and strolled in the doors.

"I can smell the alcohol off ya," Fia said.

"Coffee!" Ethan shouted. Trisha and Barry emerged
next, looking as if they'd had more sleep than Ethan, their
heads bent as they whispered to each other. Were they
forming alliances already? Martin Murphy strode in, passing everyone with gusto. He either had a good night's
sleep, or he had a natural reserve of energy. Sophia Hughes
bounced out, her bright smile showcasing the resiliency of
youth. Aoife McBride emerged next, keeping her distance
from the rest, eyes hidden behind large sunglasses. Finally,
Phil and Ronan exited the limo, looking coiffed and shiny,
and rested. It wasn't long before everyone was gathered inside, and began readying themselves for the first day of
play. Soon thereafter the townsfolk poured in, and it was
once again a cacophony of excited voices and baking sounds
infused with heavenly scents.

Siobhán was dying to hear if there was any gossip.
How had they all gotten on last night? She bit into her
banana-chocolate muffin and sipped a cappuccino as she
took in everyone's entrance. She was so focused on the
contestants, she didn't register the change in the room
until they did.

"Curtains!" Barry Ryan shouted. Siobhán whirled around
to see what he was on about. To her surprise, each kitchen
station was now hidden behind a set of red velvet curtains.

"Is someone accusing us in advance of peeking?" Barry Ryan said. "I rely on my taste to duplicate recipes, not spying."

"They're from the sponsor," Fia said. "They set them up late into the night."

"What?" Siobhán said. "Why?"

Fia shrugged. "They thought the event could use a little more drama."

"The sponsor returned after we left?" Siobhán asked.

"Yes," Fia said. "I was just locking up when he returned. He said . . ." She stopped talking and clamped her lips together as if willing her mouth to stop making sounds.

"Yes?" Siobhán prompted.

"He said he was so rattled 'by the attitude of that feisty redheaded guard' that he forgot to set up the curtains."

It was Siobhán's turn to keep her lips pressed tightly. She could feel Aretta vibrating behind her, as if trying to keep her laughter from spilling out of her.

Sophia bounced up to her station and briefly wrapped herself in the curtains. "I love red velvet," she said. "Supple, and yet so dramatic."

"Not unlike you," Martin Murphy said, openly staring at her.

She laughed and then winked. "Thank you, handsome builder," she said. "I must admit I'm a big fan of your edible skyscrapers as well." Martin Murphy wiggled his eyebrows in response.

Phil and Ronan groaned. "Leave the bad jokes to us," Phil said.

"Especially the bad and dirty ones," Ronan added.

Sophia tilted her head. "What joke?"

"Twenty minutes until showtime," Ruth announced as Charlie trailed behind her with the camera. From then on, it was a flurry of activity and soon it was indeed showtime. Each contestant stood behind their kitchen station, the curtains drawn open so the cameras could film their facial expressions as they opened their secret envelopes.

"This is so nail-biting," Ronan said. "I wish we had a glimpse of what is scribbled on each of those notes, but I suppose we won't find out until the first bake is completed."

"I was hoping we would get to watch them bake," Phil said. "But we've learned the first round is going to be a behind-the-curtains bake. They'll each have secret instructions and soon each contestant will get to choose a secret weapon." She gestured to the pile of shiny wrapped packages in the center of the room.

"At least we will get to see their faces as they read their secret messages," Ronan said. "And that starts now."

Chapter 7

"Should we have them open their secret messages one by one or all at the same time?" Phil asked. A few contestants appeared ready to rip into their messages, others were holding them at arm's length.

"Let's go wild," Ronan said. "We'll have them open and read their messages simultaneously."

"Perfect," Phil said. "Next, they will each have a number on their message." She turned and spoke directly to the players. "If your card has the number one on it, you will be the first to pick your secret weapon from the pile."

With the cameras rolling, and suspenseful music cued up, they began tearing open their red envelopes.

A large screen across the east stone wall of the mill, showed close-ups of the contestants. First came looks of concentration as the players eagerly opened the envelopes and read their private instructions. Almost simultaneously, their faces morphed into confusion. Heads popped up and they began throwing a series of perplexed glances at each other, as if trying to ascertain whether or not the others were reading something shocking as well. Sophia Hughes was the first to speak.

"Is this a joke? Are they taking the piss?"

Aoife shushed her. "You're on telly," she said. "Watch your language."

"I'm with Sophie," Trisha said. "This must be a cruel joke."

"It's Sophia," Sophia said. "But thank you for your support."

"What do they say?" Ronan asked.

Phil playfully swiped at him with a baguette she snatched from a nearby basket. "They'll be booted out of the competition if they tell," she said. "You're the one who reminded them."

Martin Murphy threw his note down on his station. "Ignore it, people," he said. "It's just a distraction."

Barry picked up a rolling pin. "Let's begin," he said. "The clock is ticking."

Ethan Brown was still reading his note. Perhaps his vision was blurry from too much drink the night before.

Sophia raised her hand.

"Yes?" Ronan said, sounding annoyed.

Sophia shook her head. "I can't do what my note says."

"I don't know what to tell you, darling. The rules are the rules." Ronan gave an exaggerated shrug then mugged for the camera.

"Now I really want to know what these secret messages say," Phil said.

"They'll never tell," Ronan said.

It was Phil's turn to mug for the camera this time with a dramatic sigh. "Who has the number one on their note?"

"I do," Aoife spoke up.

"Typical," Barry muttered.

Instead of moving toward the shiny wrapped boxes, Aoife simply pointed as if she expected the box to sprout wings and fly in her direction. "I'll take the biggest one."

"That's what she said," Ronan leaned in and said in a faux-whisper to Phil.

Aoife waited, and sure enough it didn't take long before a middle-aged woman from the crowd leapt over the red velvet rope, grabbed the largest box, and ferried it over to her.

"Thank you," Aoife said, with a tone that suggested otherwise.

"Would you sign me book?" the woman asked, holding a cookbook toward her.

Aoife glanced at it. "It's not my cookbook," she said.

"Hasn't stopped you before." The comment came from Trisha Mayweather, who seemed as surprised as Aoife McBride at her outburst.

"What's that supposed to mean?" Aoife ignored the woman who continued to hold her cookbook out for an autograph. Aoife continued to eye Trisha Mayweather as she produced a Sharpie from her apron, and signed the book with a roll of the eye. The woman stood there staring at it. "Take it and run," Aoife said. The woman nodded, then ducked under the velvet rope and melded with the crowd.

"Everyone," Fia said. "Unless you're a contestant you must stay behind the red velvet ropes." She turned and gave Siobhán the side-eye as if Siobhán were neglecting her crowd-wrangling duties.

"Maybe if she gave away more samples, I'd have the energy to chase everyone down who dares slip beyond the velvet rope," Siobhán said under her breath. Aretta laughed, cheering up Siobhán.

"I'm next." Ethan strolled over and made a production out of examining each box until he lifted the smallest one. "I don't care what this is," he said, holding it up for the camera. "No matter what *anyone* says." He turned to Aoife McBride. "My Parisian training is my secret weapon." There was a smattering of polite applause. "*Merci, merci.*" He bowed repeatedly before returning to his station.

"My turn," Sophia said, hurrying over to the pile. She slapped a hand over her eyes, stumbling and pawing at the boxes until she picked one at random. "A bit of luck got me here, and I suppose a bit of luck might get me all the way."

"That's what—" was all Ronan O'Keefe managed to say before Phil shoved a cinnamon bun in his gob.

"Number four," Trisha said.

"Grab one for me while you're at it," Barry Ryan said to her with a wink. She picked up two and hurried back.

Martin Murphy stared at the lone box left in the middle of the room. "Do I have to use it?" he asked the judges.

"Yes," they said in unison. He sighed and then jumped over his kitchen station to retrieve the final box. The audience loved the bit of action and lifted their voices in a cheer.

Ronan straightened up and cleared his throat. "Now that you all have your instructions—"

"They weren't instructions," Sophia interrupted. "They were more like—"

"Ah, ah, ah," Philomena said, wagging her finger and flashing her talon-like fingernails. "I would hate for our amateur baker to be disqualified before her very first bake."

Sophia clamped her lips shut.

"The first assignment is a free-bake," Ronan announced.

"You are encouraged to make your signature bake. Bake something that tells us a little something about the essence of you as a person."

"You must be joking," Barry Ryan said, grabbing his ample middle. "If I did that I'd be baking a jelly roll."

Ronan waited for the laughter to subside. "Give us an offering that will set you apart from all the others."

"You may only use the ingredients and supplies at your station—plus your secret weapon—and you must follow the instructions written in your secret envelope," Philomena added. "You will have a generous four hours to complete your first bake—ample time to start again if you make a mistake."

Ronan nodded. "Be free and wild, and don't forget we're also looking at the presentation. Give us some flare." He adorned the sentence by fanning out his fingers. "Adorn it with berries, icing, flavors, anything you can think of to make yours stand out. Let your baking lights shine!"

"You have two hours on the clock," Phil and Ronan said in stereo. "On your mark, get set, bake!" Applause rose from the audience and one by one the red velvet curtains closed. The crowd soon realized there wouldn't be anything to look at for the next few hours apart from contestants darting out of their curtains to fetch items from the refrigerator. To Fia O'Farrell's delight, they soon gathered around the pastry cases before wandering outside.

As the opening round started, and the excitement swelled, Siobhán swore to herself she was going to start baking. Given their family bistro was closed and the O'Sullivan Six had yet to open, it had even been a while since Siobhán had made her famous brown bread. Watching sprays of flour appear above the red curtains, knowing behind the stations spoons were stirring and eggs were cracking as these top bakers gave it their best, was inspiring. Perhaps she would bake this weekend. Macdara would be home, and he was a most appreciative audience. Her brother Eoin was an excellent chef *and* baker; not everyone had both skills, but he certainly did.

Aretta appeared beside her, bouncing with energy. "Shall we have a walkabout?"

"Absolutely." They took a stroll around the grounds and Siobhán hoped she worked off at least a few bites of all the pastries she'd consumed thus far. Lunch arrived courtesy of O'Rourke's Pub for the crew, and included Siobhán and Aretta. Declan O'Rourke had delivered some of the usual fare, ham and cheese toasties, a bag of crisps, and a mineral. *Lovely.* The weather was typical of this time of year, changing every ten minutes. Sun, clouds, rain, wind, rinse and repeat. There was enough of a break in the rain to eat at the outdoor tables, which Fia quickly dried off before everyone sat down. Charlie and Ruth kept to themselves, hunched over Ruth's clipboard as they discussed all the shots they wanted to get by the end of the day. After lunch, Siobhán and Aretta took one more stroll, and before they knew it the time was nearly up. They slipped back inside just as the judges were giving the bakers their final warning.

"Two hours left, bakers," Philomena called out. "Make every minute count." Several groans rose from behind the closed curtains.

"I don't envy them," Ronan said. "Poor pets."

"I envy them," Philomena said. "How often does one get the chance to compete against the great Aoife McBride?"

"Excellent point," Ronan said. Their heads turned to Aoife McBride's curtain, but if she heard them she did not use up any of her precious remaining time with a comment. Siobhán scanned the crowd, wondering if any of them knew their protester. Hopefully they would have an identification and cause of death sooner rather than later.

Aretta, always vigilant, picked up on Siobhán's mood shift. "What's the story?"

"I was just thinking of that poor man," Siobhán said. "Our protester."

"Is there any word on his identity?"

"The last I heard from the station, the artist's sketch will be ready by afternoon. We're going to have to pass it around to the folks here and I'm already dreading Fia's reaction." Siobhán had no desire to hurt Fia's business, and there was still a chance the man's death was accidental, but asking folks to identify an unknown corpse would not be good for business, no matter how delicately one approached it.

Aretta nodded solemnly. "Do we have a cause of death yet?"

Siobhán shook her head. "Doctor Jeanie Brady is on her way to Cork University Hospital and I've had the powder and brush sent to the morgue so the pathologist will send it on to the lab."

"Are you thinking of his death as suspicious?" Aretta asked.

"It's part of the job," Siobhán said. "But I will try to keep those thoughts at bay until Doctor Brady has come to a conclusion." Trying was not the same as *doing*, but all one could do was put forth one's best effort. It was a great frustration of life that her best never felt good enough. Especially where life and death were concerned.

"But if it was foul play," Aretta said, leaning in and lowering her voice, "doesn't that make Aoife McBride our prime suspect?" The expression on Aretta's face conveyed what a nightmare *that* would be. One couldn't just accuse Ireland's Queen baker of murder without having a motive, let alone enough evidence to back it up. And as despicable as the thought was, anonymous, evil people sometimes tampered with store products. If, and it was still a big if, there was something nefarious in that face powder, that did not mean Aoife had any clue. It could be incredibly bad luck for the protester and incredibly good luck for Aoife that she had not been the first to use it. Nothing of the sort had ever happened in Kilbane, but one could never rule it out entirely. Siobhán hoped his death was a tragic allergy, although no cause of death would not bring any comfort to those left behind to grieve.

A timer went off, interrupting their discussion. "That's it, bakers," Ronan said. "Your bakes should be in the oven, or you're going to be the one that's cooked!" Ronan and Philomena cackled as the sounds of cookers opening and closing filled the room. Siobhán consoled herself with another cup of coffee. And given there was coffee cake set up on the counter, she partook of that too—it would be rude not to. Then, she found her siblings in the crowd and loved them up against their will before calling Macdara and catching up with him, and before she knew it, the time was almost up.

"Players, it's time to reveal your bakes! And although we do like to taste as we go, we've been instructed to simply view each offering first before we get to taste," Ronan said. He threw a puppy-dog look to Phil.

"No time to waste then," Phil said. "We will open the curtains starting with Ethan Brown in station one and ending with Aoife McBride in station six."

A loud but cheerful buzzer sounded, accompanied by polite applause from the audience. Volunteers hurried over and whipped open Ethan's curtain. Lemon tarts rose from an ornate stand on his counter, shaped in an upside-down V.

"May I present the Eiffel Tart," Ethan said proudly.

"Made with lemon and blueberry filling, and dusted with crystallized sugar." The audience clapped. "If we had the right lighting, the sugar crystals would gleam like Paris at night!"

"Isn't that a gorgeous sculpture," Ronan said.

"And obviously, it reflects his Parisian training," Philomena added. Ethan grinned and took a little bow.

"Copying me already," Martin Murphy said. "Typical."

"I copy no one," Ethan replied.

"Tell that to the city of Paris," Martin said. "But don't worry, after they see mine, no one will be climbing your tarted-up tower." He winked. Ronan and Phil's heads ping-ponged between the men.

"Well, I still can't wait to get a taste of those tarts," Ronan said, turning back to Ethan with an exaggerated wink. Ethan was too busy glaring at Martin to notice.

"Station two," Philomena said. "Open your curtain!"

The volunteers scurried over to open curtain two, revealing a multi-tiered wedding cake. Siobhán counted seven levels.

"Oh, my," Ronan said. "Love is in the air."

"She finished *that* in four hours?" Philomena said. "Impressive."

Trisha beamed. "This is a tribute to my late mam, Mary Mayweather, who of course was famous for her wedding cakes, among other things. Wait until you get a taste of the fillings," she said. "Chocolate, raspberry, lemon, vanilla, hazelnut, strawberry, and shortbread. All mixed in a vanilla cake and icing made with fresh cream, of course."

"Marry me," Ronan said.

"Someone's an overachiever," Barry Ryan said in a flirtatious tone. Trisha blushed and batted her eyelashes. "Mary Mayweather would be proud."

Trisha placed her hands on her heart and nodded to

Barry. She turned away, dabbing underneath her eyes as if the waterworks were about to begin.

"On to curtain three," Phil said. The volunteers proceeded to open Martin Murphy's curtain. Siobhán was stunned to find herself staring at a chocolate replica of Pie Pie Love. It was a miniature version of the old flour mill; even the outside texture resembled limestone. It was truly a work of art. Before Martin or the judges could say a word about it, he was drowned out by applause.

"My, my, my," Ronan said. "A replica of this bakery that looks too good to eat."

"It's chocolate and hazelnut with a powdered sugar mix for the stones, cupcakes for the flowers, and a blue-dye-pudding for the water representing the creek," Martin said, flashing a proud grin.

One of the players coughed and Siobhán distinctly heard Ethan say, "Show-off."

"On to number four. What did The Sponge do this time?" Ronan asked.

They opened his curtain to reveal a giant sponge cake. More laughter and clapping. "This is a sponge cake like no other," Barry Ryan said. "With a whiskey-laced icing and traces of chocolate."

"Whiskey-laced icing," Philomena said. "I bet Ethan wouldn't mind a taste of that, now. A little hair of the dog."

"I'm fresh as a daisy," Ethan said. "Unlike most of you— I'm not ancient."

"Hurry and open the other curtains so we can get to tasting," Phil said. "Ronan here is drooling."

"I am," Ronan said. "I won't lie." He lifted his tie and mock-dabbed his chin with the end.

The fifth curtain opened to reveal a sobbing Sophia Hughes. She stood in front of a blackened pan of—whatever she had tried to bake. "It was that hateful note," she said. "It really messed me up."

"Oh dear," Ronan said. "Meltdown behind curtain five!"

Sophia picked up her note, ripped it to shreds, and tossed it into the air like confetti. "I quit," she said as little shards of paper rained down. She dashed into to the greenroom, leaving everyone openmouthed, looking left and right to see if someone was going to chase after her.

"It was risky having such an inexperienced baker stand among these greats," Phil said. "But I certainly didn't bet on her not even finishing the first round."

"I say we let her have a do-over," Martin said, staring after her like this was a dating show and he'd just lost the only eligible match.

"There are no do-overs in baking," Philomena said.

"Poor dear." Ronan did his best to sound sympathetic. "The show must go on." He gestured to the last station. All heads turned. "And last but not least, let's see what the acclaimed Aoife McBride has in store for us." The volunteers hurried over to her curtain and opened it with a flourish. It took Siobhán several seconds to process what she was seeing. Only the top of Aoife McBride's head was visible. She appeared to have collapsed onto her table. The audience gasped.

"Ms. McBride?" Phil said. She turned to Ronan, for once at a loss of words. His mouth was open, his hand was on his heart.

Siobhán rushed over, calling for everyone else to stay back. McBride's body was craned downward, and her face buried in her signature dish, no doubt her famous cherry pie. Siobhán shouted for someone to alert the paramedics outside. She tried rousing Aoife but the woman was still.

MURDER AT AN IRISH BAKERY 77

She reached for her wrist, and found it cold and without a pulse. She repeated it at the neck. Aretta hurried over and they maneuvered her gently to the ground. Siobhán listened for breath. "Paramedics," Siobhán yelled as she started CPR. She had to try. But she knew the horrific truth. Aoife McBride, the Queen baker of Ireland, had just baked her very last pie.

Chapter 8

Siobhán had been called out to numerous death scenes, but, with the exception of the protester who was arguably still alive when he was hauled off in the ambulance, she'd never been present *while* the death had occurred and she'd never had to deal with the presence of a panicked mob. "Attention," she shouted over the screams as Aretta closed the curtain up around Aoife's body. "We need everyone to clear out in an orderly manner so that the paramedics can do their job."

The paramedics had already confirmed what Siobhán already knew. It was too late for Aoife McBride, she had indeed baked her last pie. But the crowd did not need to know all the details at this moment. Backup was coming, but not in time to control hundreds of people. The townsfolk did not want to move. A few even surged toward her.

"No," Aretta said. "Out. Everyone out." For the first time ever, Siobhán and Aretta were forced to remove their batons and hold them lengthwise in front of their bodies to create a barrier against the crowd.

Siobhán took a deep breath, and made a forceful announcement. "Additional guards are on their way. Any person remaining inside the flour mill when they arrive will be arrested."

Ruth and Charlie were suddenly at her side. "What can we do?" Charlie asked.

"Help clear the mill," Siobhán said. "But keep folks here, especially our contestants, and look to see if that solicitor is on the grounds."

"Free pastries outside!" Fia yelled into the crowd. "We'll give out free pastries outside!" To Siobhán's great relief, people were listening, and a steady crowd was now flowing out the door and onto the grounds.

When the room was finally clear, Fia returned to load pastries onto a tray.

"Thank you for that," Siobhán said. "I'll look into the coffers at the garda station and we'll pay for those pastries." For once Siobhán had no appetite for them, but the guards would be delighted.

"I appreciate that," Fia said. "Times are indeed tough."

"Did you see that solicitor anywhere outside? Mr. Bains, is it?" Siobhán asked.

"I haven't seen Mr. Bains since last night," Fia said.

"If you see him I want to talk to him straightaway."

"I'll keep an eye out."

"Thanks a million." She let Fia move past her to load up the pastries. Luckily the red velvet rope that had delineated the players' area from the crowd could now also delineate their crime scene. Siobhán had this sinking feeling that whatever this was, she had been duped, starting with the protester. She'd been too distracted by sweets. *Sugar kills.* Was some master magician at work and had she been allowing him to pull the tablecloth out from underneath them?

Ruth approached the red velvet rope and waited until Siobhán made eye contact. "We could interview folks for the camera," Ruth said. "Let them talk it out, send well-wishes for Aoife McBride's recovery." At this Ruth glanced at the closed red-velvet curtain with a look that conveyed she knew it was "curtains" for Aoife McBride. The most revered Irish baker dead under Siobhán's watch—let's face it—under her nose.

But the crowd was her biggest worry right now, and perhaps if they were being filmed, it would keep them occupied. "Do it," Siobhán said. "Let them know that the gardaí might be reviewing the tapes."

Ruth frowned. "Are you saying this wasn't a heart attack? That someone might have done something to her?"

"I didn't hear her say that," Aretta said. She turned to Siobhán. "Did you say that?"

"I did not." Siobhán and Aretta gave Ruth a hard stare.

"Understood," Ruth said. She headed outside and moments later they could hear her voice projecting across the field. "We will be interviewing anyone who wishes to speak for the camera."

The bakery was now clear of its spectators, but the contestants remained openmouthed and stunned, fidgeting alongside Fia and the judges.

"I need all of you outside as well," Siobhán said. "If you want to leave the property, we are done filming for the day."

"But we'll reconvene tomorrow?" Phil asked. "We're going on with it—even though she's gone to the great bakery in the sky?"

Everyone nudged in to hear the answer.

"I do not have any predictions at this moment," Siobhán said. "You're free the rest of the day, and at some point I promise we will come out to the Twins' Inn to keep you apprised of the situation."

Ethan, his face slightly red, raised his hand. "Yes?" Siobhán said.

"Should we save our signature desserts? Will they not be tasting them?"

Siobhán briefly closed her eyes. "It's safe to say that no one will be tasting them and no one is allowed to touch anything at their stations." Wide-eyed bakers stared at her. "That will be all for today."

"I made Pie Pie Love," Martin said as they shuffled out. "Out of *chocolate*."

Doctor Jeanie Brady was on her way. One accidental death on the property was of concern; two ramped it up to a whole new level of suspicion. And it didn't take long before Siobhán made a highly educated guess as to what had happened to Aoife McBride. Although Aoife was now on a stretcher and on her way to the Cork University Hospital morgue, her kitchen station was telling a clear tale. Next to her pie, now indented with an outline of her face, was a red electric kitchen mixer. This must have been her "secret weapon." The outlet behind her station was all black, and the cord was now frayed. Tests would need to confirm it, but it appeared that Aoife had been electrocuted. There had been so much noise during the baking—not to mention music playing over the voices, and mixers whirring. Perhaps she had screamed and no one had heard it, or, it was possible that the zap had killed her immediately. But why hadn't it taken the power out to the rest of the bakery? The question was out of Siobhán's wheelhouse. They would need to get an electrician in here right away—not only for answers, but also to make sure the rest of them were safe as they processed the scene. Siobhán's heart began pattering. "The solicitor," she said. "We need to find him right away."

"And what about Sophia Hughes?" Aretta asked, emerging from the greenroom.

Siobhán felt a jolt, as if she knew something unpleasant was coming but had yet to work out what. "What about Sophia Hughes?"

"Does she even know what happened? She ran off just before we discovered Aoife was dead."

Ran off. Before they discovered her dead . . . Did the murderer just make her getaway in plain sight? "Is there anyone hiding in the greenroom?"

Aretta shook her head. "No."

"Call the Twins' Inn and see if she's there," Siobhán said. "We need to keep all the participants close until we know what's going on."

Just then, the doors opened and four guards entered. Backup had arrived. Siobhán asked one of them to contact an electrician. She gave the others a description of the solicitor and Sophia Hughes, and was about to send them out into the crowd looking for them, when a guard interrupted.

"What is the solicitor's name?" the guard asked.

"William Bains is the name he gave us," Siobhán said. "But in full disclosure it's possible he lied from the beginning."

Aretta nudged her. "You took a photo of his identification, remember?"

"Now. I certainly did." Relief washed over her. She removed her mobile and brought up the photo she took. "He's out of Dublin and his name is . . . ." She stopped, as she stared at the name on the card, and her mouth dropped open. How had she not noticed this before? She'd been too distracted.

"What is it?" Aretta asked, nudging in.

"He gave me a fake name," Siobhán said.

"How do you know?" a nearby guard asked.

"Some people have odd names," another agreed. "What is it?"

"Go on," Aretta urged when Siobhán still did not speak.

Siobhán looked everywhere but directly in their eyes. "Donut Hole."

The guard in front of her took off his cap and scratched his head, and Aretta shocked her by letting out a nervous laugh. Everyone was going to think she was a right eejit. This made two unidentified persons, one fake ID, and a dead baking diva. Something very coordinated and sinister was going on here, and Siobhán and Aretta had been played. *Timed to perfection.* Had this been the work of one of their baking contestants?

"Perhaps we should call Detective Sergeant Flannery," a guard suggested.

"Detective Sergeant O'Sullivan-Flannery," Siobhán blurted out before she could stop herself.

The guard tipped his hat. "Apologies, Garda O'Sulli-van-Flannery."

"It's Garda O'Sullivan at work," Siobhán said, realizing her hypocrisy. She was quickly losing control of whatever was happening here. Who was she kidding. She'd been out of control the minute she accepted the assignment and began counting pies in her sleep. "Someone check with the station and see if they have the sketch of our unidentified protester ready." Anger circulated through Siobhán as she headed for the exit. "Right now we need to search the grounds. And we don't stop until we find our missing guests. Mr. Donut Hole, and Sophia Hughes."

They were no one. And they were nowhere. The guards had combed the grounds and identified everyone present, and there was no sign of William Bains aka Donut Hole, or Sophia Hughes. Luckily, minutes later, Sophia was located at the Twins' Inn. One of the twins told the guards they'd found her sobbing in the gazebo, elbow-deep into a lemon meringue pie. "She didn't even have a plate," Emma (or Eileen) told them. "She was eating it with a fork straight from the tin. She didn't even offer us a slice." Via one of the twins (whichever of them had answered the phone), Sophia assured the guards she would not leave town. She expressed horror at what had transpired after she left, and had even burst into tears. Was it genuine or all an act?

Siobhán and Aretta headed back to the greenroom to have a quiet place to contemplate their situation while they waited for Doctor Jeanie Brady to arrive. Siobhán was just passing the antique sign in the greenroom when she came to an abrupt halt. Something was off. The wooden numbers marking 365 days were gone. A single digit had replaced it. It now read: 0 DAYS SINCE THE LAST ACCIDENT.

Chapter 9

Once Sophia Hughes had been picked up from the Twins' Inn and dropped off on the bakery grounds with her cohorts, Siobhán gathered them all in the greenroom. Most of them settled onto the long pink sofa. Martin perched on one of the arms on one side and Barry on the other. Ruth, Charlie, and Fia remained standing. No one knew the solicitor's true identity, nor the protester's. The sketch had arrived, but when they were shown his likeness, heads shook all around. No one had ever seen him before. Only Sophia hesitated. She cocked her head as she studied the rendering.

"I feel like I've seen him before," she said. "But for the life of me I can't remember where." Likewise, every one of them insisted they had not changed the accident sign to 0 days.

"What about cameras?" Siobhán asked Fia, holding out hope that some had been installed. "Do you have any hidden cameras?"

Fia shook her head. "I can barely afford to keep the lights on. That's why I need this show." She bowed her head. "I know this isn't the time to think about myself. But when word gets out that Aoife McBride suffered a fatal accident here, this will be the end of my family's bakery."

"We'll see to it that it's not the end," Ronan said. "Aoife McBride wouldn't want her death to close down this bakery. She was a good sport."

Trisha Mayweather snorted. When all heads snapped her way she slapped her hand over her mouth. "Apologies," she said, then crossed herself.

"Did you disagree with Ronan's statement?" Siobhán asked.

Trisha's head bowed. "There was no love lost between my mam and Aoife McBride. But that was a long time ago." She crossed herself again. "May she rest in peace."

"I'll make sure my many followers know that I'm supporting this bakery," Philomena said, swiping through her phone. The rest of the group piled on, assuring Fia they would support the bakery with a united front.

"Thank you," Fia said, tears coming to her eyes. "I can't tell you what this means to me."

One could make an argument that Aoife's death could actually bring business to the bakery, as criminals were not the only ones to visit the scene of the crime, and no doubt this was going to receive wide press followed by lookyloos. But Fia was having a genuine moment of gratitude and Siobhán did not want her cynicism to get in the way. But she wouldn't be doing her job if she didn't at least tuck the thought away to be examined later.

"I can't believe Aoife McBride is dead," Sophia said. "I knew there was something evil about those notes."

Although Siobhán had yet to reveal that Aoife had most likely been electrocuted by her secret weapon, Siobhán had nearly forgotten about the notes. Sophia had ripped hers up in front of everyone and pieces were scattered around like confetti. Siobhán felt a squeeze of pity for the guard that would eventually be assigned to taping it back together.

"We need to see all of your secret notes and secret weapons," Siobhán said. It reminded her she had not seen a note at Aoife's station. Was it tucked into her apron pocket? If only she could look, but that would not be possible until Doctor Brady arrived. Siobhán removed the notebook and Biro she always kept in the pocket of her uniform and jotted down a reminder to ask Jeanie Brady to check Aoife's apron pocket. When she looked back up, the contestants were exchanging nervous glances. "What is it?" Siobhán asked.

"Our instructions were to destroy our notes as soon as we'd read them," Ethan said. "Otherwise we would be eliminated."

"You're joking me." Siobhán had never been so furious, mostly because she was terrified. Exactly who were they dealing with here? She felt as if she was coming in last in a race she hadn't even known she was running.

"Did everyone follow these instructions?" Aretta asked. Heads began to nod.

"I burned mine," Trisha said.

"I ate mine," Martin chimed in.

Barry Ryan raised a finger. "Drowned it."

"Gave it a soap bath," Ethan contributed.

"And you saw me rip mine up," Sophia said.

Siobhán felt her temper rise with each comment. She told herself to remain calm and turned to Aretta. "Garda Dabiri, will you ask the station to send over Biros and notebooks?"

"Right away," Aretta said.

Siobhán took a deep breath and faced the contestants. "I'm sure each of you *remembers* what your secret note said, even if you ate it, soaped it, drowned it, ripped it, or burned it. When the notebooks arrive, each of you will write down what your secret note said, sign and date it, and return it to us immediately."

The contestants looked visibly uncomfortable but no one defied the order.

"I can tell you right now what mine said," Sophia said. "*Replace your neighbor's sugar with salt. Look in your righthand-side cabinet.*" Martin, who was her neighbor on one side, swiveled his head to his creation. He jumped off the end of the sofa and took a step toward the crime scene.

"You cannot go to your station," Siobhán said. "It's a crime scene."

"You put salt in my creation or Aoife McBride's?" Martin demanded.

"What does it matter now?" Sophia said.

Martin crossed his arms and glared at her. "It matters to me."

"I'm sorry," Sophia said. "I thought it was part of the game."

It was part of a game. A secret game of murder. Siobhán had the feeling that the notes were designed to keep them all busy and distracted while Aoife McBride was being electrocuted. *Diabolical.*

"That's why you needed that favor," Martin said, still focused on Sophia and what he obviously perceived as her betrayal.

"What favor is that?" Siobhán asked.

"During our bake time, Sophia opened my curtain and said she couldn't get the lid off a jam jar. I found it odd." Before Siobhán could stop him, Martin strode out of the room and defied her orders by stalking over to his creation. He stuck his finger in it.

"Stop!" Siobhán said. "Don't." Siobhán rushed over,

signaling nearby guards to join her. But Martin stuck his finger in his mouth before they could put hands on him.

He whirled around to face the greenroom. "Salt!"

Sophia turned beet red. "You should have tasted it as you were baking."

Martin glared at her. "Obviously I tasted it as I was baking and I never tasted salt, which meant you snuck it in there after I tasted it!"

"I'm sorry you have such bad timing," Sophia said. "But can you really blame me?"

"I can and I do!" Martin said.

"You cannot be in here," Siobhán said, taking him by the arm. "Everyone stay in the greenroom or I will start making arrests."

The guards who joined Siobhán hauled Martin Murphy out of the crime scene and kept him by the door. Siobhán turned to a second pair of guards. "I want crime scene tape all over the front of the bakery. I want the front entrance closed." She turned to find Fia huddling in the corner. "I'm assuming there's another entrance we can use to get into the bakery?"

Fia nodded. "There is a door off of the event space in the back. I haven't used it in ages, but I can open it for you, and I see no reason why we couldn't use it." She paused. "In fact, it's a little damp but it is a large room. We could move the baking show into the event space."

"One step at a time. Show this guard the back entrance." Siobhán gestured to a guard waiting nearby. "The rest of you get that crime scene tape up. If anyone disturbs the barrier, or their baked-goods, again, there will be severe consequences." She stared at Martin. "You go out to the ambulance and tell the paramedics you may have ingested poison."

"What?" For the first time Martin Murphy's confidence faltered.

"We do not know what or who we're dealing with here," Siobhán said. "I will not have another death on my hands."

"I feel fine. It was just salt." He put his hand on his throat as if checking for swelling. Fia hurried over and shoved a glass of water at him. He stared at it for a moment, then guzzled it down.

"Paramedics," Siobhán said. "Now."

"Fine." He whirled around and headed for the main doors, then stopped. "Am I allowed to use the front entrance?"

"Go ahead. But when you return, everyone will have to use the back entrance from now on. This one will be sealed off."

"I didn't sign up for this," Martin said as he headed for the doors. "Salt in my masterpiece!"

A thick silence hovered over the remaining group as they watched Martin leave. "I'm sorry. I'm sorry," Sophia said. "I thought this was a *game*."

"It's not your fault," Ronan said. "You were all instructed to do as your note said."

"Once we collect all of your written responses, I'm sure we'll see you weren't the only one who sabotaged another player," Siobhán said. The guilty looks on the contestants' faces and brooding silence as they took this in, proved her assertion was correct.

"What if one of them was told to sabotage Aoife McBride?" Phil asked. "I assume they'd be terrified to admit it."

"We will find out one way or another, I assure you," Siobhán said. "If you lie about your note, that is what will make you look guilty." Siobhán turned to Aretta. "Can you talk to the station and get an ETA on our electrician?"

"Absolutely," Aretta said. "I just got a text that guards

are about to pull up with the notebooks and Biros. I'll check on it."

"That would be grand," Siobhán said. Aretta headed off.

Siobhán turned to the group. "This may have started as a game, but this is not a game any longer," she said. "Aoife is dead, the solicitor who supplied you with notes and 'secret weapons' gave us a fake identity and has subsequently disappeared, and the protester has yet to be identified."

"Are you saying the protester's death and Aoife's death may have been foul play?" Ronan asked, clearly horrified.

"We don't know, but I'm not ruling anything out," Siobhán said. "I want all of you to be on high alert."

Ruth elbowed Charlie. "Start filming." Charlie raised his camera and aimed it at Siobhán.

"What are you doing?" Siobhán asked. She didn't like staring into the wide-eyed lens.

"You said to get everyone on film," Ruth said. "We're filming."

"I wasn't including the guards."

"If you want access to all my other footage, you're going to have to be included," Ruth insisted, gesturing at Charlie to start filming every time he tilted the recorder down.

Pick your battles. Siobhán did not want to engage in a petty argument in front of the people she needed to work with her. "None of the footage of guards is allowed to go public without my approval."

Ruth chewed on this for a moment, then nodded. "I can agree to that."

Aretta returned with the notebooks and Biros. She passed them out to all the bakers. "I'm going to let you take a break, but first you will write down the message that was on your secret note, verbatim. Sign and date them, then return them to me." The notebooks did nothing to ease the growing tension. "After you turn in your statements, you're free for the rest of the day."

"And what about tomorrow?" Barry asked. "Do we pack up and go home?"

"We cannot make any decisions on how or if this baking show proceeds until after we've had visits from electricians and the state pathologist. We will officially be interviewing all of you, collecting statements most likely tomorrow. No one is free to leave Kilbane unless it's been approved by us. Do not discuss this case even amongst yourselves. And be . . . careful. If anyone approaches you or anything at all doesn't feel right—listen to that little voice and call me ASAP." Siobhán passed around her calling card and gave them all one last warning. "Until we know what's going on here, I'd advise you to do nothing and trust no one."

Chapter 10

"She took a zap, alright." Doctor Jeanie Brady crouched near the body, and then the blackened outlet. "From the burn marks on the poor dear, it looks as if the current traveled through her right hand and out the other hand."

Siobhán cringed. *Horrible.* "Enough of a jolt to cause death?"

Jeanie nodded. "If it passed through her heart first, I'm afraid so." Jeanie went down to the floor and laid her hands on the stone. "It's damp," she said. She followed the trail to the large commercial refrigerator. It happened to be set up directly behind Aoife's station. She approached the fridge, knelt and felt around the base. "It's had time to dry, but it looks as if this refrigerator may have leaked." She returned to Aoife's station. "Ms. McBride plugs in her mixer, but unbeknownst to her there's water leaking from the refrigerator." Jeanie approached the outlet. The circuit was now dead, turned off by electricians. Jeanie paced out the number of steps from the outlet to Aoife's station. "She plugs it in and she's zapped. She has enough time to stumble a few feet, most likely trying to hold on to the counter, but it's too late for her poor heart." Jeanie and Siobhán stared at the crushed pie on the counter.

"Poor chicken," Siobhán said. They crossed themselves.

"This must be a dedicated circuit," Jeanie said, pointing to the outlet. "Or everyone else would have experienced a shock as well." She stood and scanned the room for additional outlets.

"Every station has an outlet," Siobhán said. One by one they checked them. They were pristine.

Jeanie Brady approached the other commercial fridge on the opposite side of the room. She felt around the base. "Dry."

"We need a professional to examine the leaking fridge," Siobhán said. Another task that would take time. Time in which a killer could get away. "Are you able to say whether or not this was accidental?"

"The appliance was brand new and the cord frayed during the incident. My guess is that the fault lay in the electrical panel, or perhaps there was some kind of conductor—standing water on the floor near the outlet, or such, and so I cannot rule out the possibility that this was nothing more than a freak accident." Jeanie sighed. "Sadly these things happen every day."

"That is true." Siobhán had once heard of a woman killed when a gargoyle fell off the top of an old building just as she was walking by. It hit her on the head and that was it—lights out. No one would have ever imagined leaving this world that way. Freak accidents happened every day. Then again, it took a human being to change the accident sign to 0—but that alone did not make one a murderer.

"Homicide is a possibility but it will be difficult to prove," Jeanie said. "In a building this age, it's not out of the question that wiring could be faulty. And the commercial fridge is not brand-new. It's not uncommon to see them leak. On the other hand, if this bakery is in compliance with the health codes she should have had them regularly checked. My impression of Fia O'Farrell is that despite the age of the mill she is diligent about keeping her equipment in tip-top shape. We'll send the kitchen mixer to an expert; if someone deliberately tampered with it, maybe there will be evidence of that, but as a layman, I'm not sure how you prove if this was accidental or if someone tampered with any of this equipment."

"The kitchen mixer is brand-new," Siobhán repeated.

"It's a good point," Jeanie said. "And anyone is capable of clogging a fridge line."

"If this was purposeful, the killer would have used the easiest and quickest method," Siobhán said.

"True. They did not have much time."

"When Aoife was killed they did not have much time. But if it's foul play, and my gut says it is—now we have to prove it." Now time was on the killer's side. Siobhán stared at the section of the floor underneath the outlet. It was a short distance and a straight line from there to the commercial fridge. "Some milk spilled earlier today but they mopped it up right away."

"That's not it then," Jeanie said. "There is definitely a leak coming from the refrigerator."

Frustration thrummed in Siobhán. "If this was foul play, the killer must have calculated how difficult this would be to prove."

"I wish I could say our task ahead was going to be easy and quick," Jeanie said. "As far as our unidentified protester is concerned, we are still waiting for results on the powder. Unless we discover he had a known allergy to a benign substance, it's likely to be some kind of poison that killed him. If I am able to rule his death a homicide—it would be more plausible that Ms. McBride was murdered as well."

"Not only that," Siobhán said. "But Aoife McBride said she bought the powder at a chemist in town. At first I was wondering if it might have been tampered with anonymously and we instructed the chemist to pull all remaining powder from the shelf."

"Smart." Jeanie Brady made a note. "If it's poison you'll hear from me straightaway so you can pick up the remaining product. Given that the powder is no doubt at chemists all over Ireland, I'm going to try to rush the results."

"The chemist has already reported the powder to . . . well, whomever chemists report to, so if it was random, let's hope they recalled them all in time."

"But you don't think it was random, do you?"

Siobhán smiled. Jeanie Brady knew her too well. "I do not . . . Someone assumed Aoife McBride would be the first to use that powder. I think it's too much of a coincidence that a second freak accident killed her."

Jeanie tapped her chin with her index finger. "You're saying, when the powder didn't do the job, it forced the killer to find another way."

"Correct," Siobhán said. "That's where the solicitor comes in. Wheeling his trolley full of weapons. They were weapons. At least one of them was." This was murder. And the poor protester was simply in the wrong place at the wrong time. And when the wrong victim went down, the killer was forced to strike again. Siobhán began to pace. "Right in front of our faces."

"Pardon?" Jeanie Brady said.

Siobhán explained how no one had been expecting Mr. Donut Hole to arrive with secret notes and secret weapons. How the players had been instructed to destroy their secret notes, and how "Mr. Donut Hole" had waited until Siobhán was gone before he returned and covered each kitchen station with red velvet curtains. Unraveling the ways in which this killer had pulled off a murder right in front of Siobhán was infuriating. The nerve. This was no ordinary killer. This was someone in full control, even cocky. The thought of the murderer enjoying the trick he or she had just pulled off, watching the guards flounder, was getting her blood pressure up. Finding this solicitor would be their top priority. "Is he the murderer, or was he a pawn, following directions?"

Jeanie listened intently, then gave it some thought. "If I may play devil's advocate?"

Siobhán greatly admired Doctor Brady, and she had learned a lot working with her. "I would expect no less."

"Is it not also a strange coincidence that Aoife McBride just happened to use the powder she purchased for herself on a total stranger?"

Siobhán took a moment to think about it. "I see your point. But it did happen. I was standing right there."

"It happened, but did it happen for the reasons you think?"

Jeanie Brady was a fantastic state pathologist, but she also would have made a good detective. "Are you say-ing—Aoife McBride suspected that poison might be in the powder and she tested it out on the protester?"

Jeanie sighed. "It sounds ludicrous when I hear it out loud."

"Welcome to my world," Siobhán said. Siobhán tried to recall every detail of her brief meeting with Aoife McBride. She had seemed jittery and flighty. But she'd also seemed genuinely surprised that the protester had been taken away in an ambulance. And even after she was told about the incident she did not appear to associate the tragic event with her face powder. Siobhán was inclined to believe her reaction was truthful.

"I'm ready to have the body removed and let the tech team do their thing," Jeanie said. They stepped out of the way as coroners arrived with the stretcher and the tech team waited behind them to finish processing any evidence. Jeanie spoke with them, giving them all the information she had on the leaking fridge, outlet, and mixer. Everything would be carefully examined and processed.

"Follow me outside for a bit of fresh air before I head off to the morgue?" Jeanie asked.

"Brilliant." They stepped outside the bakery. The skies were gray but the air was fresh and mild. "Fancy a bit of a walk?" Siobhán asked.

"Absolutely," Jeanie said. "I take advantage of any time I get in daylight."

Siobhán took her around to the side of the mill and pointed out the cast-iron waterwheel. "It would be grand if Fia could make enough money to get her running again."

"The wheel is a she, is it?" Jeanie asked in a playful tone.

"It has one job to do and it refuses to do it," Siobhán said. "Maybe it is a 'he' indeed."

Jeanie laughed. "I wish that handsome husband of yours was here," she said. "He'd be giving you one of his looks."

Siobhán laughed. "To be honest, I wish he was here too. I feel as if we need all the help we can get with this case."

"You're going to have a lot of eyes on you," Jeanie said. "The death of Aoife McBride will capture attention far outside of Kilbane."

"I've no doubt they'll bring Macdara in on the case," Siobhán said. "Lucky for us, we make a good team."

"Are you thinking that the killer is one of her fellow bakers?" Jeanie asked.

"There's also the judges, Fia O'Farrell, and a director and cameraman," Siobhán said. "But Fia O'Farrell stood to gain the most from having Aoife McBride *alive*. She needed this baking show. In addition, she's been worried that a death on her premises will be the end of her business, so I can't see her murdering the golden goose. The director and cameraman are not involved in the baking world, so I am inclined to think it's one of the seven suspects remaining." The five remaining contestants and the pair of judges.

"Good luck to you, pet," Jeanie Brady said. "I must admit, I don't envy the tasks ahead of you."

Siobhán feasted her eyes on a hill in the distance. "If we close down the show, then we might be letting our killer get away."

Jeanie nodded. "But if you keep it open, he or she may kill again."

There it was again, that double-edged sword with the sharp part aimed directly at her. It was a heavy burden, knowing one's decision could be a matter of life or death. "I'm going to have to decide whether or not this baking show will continue. If we do continue, we'll bring in extra guards to do safety checks. And we would rip down all those velvet curtains." They would also have to order brand-new stations and set them up in the event space Fia mentioned.

"I have a lot of work to do," Jeanie said. "My bag is still inside." The pair walked back to the bakery and Jeanie retrieved her bag. As she was leaving she stopped and eyed the empty pastry cases. "Where did they all go?"

"The desserts?" Siobhán was surprised to hear Jeanie

mention it; she'd lost weight and had been on a health kick ever since. "I ate them all." Siobhán said it with a straight face, that is until she saw Jeanie Brady's horrified expression, and then she laughed loud and hard. "I only ate a dozen or so," Siobhán said. "We sent some to the station, and Fia and the crew have started moving all the bits they need into the large room where they used to hold wedding receptions and whatnot. That's where they're hoping we will continue the baking show."

"Just as well," Jeanie said with a sigh as she tore her eyes away from the empty pastry cases. "Just as well."

"We can pop over to the next room if you'd at least like to have a look at them," Siobhán said, treading lightly. She didn't want to be a saboteur. On the other hand, she didn't want to *not* offer Jeanie a pastry if she wanted one.

Jeanie put her hands over her ears. "Hear no evil." She headed for the exit, then stopped. "Ms. McBride had her identification in her apron pocket."

"Her motor license?" Siobhán asked.

"Yes," Jeanie said, pondering it. "Do you find that odd?"

"I can ask Fia if they were instructed to bring their ID," Siobhán said.

Jeanie nodded. "Is her handbag here or at the inn?"

"I can have the greenroom searched," Siobhán said. "But that reminds me. Did you find any sort of note in her pocket?" Jeanie shook her head. "They all received secret notes." Had she followed instructions and destroyed hers?

"Perhaps it's in our missing handbag," Jeanie said.

"We'll be sending guards over to the Twins' Inn to check Aoife McBride's room, but we'll have to wait on a judge's order."

Jeanie said her goodbyes just as Siobhán received a text. It was from Macdara. He was on his way back to Kilbane

and would, as predicted, be heading the case. In the meantime, Siobhán and Aretta were cleared to start processing
the remainder of the kitchen stations. Electricians would
be arriving to check out the event space where, if it was
decided the show must go on, new stations and fridges
would be delivered. They had quite a challenge of their
own ahead of them, and Siobhán knew it would be anything but a piece of cake.

Chapter 11

"Station one," Aretta called out. "Ethan Brown." Siobhán and Aretta stood in front of Ethan's Eiffel Tart, admiring the impressive structure. Forensics had finished processing Aoife McBride's station and they were cleared to begin their work. They were gloved and suited up, and intended on treating each station like a possible crime scene. Ethan's tower may have been pristine, but his station looked like the aftermath of a child's birthday party. Every inch was covered in something sticky or white, dirty bowls were piled in a corner, spatulas and spoons lay sideways where they were dropped. Ethan Brown may have had French training but he could learn a little bit about sparking joy. *Messy.* Having helped run her family bistro most of her life, Siobhán had learned that you clean as you go, or you'd be faced with hours of wash-up after a shift. She was suddenly grateful for her mam's sage advice and teachings. Whenever she slid something into the cooker, she would pivot to cleaning up the mess she just made. Granted, this had been the first challenge and, other than Siobhán, no one was going to be judging the lad on his cleanliness.

"Read me his secret note," Siobhán said.

" *'Time is of the essence. Trisha Mayweather does not work well under pressure. Switch her timer. Ten minutes less should do it.'* "

"And his secret weapon?" Siobhán asked, although she had already guessed.

"A timer."

"I wonder if he followed through with it," Siobhán said.

"We only asked them to write down their secret message and secret weapon," Aretta said. "We forgot to ask them to write down whether or not they followed through with it."

"Given this is a competition and no one but the real killer would have suspected their actions would end in someone's death—I'm going to assume they all followed the instructions. But you're right—we need to ask them all face-to-face." Siobhán crossed to Trisha's station, where she found a red timer. Each station had been given a timer in a different color. She crossed back to Ethan's station. A blue timer sat on the counter. She poked around in the cabinets until she found what she was looking for: Stuffed under a spare apron in the back of the counter was a red timer.

"What's that?" Aretta asked.

"I'm guessing he did follow the instructions and this is Trisha's original timer. The one he switched must have been altered to shorten her time, and amp up her stress."

"Someone put a lot of thought into this," Aretta observed.

"And money." Siobhán picked up the spare apron that had been hiding the duplicate timer, and mainly out of habit from raising her younger siblings, she checked the pocket. There was something in there. Siobhán pulled out a yellowed and fragile piece of paper. It looked ancient. On it was a handwritten recipe penned in black ink.

"What beautiful handwriting," Aretta said.

"Indeed." It was in cursive but the letters so perfectly formed that it was as easy to read as print. *Gorgeous*. But the paper itself was not in good condition. It was marred by sticky spots and smudges. It appeared to have been ripped from a small notebook. There was even a thumbprint visible in the corner. The title read: *Porter Cake*.

Underneath it in slightly different handwriting was a note: *Need a Twist—A.M.* "A handwritten recipe," Siobhán said. "With an added note as if the recipe wasn't quite finished."

"A baker's note," Aretta said. "It looks like it's been in Ethan's family for a long time."

"Or someone's family." Siobhán pointed out the initials.

Aretta's eyes widened. "Are you saying that stands for Aoife McBride?"

"That is definitely something we'll need to find out," Siobhán said. "And if it is her recipe, I have a feeling she didn't intend it to be in one of her competitors' hands. We need to put this in an evidence bag."

"I don't understand," Aretta said. "Did everyone have a spare apron?"

"Can you do a quick check of everyone's cabinet?"

Aretta nodded and one by one began checking them. "They all have a spare apron, but all the pockets are empty."

Siobhán examined the recipe. There was a faint indentation of a circle imprinted on it. She picked up the spare timer in Ethan's cabinet, the one she presumed was Trisha's original. "What if—when Ethan took Trisha Mayweather's timer, the recipe was stuck to the bottom?" Siobhán said.

"Does that mean Trisha Mayweather stole a recipe from Aoife McBride?" Aretta asked.

"Stole—or maybe it was *her* secret weapon?"

"A lot of maybes."

Siobhán nodded. That was the burden of detective work. One had to examine any number of possibilities. "Let's go with our theory that this recipe was stuck to the bottom of Trisha's timer. Ethan must have glanced at it, realized what it was, and stuffed it in the apron pocket."

Aretta considered this. "It seems Mr. Ethan Brown forgot to mention it."

"It does indeed." It was also possible that the recipe had been sitting on Ethan's station. Perhaps when he grabbed Trisha's timer, he placed it on his own messy counter. But when he went to shove it in the cabinet, the recipe was stuck to the bottom. Siobhán shared her thought with Aretta.

"That would explain why he didn't mention it," Aretta said. "He must have noticed it as he was putting the timer away, and all he had time to do was shove it in the pocket of the spare apron and pray no one would be the wiser."

Siobhán went from being proud of them for sussing out the possibilities to wondering if it mattered at all. "Even if Ethan Brown did steal a recipe from Aoife McBride—is that a motive for murder?"

Aretta was used to the back-and-forth process of endless what-ifs, and played along. "Perhaps Aoife McBride found out he stole a recipe and threatened to have him eliminated from the competition?"

"That is a stronger motive," Siobhán said. Not only would Ethan be eliminated from the competition if it had been proven he'd stolen a recipe from another player (let alone Aoife McBride); given the televised nature of the event, the media attention would have been immediate. It's not just the twenty-thousand-euro prize he would have stood to lose, it was his entire reputation and therefore career. Thank goodness she checked the pocket of his apron. Siobhán was suddenly thankful for all her siblings and their tendency to leave things in their pockets. "And then we closed off the entire area as a crime scene so he didn't have time to return for it," Siobhán continued. If this was indeed an original recipe by Aoife McBride, how did Ethan or Trisha acquire it?

Was porter cake one of the upcoming challenges? If this recipe had been stolen from Aoife McBride, how was it done? The paper on which it was written showed its age. Had Ethan or Trisha purchased it on some kind of recipe black market? Snuck into Aoife McBride's room at the inn? Perhaps her handbag wasn't just missing, perhaps the killer had stolen it. Or was Siobhán just howling into the wind? "Maybe we can get approval to look into recent financial transactions of both Ethan Brown and Trisha Mayweather," Siobhán said. "But first we'd have to prove that that is indeed an original Aoife McBride recipe. Even then we'd need more evidence to get approval to snoop into their finances."

"Besides ingredients and baking supplies, I don't see anything else," Aretta said. Siobhán nodded, but before moving on to station two, she opened the cooker. Empty. "Looking for runaway tarts?" Aretta teased.

"Can't hurt to look." Last, Siobhán removed a chunk of tart from Ethan's creation and plopped it into an evidence bag. There was a chance that headquarters wasn't going to be thrilled testing every single baked good for poison, but

Siobhán knew the only way she was going to catch this particular killer was to turn over every stone. Or tart. They moved on to station two.

Unlike Ethan's messy station, Trisha's was pristine. Siobhán took a moment to take in Trisha's seven-layer wedding cake, with all the filling. She bent down to examine the timer. Sure enough, she could see sticky splotches and flour on the sides. "It certainly looks like Ethan switched the timers," Siobhán said. "It's the only thing at Trisha's station that isn't wiped down." Did Trisha not notice the white smudges on the timer once it was switched? Siobhán re-examined the red timer they'd found stuffed in Ethan's station. "This one is messy too. I'm guessing Ethan set it on his own messy counter before putting it away. And that means . . ."

"The recipe was in Ethan's possession," Aretta said. "It too has smudges."

"Exactly. Had this recipe been with Trisha, I'd expect to see the ring from when Ethan placed the timer on it; however, I wouldn't expect to see smudges all over it."

"Couldn't he have smudged it *after* he accidentally ferried it over to his station on the bottom of the timer?" Aretta pointed out.

"Yes, that's possible too." They were going in circles on this one.

"Do you think she noticed the switch?" Aretta asked.

"Given red is such a dominant color, and if she suddenly thought she had a ten-minute deficit and started to panic, it could explain why she didn't notice it."

Aretta stared at the towering cake. "This was such an ambitious bake."

"And she pulled it off," Siobhán said. "At least it presents beautifully."

"Even if she did notice the timer switch she wouldn't have had time to deal with it," Aretta said.

"And if Ethan was quick about it, which, given the smudges, it looks like he was, it's possible it escaped her attention."

Aretta took a moment to glance between the stations. There was only a few feet between each of them. "Given all the stations were hidden behind curtains, how do you think he managed the switch?"

"He could have switched it when she made a trip to the fridge." The closest refrigerator to Trisha was the one located a few feet behind Ethan's station, although players were free to use either one. "With all these fillings Trisha was preparing for her cake, she would have needed to make several trips, giving Ethan ample opportunity to sneak in and replace the timer when her back was turned."

"It's as if someone knew he would have time to do it," Aretta said.

Someone knew absolutely everything. "We need to find that lying solicitor," Siobhán said. "His client—the sponsor—is our killer."

"And they might be one and the same," Aretta noted.

"That is a possibility," Siobhán said. "The sooner we identify him, the better." Unfortunately, Siobhán was starting to think everything about the man was made up, including that he was a solicitor. Guards were working on tracking him down, but she had a feeling someone had covered his tracks very well.

"Even if our solicitor is not the killer, he certainly knows who hired him," Aretta said.

"Yes," Siobhán agreed. "The mysterious benefactor." This entire baking show had been planned to commit a murder in full view of the public eye. Given that was such a specific and elaborate plan, there had to be a compelling reason.

"Perhaps our mystery man is in the wind because he's afraid he's next?"

"And don't forget our protester," Siobhán said. "I still haven't figured out if he was a part of the plan or an unhappy surprise."

"This one is a head scratcher," Aretta said.

Indeed. "What does Trisha's secret note say?" Siobhán asked. Aretta read it to herself and frowned. Siobhán nudged in. "What?"

" '*Did you forget what Aoife McBride did to your mother?*' "

"Interesting," Siobhán said. She thought back to when the bakers were first introduced. There had been something mentioned about Trisha's mother. "Mary Mayweather." She'd made a remark insulting Aoife McBride's icing—how fresh cream was a better choice. But in that case, Mary Mayweather was insulting Aoife McBride. What did the note mean? Did Aoife retaliate in some way? If so, Trisha Mayweather conveniently decided not to mention it.

"Ethan received a direct suggestion to harm Trisha by replacing her timer," Siobhán said. "But Trisha only received a vague prompting?" This was maddening. If Trisha did not work well under pressure, which is what the secret note to Ethan suggested, then why did the writer of the note think Trisha would stop her baking just to come up with some "revenge" against Aoife McBride for whatever this past incident was between herself and Mary Mayweather? "If Trisha retaliated in some way she would have had to stop baking and figure out how to sneak all the way over to Aoife's station."

"Or," Aretta said, as she contemplated it, "she snuck

over and tampered with the refrigerator behind Aoife's station."

"I think it's plausible that any one of them could have done that," Siobhán said. "But if Trisha already thought she was ten minutes behind, and the note is terribly vague about exactly what she should do—I don't see how she had time to make this elaborate layer cake and sabotage Aoife McBride."

"I see your point."

Siobhán pinched the bridge of her nose. She needed headache tablets for this one. "What was her secret weapon?"

Aretta glanced at the sheet. Her eyebrows shot up in surprise. "You're not going to believe this."

"You'd be shocked at what I'd believe." It came with the job.

"A handwritten recipe by Aoife McBride for porter cake."

"What?" Siobhán was used to the unexpected, but this one had her thrown. She was so sure the recipe had been stolen. It was another humbling lesson of police work. Playing what-if was grand as long as one remained open and didn't manipulate the evidence to fit his or her theory. Given that, how did this new piece of information change the story? "This means either the recipe was already stuck to the bottom of Trisha's timer when Ethan switched them, and when he noticed it he simply shoved it in the apron pocket of the spare in his cabinet . . ."

"Or Ethan nicked the recipe when he switched the timer?" Aretta filled in.

"Those seem to be the options," Siobhán agreed.

"Trisha Mayweather did not mention anything about losing her secret weapon," Aretta pointed out.

Siobhán nodded. Perhaps that was because, unless

Trisha Mayweather planned on making porter cake later in the competition, it was not much of a secret weapon. But at this point of the game none of the players could grumble because they had no idea what the others had received. Aoife McBride had chosen first. It couldn't have been dumb luck that Aoife McBride chose the one item that would kill her, could it? If that was the case then this wasn't a murder at all, it was a freak accident. It meant that any baker who chose the mixer would have been electrocuted by this killer. If not for the protester's death it was possible that the killer didn't care who his or her victim was—perhaps he or she even enjoyed the randomness of killing the unlucky sap who chose that secret weapon. But when you factored in the face powder, it pointed to Aoife McBride as the target. So if Aoife McBride was the intended victim, as Siobhán assumed, how had the killer ensured that she was the one who chose the kitchen mixer?

"Who knew baking would be so complicated," Siobhán said with a sigh. Ethan Brown had some explaining to do, and depending on his answers so did Trisha Mayweather. Siobhán put a star and a little note next to their names. "Despite all the smoke and mirrors the killer has erected, murder, at its heart, is very basic. There are only so many motives. Someone is going to an extreme here. Who among the suspects had the biggest motive to kill Aoife McBride?"

Aretta shook her head. "I haven't the faintest idea."

"Neither do I," Siobhán said. "Crime of passion. Greed. Revenge. All of our players are competitive, that's a given, but all but Sophia Hughes already enjoyed a modest amount of success with baking. At her age I would guess that twenty thousand euro is quite a large sum of money. Otherwise— is the prize money enough to entice someone to kill off the competition?"

"It seems we'd benefit by looking into all of their finances," Aretta said. She paused, twirling her Biro as if debating whether or not to say something.

"Go on," Siobhán urged.

Aretta's Biro stilled. "Has it occurred to you that someone might not tell the truth about their secret note?"

"I'm counting on it," Siobhán said. "I'm counting on at least one of them to lie."

Chapter 12

As they moved on to Barry Ryan's station, Siobhán made a note that she would do an internet search on any rivalry between Trisha Mayweather's mother and Aoife McBride. But their best chance at cracking this, or at least putting a little crack in the case, was during their interviews. Would Ethan confess to stealing Trisha's recipe? Did Trisha realize the recipe may have been written by Aoife McBride? Would Trisha confess what Aoife had supposedly done to her mother? And if Trisha had retaliated against Aoife during this competition, why hadn't Trisha mentioned it?

"The judges made a point of stirring up trouble between Aoife McBride and all of the contestants," Siobhán said. "Trisha's note is yet another layer of the same tactic."

"Much like a layer cake," Aretta said. "Speaking of which—I forgot to get a sample." She returned to Trisha's station with an evidence bag, cut a small slice from the top tier, and dropped a melting slice of cake into the bag. She glanced at the rest of the layers. "Do I need to remove a slice off of each layer?"

"Not at this point. But we can freeze the rest of the cake

and if anything nefarious is found in any of the samples then we can always lop off another slice."

"Someone really wanted that poor woman dead," Aretta said as she sealed the bag. "Would we be testing all of these desserts if not for the protester being potentially poisoned?"

"Probably not," Siobhán said. "But it's better than a half-baked approach." Aretta laughed, and Siobhán enjoyed the moment of levity before turning back to Barry Ryan's station. A large cake, shaped like a sponge, took over the counter. The texture looked so real that Siobhán wished she could remove her gloves and squeeze it.

"Given that they were tasked with making their signature dish, I suppose with his nickname he had no choice but to make this," Aretta said. "But it doesn't look very appetizing."

"I know," Siobhán said. "But I want one this size to scrub me house down." Siobhán paused. "Not to mention me brothers."

Aretta threw her head back and laughed. There was no better sound in the world than that of laughter. Even during such troubling times, or maybe because of such troubling times. They soon settled down and went back to staring at the giant sponge cake. A bottle of Irish whiskey sat on the counter next to mixing bowls. Siobhán bet the whiskey-laced icing was delicious. Or used to be. "Note and weapon?"

Aretta had anticipated the question. "*Use the refrigerator behind Ethan. Open the one behind Aoife a crack. It's getting too hot in here.*"

Siobhán shook her head, disgusted that all of the players took these notes as part of a game. She supposed that was due to the plethora of survival games flooding the telly. But did none of them question it at all, other than Sophia? Didn't they realize this was extreme for an Irish baking show?

"He says he didn't do it," Aretta said, as if reading her mind.

"May I see?" Aretta handed her the sheet. *I did not use the fridge behind Ethan, nor did I prop open the fridge behind Aoife!* "Good for him," Siobhán said. "A man with a conscience." Unless of course, he was a liar and a killer . . .

She scanned down to see his secret weapon. It was the bottle of Irish whiskey. He had added another note: *I hadn't planned on making a whiskey-laced icing, but it was brilliant. I've no doubt mine would have won the first round.*

"Confident, isn't he?" Aretta said.

"He's either a stand-up guy, or his story is like a sponge," Siobhán said.

Aretta raised an eyebrow. "Squishy?"

"And full of holes."

Martin Murphy's station was next. Both Siobhán and Aretta stared at his sculpture: Pie Pie Love made out of chocolate. It was truly a work of art. "I don't know how he did this in four hours," Siobhán said. "He must have practiced it loads at home."

"Chocolate practice," Aretta said. "That sounds like the perfect job for Siobhán O'Sullivan."

Siobhán laughed. "I'd eat more than I'd create," she said. "I'd be booted out of the competition straightaway."

"I can imagine he was furious at Sophia," Aretta said. "Salt in a structure this grand?"

"Not to mention the note to mess with it was given to the youngest, most naive contestant," Siobhán mused. "Perhaps that was deliberate." She paused for a second, knowing what Macdara would say if he was here: *C'mere to me. Say more about that.* "Imagine if Barry Ryan had sabotaged Martin Murphy's sculpture. Perhaps it would have come to fisticuffs."

"You're saying our killer wanted to prevent a violent reaction?" Aretta tilted her head. "A murderer with a conscience?"

"That does sound ludicrous." But Siobhán couldn't help but feel everything this "puppeteer" was doing behind the curtains had a purpose. Including who received which note. "Let's circle back to that sometime," Siobhán said. "Until a case is solved, everything is possible."

Aretta bend her head and wrote in her notebook. "Even if it's not plausible?"

"Sure, lookit. I'd prefer both, but right now I'll take what I can get." Enough admiring the salted chocolate replica of the mill. Siobhán moved around to examine Martin's station. His was a combination of messy and neat, bowls that needed washing stacked in the sink, spatulas and spoons hanging out on the righthand side, and chocolate smears and the molds he used to form the chocolate in the center. It took a moment to see it, but in the middle of the flour still visible on the counter, someone had drawn a heart.

"A crime of passion?" Aretta quipped when Siobhán pointed it out.

"I didn't peg Martin as the heart-drawing type," Siobhán said.

"Perhaps it was Sophia," Aretta said. "Apologizing in advance for sabotaging his creation?"

"Now that is entirely plausible," Siobhán agreed. She made a note to ask Sophia about it. "Let's hear his secret note."

" '*The ginger lass next to you may be young and pretty, but wanna bet she won't notice if you nudge the heat up on her cooker . . .*' "

"That's why her pan was blackened," Siobhán said. "And yet when she confessed to sabotaging Martin, he certainly didn't admit to his own wrongdoing."

Siobhán thought over all the notes. Ethan was instructed to mess with Trisha. Trisha's instruction seemed to be a reference to a past grudge, but there was no direct message on how to retaliate. Barry's instruction was quite mild—even if he had cracked open a refrigerator door, surely someone would have come along and closed it. But turning up the heat on one's cooker was certainly playing extremely dirty, not to mention dangerous. And had Sophia been paying attention, there was a good chance she would have noticed that the dial had been cranked up. But the time pressure and stress of the competition had them all befuddled, and the killer had been counting on that. Siobhán figured the main reason for the notes was to keep everyone distracted while the killer was arranging the attack.

"I bet Sophia Hughes would have drawn a dagger in that heart had she known Martin was turning up the heat on her cooker," Aretta said.

Siobhán agreed. She made a note to ask both Sophia and Martin about the heart and snapped a photo with her mobile phone. "What about his secret weapon?"

"Specialty chocolates," Aretta said.

"Does he elaborate?" If Siobhán could do her job and get a hot tip on chocolates, she saw no harm in it.

"He did not."

Siobhán made a note by his name. *Did not divulge name of specialty chocolates. Selfish.* She'd have to use her interrogation skills and get it out of him yet.

Aretta stood over his sculpture with a large knife. "I hate to do this."

"I know," Siobhán said. "Might as well just chop off the wheel, it doesn't work anyway."

Aretta took the knife to the wheel, and bagged it. They moved on to Sophia's station. The blackened pan stared at them from the counter. Although the cooker had long since been turned off, to create this kind of disaster the dial must have been cranked all the way up. "We're lucky she didn't start a fire," Siobhán said.

"We already know what her secret note read," Aretta said. "Although putting salt in chocolate is less damaging than this."

Siobhán surveyed the area and soon spotted a large container of Morton Salt. "It depends on how much salt," Siobhán said. "But I agree—a touch of sea salt in chocolate is heavenly, but she used Morton's. And her weapon was a new pan." Aretta pointed to the blackened heap on the counter. "Not much of a weapon."

Siobhán sighed. "I don't think there's even any use trying to test her dessert." She edged over to Aoife's station. "Unless we count Trisha Mayweather, nobody admitted to having a note that instructed them to sabotage Aoife McBride." She glanced at the blackened outlet, and the space where the mixer once stood. The Technical Bureau secured the outlet, but they were waiting on the electrician. Although there were plenty they could call out at a moment's notice, the expert needed to be approved and documented by An Garda Síochaná, so it was taking some time. He or she would also start their examination with the mixer itself, which had been sent to the evidence room at the station.

A thought dawned on Siobhán as she stared at the kitchen mixer and thought about those secret messages. "They were instructed to open their notes first," Siobhán said. "The notes also included numbers. The order in which they would pick their secret weapons."

"Aoife was number one," Aretta said.

"Look at all the secret weapons aside from Aoife's. A timer. A recipe. A bottle of whiskey. Chocolates. A pan. What makes Aoife's different?"

"It's very dear while the others are cheap?"

"True. But imagine them wrapped up as they were—"

"It's large," Aretta said, copping on straightaway.

"It's large," Siobhán confirmed. "Perhaps her secret note instructed her to pick the largest box from the pile."

"If that's the case," Aretta said, walking over to the refrigerator, "was the killer standing behind this fridge, nudging it to spring a leak?"

"That's an excellent question." She looked back at Sophia's blackened pan. "What if Sophia let hers burn on purpose?"

"Because she was too busy fussing with the fridge," Aretta said.

"Indeed." Siobhán made note of this by Sophia's name.

"We can assume that Ethan and Trisha used the fridge behind Ethan. Barry and Martin would have been an equal distance from both refrigerators, and Sophia would have used the leaky fridge for sure."

Siobhán gave a brief thought about checking each refrigerator to document the stored items, but every contestant would have used similar ingredients, and both refrigerators had most likely been stocked equally. There had also been no rule about who was to use what fridge, so even if contestants had swapped there wasn't anything to be learned by it. Their best evidence would have to come from the technician who examined the refrigerator to determine what had caused it to leak. But Siobhán had a feeling they already knew the answer—the killer. Not only had they set up the refrigerator to start leaking, they positioned it so the water would flow directly underneath the outlet that Aoife McBride would have used once she unboxed her secret weapon.

Aoife's station was the most organized. Extra gloves, hair nets, and printed instructions labeled "My Signature Cherry Pie." They checked every nook and cranny but found nothing out of the ordinary. In the cabinet they found three of Aoife's best-selling books. Had one of the other contestants had them it might have been grounds for dismissal. But Aoife could certainly consult her own books. Had she really needed them? Or were they for bragging rights?

"She chose first," Siobhán repeated. "She asked an audience member to fetch her the biggest package." That had to be the instruction on her note. This killer had messed up once. He or she wasn't going to let that happen again. The reason neither Fia O'Farrell nor Ruth had never met this solicitor or had a heads-up about secret notes and secret weapons was because it was a last-minute concoction when Aoife McBride decided to powder someone else's nose with her poisonous compact. It could only be a theory until the tests came back on the powder, but the pieces fit. If only the protester had sorted himself out and stopped screaming, he might still be alive. She shared her thoughts with Aretta.

"If that's the case, what about our mysterious solicitor?" Aretta asked.

"Mr. Donut Hole is either our killer, or he was hired by our killer at the last minute." If he was innocent, he'd surely heard about the death of Aoife McBride by now. Perhaps he knew he was in danger. After all, he could identify whoever asked him to bring in the packages and secret notes, aka the killer. But that wouldn't explain why he had given them his name verbally but used Donut Hole on his fake ID. And why he was twisting in the wind? Had he unknowingly been snared in a web and was trying to figure it our, or was he the guilty party? . . . If he was the killer, Siobhán had not only let a killer walk in with the murder weapon, she'd opened the door and invited him in.

Chapter 13

"I know I shouldn't be happy about being called back for this assignment," Macdara said.

Siobhán laughed and shook her head. "And yet you are."

"My stomach cannot lie," Macdara patted his stomach and grinned.

"I've heard it fib now and then," Siobhán said. She and Macdara stood outside their dairy barn, watching the builders make progress on the O'Sullivan Six. Macdara had been asking her nonstop about the baking show, but instead of the particulars of the deaths, most of his questions had been focused on the baked goods.

"We've got a possible murderer or two running around, and you keep asking me about pies." She said it lightly; she knew he would soon get his mind on murder, where it belonged.

"I didn't specifically say pies—were there pies?" He flashed her a hopeful grin.

"Aoife McBride ended up facedown in her cherry pie."

Macdara grimaced. "We cannot let this murderer stop the show," he said. "Or the baking."

"It was supposed to be such a sweet assignment," Siobhán said with a sigh. "Now it's all twisted up with—whatever this diabolical plan is."

"It does sound perplexing. Two possible victims of foul play and a missing person."

Siobhán made a face. "I have a feeling Mr. Donut Hole is more of a hiding weasel than a missing person."

"Why do I get the feeling that you enjoy calling him Mr. Donut Hole?"

Siobhán made a fist and shook it. "He handed me identification with that ridiculous name on it and I didn't even cop on." He'd made a fool of her. "Wait a minute . . ." Siobhán stepped away from the dairy barn and began to have a walkabout. Macdara didn't follow. He was used to her way of processing things. When she returned, he waited patiently for her to speak. "At a quick glance the identification looked legitimate. So much so that instead of stopping to read it carefully I simply snapped a photo." There had been so much going on at the time and she'd had no inkling of what was to come, but there was no use rattling on with excuses. She'd mucked it up and that was all there was to it. "I'm convinced that these secret notes and weapons were a last-minute addition when the powder killed our poor protester instead of Aoife McBride."

Macdara considered this. "Last minute means mistakes could have been made."

Siobhán crossed her fingers and held them up. "We also need a warrant for the Twins' Inn," Siobhán said. "I'd like to search all their rooms, but we'll have to hope there's something in Aoife McBride's room that points to her killer."

"You could dress up in a French maid's uniform and sneak into all the rooms," Macdara said with a devilish grin.

"Cheeky and misogynistic," Siobhán said.

He laughed. "I beg your pardon, wifey. But a man can dream."

"If you call me wifey I'm going to call you hubby."

"I'll answer to anything as long as it's coming from you." His eyes locked with hers, and they shared a rush of energy.

"When do you think this honeymoon phase will end?" Siobhán asked, leaning in for a kiss. "It's terribly distracting."

"It's disgusting is what it is," James said, coming out and startling them. He clapped Macdara hard on the back. "If you have nothing better to do than stand grinning at each other like someone walloped you each to the side of the head with a two-by-four, I can certainly put you to work."

Macdara looked around as if he suddenly did not know where he was. "We do own this property, do we not?"

James laughed, and punched Macdara playfully on the shoulder. "She's still my sister." He was handsome, the oldest of the O'Sullivan Six, and sobriety looked good on him. If only he would find a woman who made his heart sing. He'd been broody since breaking it off with his fiancée, Elise, well over a year ago. Siobhán hadn't been particularly fond of her, but she hated seeing her brother so unhappy. He wouldn't be easy for any woman, but perhaps that could be said for all of them. Not everyone was lucky enough to find the kind of love she shared with Macdara. It was not only a solid friendship and fierce respect they had for each other, but it was a once-in-a-lifetime kind of love, and she vowed never to take it for granted.

"We have to get back to the bakery," Siobhán said to James. "But I wanted Dara to see the progress you've made."

"Shaping up to be a real beauty," Macdara said.

"It's definitely shaping up," Eoin said, coming out to join them. He had "product" in his hair, something keeping it spiky. No doubt at the urging of Gráinne.

"What's the story with the bakery?" James asked. "Any word on who is targeting the bakers?"

"Unfortunately, we're just getting started," Siobhán said. "This one is a bit complicated."

"Is the baking show going to be canceled?" This came from Ciarán, rounding the corner of the barn and startling all of them. He had his fiddle in hand; lately he'd taken to practicing while wandering around their property. Trigger, their Jack Russell terrier, was trotting after him. Siobhán scooped up the little beast and scratched him behind the ears as she fought the urge to tell Ciarán to stand up straight and brush the fringe out of his eyes.

"We're weighing our options," Siobhán said as she set Trigger down. He ambled to a nearby tree, curled up and was snoring in a matter of seconds. She'd never wanted to be a dog more in her life. She forced her thoughts to return to the matter at hand. Even if they continued filming, it was too dangerous to allow the audience to return. If both deaths were indeed murder, the killer had used the crowds and chaos to their advantage. It was possible that the killer was long gone. But if not, boiling their crowd down to the essential suspects was the smartest move. Macdara leaned in.

"I hear your wheels turning," he said. She laughed, then shared her thoughts. "You're right," he said. "We should continue the baking show, but remove the audience and increase the presence of the guards."

"The town is going to be up in arms," Siobhán said. "This was the event of the decade."

"You could livestream it." The suggestion came from Gráinne, who had exited the dairy barn, her arms loaded with fabric samples.

"How ya?" Siobhán said with a nod to the fabrics.

"Grand. We've got the curtains and the tablecloths sorted."

"Brilliant." Siobhán had no doubt they would be perfect. Each member of the O'Sullivan Six was so different. It was as if they'd all come into the world with fully formed talents and personalities. Sometimes they drove her mad, but with each passing day she appreciated them more and more. It wouldn't be long before they all had families of their own. "What's that about a stream, pet?"

"You could livestream the baking show. People can gather in O'Rourke's Pub, or anywhere really, to watch it online."

Siobhán studied her pretty sister and nodded. "That's not a bad idea."

"That's class," Ann said. She was the last to emerge from the construction site, a yellow hardhat perched atop her blonde head. Siobhán felt a squeeze of envy; she was missing out on the build.

"I know," Gráinne said, tossing her head. "I only have fabulous ideas."

"Livestream?" Fia said. "How will folks buy pastries over a livestream?" Her outrage was palpable. They were gathered in the back section of the flour mill that used to host weddings. It was a cavernous space, and a chill emanated from the gaps in the old limestone, but there was plenty of open space. Contestants came prepared, layered up in wooly jumpers, and ready to bake. New kitchen stations and refrigerators had been set up, and a team of electricians and contractors had checked out the wiring and surrounding area for safety concerns or vulnerabilities. The electricians confirmed that all of the electrical panels were up to code, which meant the fault had been a deadly combination of the mixer and a leaky fridge. The refrigerator repairman found a clog in the water line. Although it was a common occurrence, the manufacturer swore up and down that he checked out the refrigerators before sending them, and that they had been brand-new and clog-free. Siobhán was sure someone had deliberately tampered with the line. Finding the so-called solicitor was still their top priority. Guards were now canvassing town with two sketches, their protester and Mr. Donut Hole, along with contacting all local businesses, the inn, limousine services, the chemist, and restaurants and pubs. If either of them hung around town at all, someone would recognize them.

In the meantime, Siobhán wanted to keep an electrician on hand to examine every piece of equipment before anyone plugged it in or turned it on. From now on everything would be triple checked. But even then it was obvious that the players and judges were on edge. They were huddled in the back corner, whispering amongst themselves. Siobhán needed to break that up before they formed some kind of a pact and agreed to one particular story. Fia was still bemoaning her bad luck.

"I'll buy your pastries," Macdara said. "On behalf of the Kilbane Gardaí Station." Siobhán resisted the urge to wipe drool from her husband's mouth.

"That's very kind of you, Detective, but you can't buy enough to make up for the loss," Fia said. How little she knew Macdara Flannery.

"We can hire a few volunteers," Siobhán said. "People can order online and have their pastries delivered to wherever they're streaming the event." Fia didn't look convinced, but the more Siobhán thought about it, the more sense it made. This would also be a boost to the local shops and businesses who had been expecting to be ghosted most of the week. "I think this can be a positive turn of events. There's not one venue in town big enough to host everyone who wants to watch. We will fill multiple venues with spectators and each venue can put in an order for pastries each day." O'Rourke's Pub, Gordon's Comics, Turn the Page bookshop—those were at least three establishments off the top of her head that would be eager to join in.

Fia seemed to be catching on. "I suppose that might work. Do you think all these venues will agree to it?"

"They'll be over the moon. Otherwise they'd have no business at all this week."

"A small daily purchase could be a requirement to watch the livestream feed," Macdara added. "And who doesn't want to eat baked goods while watching a baking show?"

Fia looked visibly relieved. "I suppose it's better than nothing."

"It's better than shutting down the production entirely," Aretta said.

Fia slapped her hands over her ears and walked away. Ruth barged up next, barking at Charlie to follow. "Tell me we start again in the morning."

"If we can get through all the safety checks and interviews today, that's possible," Siobhán said. If any of the players knew anything about this case, the only way of keeping them in town was to continue with the production. While they were sifting through flour, she could sift through their backgrounds. The protester had hidden his true identity. William Bains had done a bit of both. Given them his name but then used a ridiculous I.D. Siobhán was starting to think that as simply a joke, meant to add levity to the baking show. Or it was devised by the killer as a smoke screen. Either way, who was to say that another one of their contestants wasn't also fudging or hiding his or her identity?

"Let's get started then," Ruth said. "We can film the interviews with the gardaí."

"No, you cannot," Macdara said. "We'll be recording our own interviews. But we can set up a table here to conduct our interviews instead of dragging everyone into the gardaí station one by one."

"How does that help me?" Ruth asked.

"The interviews will take less time," Siobhán said. "Allowing you to get back to the production sooner." She finished it with a stern look.

"I suppose that works," Ruth said, as if she had any bargaining power in this at all.

"May I make a suggestion?" It came from Barry Ryan, and the rest of the players were standing behind him as if they were offering moral support.

"Why not," Macdara said, somewhat perturbed. No doubt he would need a pastry soon.

"I understand that you'll need to speak to each of us, we all understand that. But in the meantime, could we not start practicing our bakes? This is still a competition isn't it?"

"You want to practice baking while we interview folks?" Macdara said. Only Siobhán could hear the hopeful tone in his reply.

"We still have the curtains that kept our stations private," Trisha Mayweather said. "You could use them to put around your interview station. And I agree—otherwise we'll just be sitting around, twiddling our thumbs, wondering which one of us might be a cold-blooded killer."

"And we could share our creations," Ethan Brown said directly to Macdara, as if he'd already sussed out his weakness.

"I don't see why you couldn't all practice while we're doing the interviews," Macdara said. "We can figure out an order and time slots so that no one is in danger of burning his or her cakes."

"Or they or them," Philomena said from the corner of the room where she stood stroking her fingernails.

"May I be interviewed first?" Sophia said. "If I have to wait and watch everyone else go before me, it's going to make me very tense."

"Everything makes you tense," Martin Murphy said under his breath.

"I can't help it," Sophia said. "I'm the nervous sort."

"My apologies," Martin said. "By all means, let the guards interview you first."

"I hope you don't expect me to thank you," Sophia said. "You're not in charge."

"Believe me," Martin said, "I don't expect a thing from you, or anyone else here for that matter."

"Enough bickering," Ronan said. "We expect all of you to be good sports and cooperate."

"All except the killer that is," Trisha Mayweather said, flicking her eyes over each contestant as if she could suss out the guilty party.

"Killer, killer, killer," Philomena said, joining the group. "People get electrocuted all the time. It's horrible, but it happens. Why is everyone so sure there is a killer?"

"Because a protester also died mysteriously after using a powder meant for Aoife McBride," Ruth said.

Siobhán wished she could stuff a croissant into the woman's gob. This was the problem with having a director and cameraman at your crime scene. There were no secrets.

"And someone changed the accident sign to *zero days*," Fia said.

"For everyone's safety, we must assume that there is indeed a killer among us," Siobhán said reluctantly. "But rest assured, we have guards and eyes everywhere now."

"And Aoife is already dead, so why should we be worried?" Ethan asked.

"Maybe it's a serial killer," Barry said. He sounded excited at the prospect.

"Everyone calm down," Macdara said. "The guards are here now. When you're in this mill you are protected. But I'd suggest walking in pairs and if anyone says or does anything that does not feel right, you need to trust your gut and notify us immediately."

Heads slowly nodded as the contestants all began eyeing each other.

"I'm watching you," Martin Murphy said. "All of you."

"We'll set up the interview station and decide an interview order shortly," Siobhán said. "In the meantime, ready, set, practice-bake!"

Chapter 14

Sophia Hughes sat eagerly in front of them, like a child on her first day of school. They were set up at the end of the large hall with a table; three chairs on one side for Siobhán, Aretta, and Macdara, and a single chair on the other for the witness. The red velvet curtains had been set up between them and the relocated kitchen stations. From the other side, sounds of baking filtered over, along with the scents. Siobhán found it comforting. Siobhán had the sketch of the protester and another one of William Bains in front of her. The artist had done a marvelous job rendering their faces. Although each one of them had seen the so-called solicitor in person, it had been a chaotic time and the sketch could help trigger their memory. Hopefully that evening wasn't the first time someone had caught a glimpse of him, and if he was still in Kilbane, maybe someone would spot him and notify the guards. They would present Sophia with the sketches after they'd asked all their pertinent questions.

Macdara started them off, offering a smile and a nod. "How did you get involved in the baking show?"

"I just got lucky, I guess," Sophia said, twirling a strand of hair around her finger.

They waited for her to offer more; she did not. "What was the process for applying?" Siobhán asked. Sophia seemed to only register Macdara at the table. Siobhán knew her husband was handsome, and if Sophia only wanted to stare at him and address him, so be it, but Siobhán was still going to ask questions.

"Let's see," Sophia said, as if she couldn't quite remember this momentous event. "I suppose it doesn't hurt to tell the truth now." She leaned back and grinned at Macdara. "I read all of Aoife McBride's books. She has a memoir coming out in a few months, did you know that?"

"*Bake Me*," Siobhán said reflexively. "My mam owned all her books. We have them in the kitchen." A thought occurred to Siobhán and she jotted it down: *Contact Aoife McBride's publisher . . .*

"We?" Sophia asked, sounding horrified.

Siobhán placed her hand over Macdara's hand. "We're newlyweds," she said. "Nearly a year in and still madly in love."

Macdara gave her another look. "Or just plain mad," he said. Siobhán kicked him under the table. He chuckled.

Sophia slumped in her seat. "Typical," she muttered. She twirled a strand of red hair around her finger. "I heard the memoir contains some kind of shocking confession."

This got Siobhán's attention. "Where did you hear that?"

"That's the gossip. I heard that Aoife was scrambling to add something shocking at the last minute."

Siobhán fell silent, mulling this over. Perhaps, just like this baking show, her publishers wanted conflict, conflict, conflict. It was a sad world when just plain sweets weren't enough.

"And you do a lot of baking yourself?" Macdara asked.

"I do, of course," Sophia said. Either she suddenly had

dust in her eyes, or she was deliberately fluttering her eyelashes. "I can bake you anything you want."

"What does reading Aoife's memoir have to do with my husband's question?" Siobhán asked.

"Oh," Sophia said, fidgeting in her chair. "Right, so. In her memoir she said she's passionate about supporting new bakers. The young ones like me." She stopped to grin.

Siobhán folded her arms and glared at her until she wiped it off her face. "For a book that hasn't been released you seem to know an awful lot about this memoir."

"I'm just telling ye what I heard at the Fan Club Appreciation Day."

"What's that?" Macdara asked.

"The Fan Club Appreciation Day?" Sophia asked. Macdara nodded. "It was an event held a few months back at a bakery to celebrate Aoife McBride."

Siobhán leaned in. "You were there?"

"I certainly was there." Sophia sat up straight. "It was a grand event, held in Donegal."

Siobhán was eager to hear more but tried to keep her tone neutral. "What exactly went on at the Aoife McBride Fan Appreciation Day?"

"Fans came from all over Ireland dressed up as Aoife McBride. We swarmed the local bakery to hear her read an excerpt from her new memoir. I was smart. Most of them came as the old Aoife McBride. I dressed up as a young Aoife McBride. Can you even imagine me old?" She placed her hand on her chest as if the thought physically hurt.

Fan Appreciation Day. Siobhán felt a humming in her bones. "Did you meet Aoife at this event?"

"We were all hoping to meet her, of course," Sophia said. "But she never showed up." Sophia crossed her arms. "I spent loads of money and she doesn't even show up to greet her fans. But a measly twenty-thousand-euro prize along with a show on telly, and here she comes!" It took Sophia a minute to remember exactly how that worked out for Aoife McBride and when she did, she gasped. "I'm so sorry. It's terrible what happened to her. Just terrible!"

Siobhán nodded, but either Sophia Hughes was as clueless as she behaved at times, or she had just delivered two bold-faced lies. One, Siobhán very much doubted that Sophia Hughes would consider twenty thousand euro a "measly" amount. Two, she hadn't recognized the real Aoife McBride when she walked into the room. Because Siobhán knew for a fact that Aoife McBride was present at the fan appreciation day event. It was well-known garda gossip that *after* this fan appreciation day—which Siobhán and Macdara knew all about, despite pretending otherwise—Aoife McBride had actually filed an incident report with the Donegal Gardaí Station claiming that someone had been stalking her. Unfortunately, she hadn't supplied the guards enough to go on. It was more of a feeling that someone was behind her wherever she went, but she couldn't even say if it was a man or a woman. The guards didn't know what to make of it, but in retrospect, the claim was becoming more and more plausible. Was the killer also at this event? Was the killer sitting in front of them?

"What does this Fan Appreciation Day have to do with you getting chosen for this competition?" Aretta asked.

"It was at that bakery that I saw the notice about the competition," Sophia said. "On the bulletin board."

"Did you ever find out why Aoife McBride didn't show up?" Macdara asked.

Sophia let out a huff of air. "I tried asking her. That night we all went to the pub." She shook her head at the memory. "I tell you, I think Aoife McBride may have been experiencing health problems." Sophia tapped her head. "You know. Mental ones."

Macdara leaned in. "Why is that?"

"She looked me straight in the eyes, and said, 'Whatever do you mean? I was there.'" She looked at them as if hoping to see a reaction. "Can you imagine? I would have known if she was there."

"How many fans were in the bakery dressed like Aoife McBride?" Siobhán asked.

"I'd say there were at least sixty. And I was the only one who was able to dress young. You know. Because they were all old."

"Is it possible she was there and you didn't recognize her amongst all the other Aoife McBrides?" Siobhán asked.

Sophia chewed on her lip and thought about it. "Well, I didn't fingerprint them or anything, but if she was there, she certainly was pretending *not* to be there."

"Right," Siobhán said. Now that was entirely possible. But if that was the case then *someone* recognized Aoife, otherwise why would she fill out a police report claiming someone from the event had been harassing and stalking her? Was Sophia herself the stalker? Was that why she was pretending she hadn't seen Aoife at the event? After all, Sophia knew with the number of attendees at the event and her face now on a televised baking show that someone would have eventually reported that Sophia Hughes was there. She had just admitted she'd been dressed differently than the rest, a younger McBride. She would have been impossible to miss. And her bake was ruined—burned— but what if there had been no bake at all? Just enough to make it look like a charred mess when Martin Murphy followed *her* secret instruction to turn up the heat on her cooker. In this scenario, Sophia Hughes had time to sneak over and sabotage the refrigerator while Aoife's back was turned.

Sophia began to squirm under the silence. She tilted her head and concentrated. "Do you think she was just hiding amongst us *pretending* not to be there? I read that she hates signing autographs."

"She does?" Siobhán felt a pinch of guilt. She'd asked Aoife for her autograph straightaway. In her garda uniform. Aoife had been kind and agreed to sign a book for her, but perhaps that had been terribly rude of Siobhán, especially given her official role. Not that she managed to get one of her books signed, given the horrific events that followed.

"What's the name of the bakery that held the event?" Macdara asked.

"Pretty Baked," Sophia said. "The owner is a Michelin-trained chef." She looked up and shouted at the curtain. "Did ya hear that, Ethan Brown?" She shook her head. "He thinks he's better than us."

"Now," Siobhán said. "You are rather new at this, so technically he is better than you. You know. Because you're *so young.*"

Sophia frowned, then smiled, then frowned again.

Siobhán couldn't hide her grin. "You must have been very upset you didn't even make it to the first round."

Sophia shrugged. "It's because of that note. Because I'm a decent person."

"And yet you added salt to his creation anyway," Aretta pointed out.

She crossed her arms. "It's a competition. A game. I had no choice."

"What was your signature bake supposed to be?" Siobhán asked.

"An Irish apple cake," she said. "It would have won."

"Do you know why it burned?" Macdara piped in.

Sophia shook her head. "I guess I was too distracted. I felt awful adding salt to Martin's sculpture. But how is that even fair competition? It was chocolate. He didn't hand-make the chocolate, now did he? He just carved it. I mean, yes, it was gorgeous, but it was hardly a traditional Irish baked good."

Macdara took the next question. "Are you saying you had no idea that Martin Murphy's note instructed him to turn up the heat on your cooker?"

Sophia's smile evaporated. "What?" She rose from her seat. "What?" Her face flushed with anger. "Martin Murphy!" she yelled. "How dare you."

"Sit down and lower your voice," Macdara said.

Sophia slumped back down in her seat. "I can't believe it. It wasn't my fault at all then."

"You might have glanced at the dial and noticed it," Siobhán said. This time Macdara kicked her under the table. She couldn't help it, the lass got under her skin. "It's a competition, a game, remember?"

"It's a good thing we're starting over," Sophia said. "Mark my words. I'm going to win."

"What was your secret weapon?" Siobhán asked, hoping a change of direction would open her up.

"What does it matter now?" Sophia said.

"Drop the attitude and answer the question," Macdara said. Siobhán's insides warmed up. She was going to bring him breakfast in bed for the rest of his life. Or at least once.

"A cake pan," she said. "Not much of a weapon. But I guess that's better than a kitchen mixer that kills."

Siobhán sat up straighter. "How did you know what Ms. McBride's secret weapon was?" The stations had all remained behind red velvet curtains. The guards certainly hadn't spoken to them about everyone's secret weapon. But they had passed out notebooks for each contestant to write down their secret note and weapon. However, Aoife, of course, had not been alive to write hers down. How did Sophia know?

"I know what a kitchen mixer sounds like," Sophia said. "And why else would electricians be crawling all over the place, not to mention that blackened outlet? And before you get mad at me, everyone knows. It's all anyone can talk about." Siobhán supposed that was bound to happen. She'd been foolish to think the others didn't know. "She was electrocuted, wasn't she?" Sophia continued. "How could that even happen?"

"We cannot confirm any of those details," Macdara said. "What else was 'everyone' talking about?"

"You want me to talk out of school?" Sophia glanced at the curtains, as if worried the other players could see through it. "After they graciously let me back into the games and forgave me the error of my ways?"

"We'll be asking everyone the same questions," Siobhán said. "And we'll either mark you down as compliant or suspicious." That wasn't really a thing, but Sophia didn't need to know that.

"I'm sure she's compliant," Macdara said. "She did follow the directions on the note, after all."

"I'm no gymnast," Sophia said. "But I'm willing to be helpful."

"Was there anything out of the ordinary since you've arrived?" Aretta said. "Anything at all?"

Sophia placed her index finger to her lips and began to tap it. "I did see that funny little man at O'Rourke's."

Siobhán pushed the sketch of William Bains forward. "This funny little man?"

"That's the one," Sophia said.

"He was at O'Rourke's?" If he had returned to the bakery to set up tents, it must have been rather late by the time he showed up at the pub. O'Rourke's stayed open until half two in the morning.

Sophia nodded. "He was arguing with someone."

"Who?" Siobhán was trying not to sound eager, a difficult task given she wanted to leap across the table and shake Sophia until the answers tumbled out.

"I have no clue. They were huddled in the back near the jax, and I didn't even see the person he was arguing with." Siobhán sighed. If one wanted to hold a private conversation in a pub, lingering around the bathrooms was a perfect way to keep others at bay.

"Did you hear any of their argument?" Macdara asked.

"Only one sentence." It must have been good, for she waited for them to ask with a cheeky look on her face.

"It would help if you told us what you heard him say," Macdara said. From the tone of his voice, he too was losing patience with Sophia.

"He said something like—'he or she will pay for this.' "

"Which was it?" Siobhán said. "He or she?"

Sophia shrugged. "It was loud, the trad band started to play. I don't know."

"Are you sure?" Siobhán asked.

"Pretty sure. And I saw his face. He was angry."

"Did you talk to him?" Macdara said.

Sophia shook her head.

"One more question," Aretta said. "Did you draw a heart in the flour on Martin Murphy's counter?"

Sophia bit her lip, then nodded. "But if I'd known he was the one who turned up the heat on my cooker, I would have drawn a broken heart."

Chapter 15

By the time they showed Sophia the sketch of the protester (she said she had no idea who the man was) and were about to call the next contestant, the bakers were so immersed in their practice that Macdara decided they should speak with the judges and Fia next. After that it would be time for lunch, at which point Siobhán would head to O'Rourke's to speak with Declan and Maria about that evening while Macdara and Aretta canvassed the town with the fliers of the protester. Philomena Lemon seemed to float into her chair, a portrait of lips and nails, both in shocking red. She noticed the sketch of the protester before they could even begin the interview, placed a long talon upon it and slid it closer.

"Who is this?"

"Do you recognize him?" Siobhán asked.

She tilted her pretty head. "Should I?"

Siobhán was already losing patience. "Try answering the question."

Phil's head shot up. "There's no need to be rude."

"Too much sugar can make one irritable," Aretta said matter-of-factly. Philomena laughed and the tension eased, which was the only thing that stopped Siobhán from denying it.

"Is he a baker?" Phil said, still studying the picture.

"If he is, I wouldn't want to try one of his creations," Siobhán said. "He was anti-sugar."

"Perhaps he should try ones with stevia, or molasses, or honey, although it's never the same as the good stuff."

"He won't be trying anything anymore," Siobhán said solemnly.

Philomena slid the sketch back over the table. "That's a shame. I take it he's the gentleman who was taken away in an ambulance shortly before we arrived?"

"Indeed," Macdara said. "He had no identification on him, and we're trying to find out who he is so we can notify his family of his passing."

"Who could have imagined that we'd have two deaths at a baking show?" Philomena said.

The killer . . . Siobhán thought, but kept it to herself. "Apart from the filming, did you have any interactions with Ms. McBride, or the solicitor who delivered the secret notes and weapons?" Macdara asked.

Philomena shook her head. "I *tried* to have an interaction with Ms. McBride. I wouldn't call it successful."

"What's the story?" Siobhán tried to keep her voice pleasant.

Philomena shifted in her chair, then leaned in. "Ronan and I paid a visit to her room to drop off a little welcome package. We were so thrilled she agreed to be a part of this."

"When you say 'her room'?" Siobhán asked.

"At the Twins' Inn," Philomena said.

Siobhán nodded. "When was this?"

"After Ronan and I arrived," Philomena said. "We wanted to leave it in her room so that it would be the first thing she saw, but she had already checked in. The twins insisted on leaving it in her room for us." Philomena frowned. "Can you imagine? It's not like we were going to snoop."

"I can imagine," Siobhán said. "The twins do run a tight ship." What Siobhán really wanted to say is, why did Philomena think she had the right to go into anyone else's private room? Perhaps she was a snoop . . .

"What was in this welcome package?" Macdara asked.

"Flowers, cards, and champagne." Philomena gave them a look that conveyed what a generous gift it was.

"Lovely," Siobhán said.

"Right?" Philomena said. "That's how she should have reacted." She folded her arms and shook her head at the unpleasant memory.

"Please, take us through it," Macdara said.

"She wasn't in her room. I tried to get the innkeepers to let us in, but those twins were very protective of her privacy."

An image of Emma and Eileen flashed in Siobhán's mind. It was true, they were very protective of all their guests, which was good for those checking in, but bad for those wanting to check things out. *Double trouble.* The guards wanting access was one thing, but Siobhán found it odd that Philomena expected to be let in. "Did you really think they would let you sneak into her room?"

"Sneak? We only wanted to set the flowers, champagne, and cards on her table. While they stood and watched. As I said, we were hoping to do it before she checked in. It's not like we planned on snooping around."

"When did you first have an interaction with Ms. McBride?" Aretta asked.

"It wasn't really an interaction, more of a reaction. From her, that is." Phil sat back and shook her head. "She stormed right past our window, holding the vase of flowers away from her as if it were a bomb. The face on her! She was furious. We were so shocked we followed her outside. She stormed into that little cottage where the twins live. I don't see how they live and work together without going mad."

"Do you know why the flowers upset her?" Aretta asked.

Phil waved her hand as if it didn't matter. "I can't imagine why. Either she was allergic to them, or she has something against people lavishing her with gifts."

Siobhán jotted down a note. Now in addition to O'Rourke's Pub they would need to go to the inn and speak to the twins.

"Perhaps she does not like to see living things cut down only to die in front of her days later," Aretta said wistfully.

All heads turned to Garda Dabiri. Siobhán made a mental note never to give Aretta a bouquet of flowers. "Any other interactions?" Siobhán asked.

"Unfortunately, there was one more somewhat embarrassing incident," Philomena said. She crossed her arms and stared at a spot in the distance.

Siobhán perked up. Embarrassing incidents were always of interest when one was not the subject of them. "What is that?"

"At that little pub we congregated in on our night off," Phil said. "I just happened to be standing by Aoife when a young man came up to ask for an autograph." She waited, looking at them expectantly as if waiting to see if they could guess the ending. "You see Aoife thought he wanted *her* autograph, poor dear." She leaned back in her chair. "He wanted *mine*."

"Did that make her angry?" Macdara asked.

"I would say so. She took off in a huff."

"Did you speak with her after that?"

A smile appeared on her face. "I'm afraid after that there was a line of young lads who wanted my autograph."

Siobhán slid the sketch of the protester forward once more. "Are you sure this man wasn't one of your many fans?"

Philomena shrugged. "It's possible." Silence descended.

"That will be all for now," Macdara said. Philomena rose.

"What about the solicitor who brought in the secret envelopes and weapons?" Siobhán said. "Mr. Bains."

Philomena placed a finger across her lips, then abruptly sat down again. "I did run into him at O'Rourke's."

Siobhán perked up. This verified Sophia's sighting. "Was he with anyone?"

"I saw him standing in the corner on his phone." She shook her head. "There was a trad band playing, I don't know how he could hear a thing."

Had Sophia overheard him arguing with someone on the phone? *He or she will pay for this.* Who was "he" (or she?) and what had he or she done?

"To be honest, he didn't look well," Philomena said, interrupting Siobhán's thoughts.

"He was ill?" Macdara asked.

"Either that, or he'd smoked a certain weed, if you know what I mean."

"Marijuana," Aretta said plainly.

Philomena nodded.

"You smelled it?" Siobhán asked.

"No," Phil said. "But he was acting paranoid."

"Paranoid how?" Macdara asked.

"He asked me if I knew why Aoife McBride agreed to do this baking show." She tilted her head up. "As if it was too good for her and he was sorry he got involved."

Did this mean he really was a solicitor? Had he begun this endeavor thinking this was a high-profile assignment and now he'd realized he'd been played? Or worse—was he now in a killer's crosshairs? If anyone knew too much, it was him. Siobhán did not want to come out and ask Philomena if she thought he was a legitimate solicitor, for she didn't want to give away their theories on the case.

"He was sweating profusely and I wanted to get away from him," Philomena was saying. "That's when he grabbed my arm." She slid up her sleeve, and sure enough her arm sported bruises in the shape of a thumb and fingers.

"Why didn't you report that?" Aretta asked.

"I honestly didn't feel he was attacking me. He seemed as if he was trying to warn me."

"Warn you," Siobhán said, mostly to herself. He was frightened. Or . . . he was vengeful . . .

"Did he say anything else?" Macdara asked.

Philomena nodded. "He said I should go back to the inn, pack up all my belongings, and get as far away from this so-called baking show as I possibly could."

Ronan O'Keefe looked uncomfortable in the chair. It was either too small for him, or he had a deathly fear of speaking to the guards, for he wouldn't stop fidgeting. He looked back at the curtain. "What did Philomena tell you?" he asked.

Siobhán found that a very interesting question. "What do you think she told us?"

He fidgeted some more. "I haven't a clue, that's why I asked."

Macdara slid the sketch of the protester in front of him. "Do you recognize this man?"

Ronan gasped. "Is he a murderer?"

"No," Siobhán said. "He's the anti-sugar protester who seemed determined to stop the show."

Ronan covered his mouth with his hands, then dropped them. "Do you think he knew something horrible was going to happen to Aoife?"

Another odd statement. "Why do you say that?" Siobhán asked.

Ronan shrugged. "From what I heard he was in a right state. Before the baking show had even begun."

"Do you recognize him?" Macdara repeated. It never failed to surprise Siobhán how many suspects tried to pry information out of them instead of just answering questions. Ronan, it was quite apparent, was a mad one for the gossip. Ronan was suddenly enthralled with a speck of dust on the table. "I will only ask this one more time," Macdara said. "Have you ever seen that man before?"

"If I have, Detective, I assure you, I do not recall." His gaze swiveled to Aretta, then Siobhán. "I do meet so many folks, I couldn't possibly keep them all straight." Finally, he turned to Macdara. "I'm very good at reading people too. I'd say you're a lemon meringue man, am I right?"

Macdara shifted, doing his best not to glance at Siobhán. "He hasn't met one dessert he doesn't like," Siobhán said. "Including lemon meringue."

"I don't like fruit cake," Macdara said.

"Heavens, life is too short for fruit cake," Ronan said. "I'll bake you one of my famous lemon meringue pies. It's the least I could do."

Was he trying to bribe them with pie? *Genius.*

"Lemons are a fruit," Aretta said.

Ronan held up a finger. "But they are not used in fruit-cake."

"They certainly are not," Macdara said. "I dare say. I *am* a lemon meringue man."

Ronan slapped his hands on the table. "I knew it," he said, grinning and jabbing his finger at Macdara. Macdara glowed as if he'd just won a trophy.

Philomena Lemon might be a stunningly beautiful woman, but Siobhán knew it was Ronan who had just captured

Macdara Flannery's full attention. Siobhán wanted to mess with Macdara and tell Ronan that they could never accept such a thing, but if she did and he took her seriously, she would miss out on the pie, so she kept her gob shut.

"Let's put the pie aside for a moment, although if you need a taster, we aim to please," Macdara said. "We'd like to know first if you've had any interactions with Aoife McBride apart from the bit of filming you've done so far."

"There was a faux pas with the flowers, did Philomena mention that?"

Macdara nodded. "She did."

Ronan sighed. "Since then I haven't spoken to her, or any of the contestants. It's not a good idea to be seen chatting with any of them when there's a cash prize involved."

"You didn't think the flowers could be seen as favoring one particular contestant?" Aretta asked.

"We sent them before any of the filming began. I suppose in retrospect it was inappropriate. But when it comes to judging, we're only basing our decisions on presentation and taste." He sighed. "Or at least we were. I cannot believe she's gone. What a horrible, horrible turn of events."

"That's all I the questions I can think of for now," Siobhán said. She glanced at Aretta and Macdara.

Macdara nodded. "We appreciate you speaking with us, along with the offer for the lemon meringue pie."

"The pie," Ronan said as if he'd forgotten. "I wasn't thinking this through; there are no available kitchen stations."

"Good thing we have a house nearby," Macdara said. "And it has a lovely kitchen that no one is using."

"Oh?" Ronan said, flicking a look to Siobhán.

"We're using it," Siobhán said. "And I make a mean brown bread if you must know."

"Must I?" Ronan said. "Know it?"

"Right?" Macdara said. "It's brilliant, but we could use a little lemon meringue action." Ronan made a finger-gun and pointed it at Macdara with a wink.

Siobhán stared at her husband until he stopped grinning. "I'm only now just realizing we need a new freezer," she said.

"We do?" Macdara said. "Why do you think that?"

"It's not nearly big enough for your dead body."

By the time they finished interviewing Philomena and Ronan, everyone was due for a lunch break. The contestants and judges were dismissed and instructed to return in two hours. This would give Macdara, Siobhán, and Aretta time to go back to the station and see if there was any progress on identifying their protester.

"Let's hit O'Rourke's first," Macdara suggested. "We can get Declan's account of Aoife McBride and the rest of our contestants that evening, and have a spot of lunch."

"Brilliant," Siobhán said.

The familiar yeasty smell of O'Rourke's Pub wrapped around Siobhán as she entered. Her bestie Maria was behind the bar, along with Declan, the larger-than-life publican who was a familiar fixture to everyone in Kilbane. They slapped playing cards down on the counter, and Declan must have lost, for he yelled out, "You got me again, you little cheat, ya!"

"You're just getting too old to keep up with me," Maria gave back. They both howled with laughter and only stopped when they spotted Siobhán and Macdara waiting patiently before them.

"You're here!" Maria exclaimed. She was a short woman with a booming voice. Her dark hair was pulled back with a band, and she was wearing a T-shirt that read: THAT'S A HORRIBLE IDEA. Underneath it: WHAT TIME?

Maria turned to Declan. "You owe me fifty euro."

Declan huffed. "Prove you're not cheating and I'll pay."

Maria shook her head. "Are you here for lunch, luv?" she asked Siobhán.

"She is," Macdara answered. "And she brought the husband."

Maria threw a glance at the door to the kitchen. "Ham and cheese toasties coming up," she said.

"I wanted to look at the menu," Macdara said.

"And I wanted to marry an astronaut," Maria replied. "We've been jammers and all we have left are ham and cheese toasties. We've got bacon and cabbage and shepherd's pie for tonight, but you're stuck with ham and cheese toasties and crisps for lunch."

"We'll take two," Siobhán said, looping her arm through Macdara's and guiding him to a nearby booth before he could barge into the kitchen and suss things out for himself. "It's good they've been busy," Siobhán said.

"She'd need to marry an astronaut," Macdara said. "I bet he'd still be able to hear her from the moon."

Siobhán looked around. There were only a few folks scattered about the place. "Good thing we beat the rush."

Macdara suddenly leaned in. "Is Maria cheating at cards?"

"Of course she is," Siobhán said. "But Declan will never prove it."

On the wall across the way, a large new telly had been mounted on the wall, and it was streaming the Internet channel that was broadcasting the baking show. Siobhán pointed it out. "I hope we can investigate these deaths while still keeping the event alive," she said. "It means a lot for the town."

"I agree," Macdara said. "I still think there's a small chance they could be terrible accidents."

Siobhán shook her head. "We have two dead bodies and two mysterious missing people. Someone changed the sign to ZERO DAYS SINCE THE LAST ACCIDENT."

"People die from allergic reactions and faulty wiring every single day," Macdara said. "And as cold-hearted as it sounds, someone may have changed that sign after Aoife died—and it makes them a right eejit—but we still have no hard evidence of a crime."

"Where is Mr. Donut Hole if there's no foul play involved?" Siobhán realized too late that the few heads in the pub craned her way at this last utterance. She smiled and waved until they looked away in embarrassment. A commercial boomed from the telly. The sounds of someone thoroughly enjoying a chocolate croissant filtered from a commercial. Siobhán glanced at the melodramatic commercial, then stared in the direction of the kitchen, dreaming of ham and cheese toasties. She was so hungry she could eat a small horse. She'd noticed that whenever her stress ratcheted up, so did her desire for comfort food. But she couldn't imagine anyone, including her hubby, enjoying a pastry as much as the actor on the telly. Siobhán stared at the man. There was something familiar about him.

"I'd marry this croissant if I could," the actor bellowed. He brought it up to his mouth, kissing it. "You're beautiful, you sugary slice of heaven. You're gorgeous." She knew that voice. Where had she heard that voice?

Maria interrupted the man's intimate moment, carrying two plates with toasties and bags of crisps. Siobhán got barbecue and she tossed Macdara a packet of cheese and onion. As Siobhán knew he would, he switched them when her glance flicked back to the telly.

"Not that obnoxious guy again," Maria said. "I want to punch him in his big fat piehole. Better yet, I'd like to choke him with that croissant, stuff it into him until he can no longer annoy me with that grating voice that's way too enthusiastic about a croissant."

Siobhán stood. "There's no need," she said, recalling the familiar face on the commercial. She would know that booming voice anywhere. *Sugar kills.*

Maria's eyes narrowed. "Why's that?"

"Because," Siobhán said, "the lad is already dead."

Chapter 16

"An actor," Macdara repeated for what seemed like the umpteenth time. They were at the Kilbane Garda Station in the large conference room with their takeaway lunches from O'Rourke's. On the whiteboard at the front of the room, Siobhán had written their victim's name: George O'Leary. An actor from Dublin. It was a positive development in the sense they had been able to quickly locate his family, including a fiancée, to whom Siobhán unfortunately had to break the news of his death over a video chat. They learned he had no known allergies. Siobhán called Jeanie Brady to update her.

"No allergies?" Jeanie repeated.

"Correct."

Jeanie made a noise, as if she had an idea. Siobhán waited. "Strychnine," Jeanie finally said. "It causes spasms as we saw in our victim before he died, and it comes in a crystal form which could have been mixed up with face powder."

"It can kill on skin contact?" Siobhán asked with a shudder.

"It can get into the nose membranes," Jeanie confirmed. "A small amount inhaled could cause death."

"She powdered his nose," Siobhán said. "Aoife McBride . . . do you think she *knew* what she was doing?"

"If Aoife McBride killed this actor—the first question is why," Jeanie said. "And the second . . ."

"Who killed Aoife McBride?"

"Exactly."

"I still think the powder was meant for Aoife all along."

"You think powdering his nose with a deadly poison was a coincidence?" It was obvious from Jeanie's tone that she found it a stretch.

"I don't know."

"You know what I like about you, O'Sullivan? You're not afraid to admit when you haven't got a clue." She laughed long and hard at her own joke. "I'll submit a test for strychnine."

"It's banned in Ireland, is it not?" It used to be a pesticide, primarily rat poison, but it was banned ages ago.

"Officially banned in 2006, sure," Jeanie said. "But not impossible to get one's hands on it if one is determined." There was a pause in the conversation but Siobhán could hear Jeanie thinking. "It was often used in rat and gopher poison."

"The flour mill," Siobhán said. "I wouldn't be surprised if there is some in the older parts of the mill."

"I concur. Where there are sweets, there are rats."

It was true on so many levels.

"You'll be sending in all the powder samples from the chemist to check them out as well as the toxicology on George O'Leary?" Siobhán knew that Jeanie had it handled but repetition helped Siobhán keep things straight.

"Now. I will, so. Can't have the ladies of Kilbane waiting around too long with shiny noses, now can we?"

"Not unless it's Christmas and the panto is Rudolph,"

Siobhán quipped. Jeanie laughed, and they ended the call. Siobhán returned to the briefing room. Macdara was at the front of the room ready to give an update. "We need to search the flour mill for strychnine," Siobhán said, whispering in his ear.

"Talk that love talk, wifey," he said. She swatted him and filled him in on her call with Doctor Brady. "Let's finish this briefing and get word to the contestants that they'll get a longer lunch break," Macdara said.

"Do we mention the reason why?"

"No," Macdara said. "They need their full concentration on their bakes."

Siobhán laughed. It was true that they didn't want to tip their hand concerning a probable murder weapon, but Macdara also wanted the bakes to be delicious. As he briefed the room, she mulled over the case. It was downright perplexing. Who hired George O'Leary to stage a fake protest outside of Pie Pie Love, and why?

Siobhán was jotting down her thoughts as fast as they came.

He was used as a distraction.

While he was making a fuss outside, what was the killer doing inside the bakery? Looking for strychnine and putting it in Aoife's powder? Anyone who had toured the mill in the past might have seen bottles stored somewhere, covered in dust. Was the killer Fia O'Farrell and she *knew* the bottles were in the mill? Had she ever mentioned they were there and the wrong person overheard her? And even though they no longer gave official tours, wasn't it possible that someone could have entered the bakery, then snuck around the mill when no one was looking? There were numerous "what ifs" that convinced Siobhán it wasn't out of the realm of possibility that the poison had been found nearby.

Why did Aoife McBride arrive ahead of all the other contestants that day?

Was Mr. Donut Hole an actor too?

When the debrief was over, Siobhán approached Macdara and Aretta. "Do we have the name of George O'Leary's agent?"

"We do," Macdara said. "He's out of Dublin."

"We'll need to schedule a video call. I want to show him the sketch of the man we know as Mr. Bains."

"Let's call him after the tour of the mill," Macdara said. "I'll have the clerk call him now and tell him to clear his schedule for us."

"I have to call the bookshop and postpone our chat with them until later," Siobhán said. The case was heating up, and as Murphy's Law would have it, everything was happening at once. They found Fia O'Farrell waiting outside of the mill to take them around.

"Strychnine," she said when they explained what they'd be looking for. Her facial expression told them what they needed to know.

"Ground floor," Fia said. "Me father used to put it down to kill the rats. If there's any still around that's where we'll find it."

Siobhán and Macdara followed Fia as she unlocked and opened the door leading to the working part of the mill. "We're going down to the first floor," Fia said. "It's known as the ground floor, where the flour used to slide down the shaft and into waiting bags. Above we have the middle floor, where the stone wheels used to do the grinding, and finally the top floor, where the wheat was poured into the shaft."

As they descended, the smells of water and earth grew pungent. Soon a light flickered on and Fia's face was shrouded in an eerie glow as she stood beside the swinging chain of a dim lightbulb. She pointed to another chain nearby, this one much larger and sturdier, as it did more than bring forth light. "My father used this chain to hoist bags of wheat up to the top floor, and had it set up so that the bag could be tipped into the shaft, all manipulated from below." She paused, then glanced at the empty shaft. "I haven't been down here in ages. It makes me sad."

She turned to a back corner. "My father used to put rat poison along the edges of the walls." Siobhán and Macdara edged forward; there was no visible powder, thankfully.

"Do you know where he stored the poison?" Macdara asked.

"There's a small room in the back." Fia produced a torch and turned it on. "I haven't turned the light on in there in ages, so just in case." She led the way, and Siobhán and Macdara soon found themselves in a small storage room. Seconds later a light flickered on. The room was mostly emptied out except for a dusty old shelf. "All the cleaning products and pesticides were kept in here," Fia said. "Top shelf where young ones couldn't reach."

The top shelf was not illuminated under the single bulb. "Shine the torch for us, will ya please?"

Fia aimed the light at the top shelf. Five brown bottles were lined up on the top shelf with a DANGER label in red, complete with a skull and the word POISON. In the middle of the bottle was a photo of an unsuspecting gopher. The words GOPHER BAIT and STRYCHNINE were also clearly visible. There were five bottles on the shelf with a gap in the middle. Siobhán turned to Macdara. "Do you have your gloves?"

"I do." He removed a pair of blue gloves from his pocket and she did the same. They gloved up.

"Can you give me a lift?"

"I can." Macdara laced his hands together and Siobhán stepped into them. She grabbed the top shelf for balance. It wobbled.

"Careful."

"It'll hold." She directed Fia to aim the light higher. There, in the middle of the line of bottles was a faint circle in the dust. "There's one missing alright," Siobhán said. Macdara lowered her.

"We need to get our technical team back out here. This storage room is now a secondary crime scene."

"Not again," Fia moaned. "Don't tell me this will affect the production?"

"It's far enough away from the baking show," Macdara said. "But these bottles will need to be removed and the room checked for clues."

"Maybe we'll get lucky and our thief will have touched all the bottles with their bare hands," Siobhán said. "But from the layers of dust up here, I don't have high hopes."

"Neither do I," Macdara said. "But now we know where one of the murder weapons came from, and perhaps just knowing this will lead somewhere."

They exited the room quickly and headed back to the main area of the ground floor. "I've texted the station and the tech team will be out within the hour."

"While we're here, why don't you give us the rest of the tour," Siobhán said.

"Why not," Fia said. "I warn you, I'm out of practice."

"Are you?"

Fia stilled. "What do you mean?"

"Are you telling me that no one else has taken this tour recently?"

"I did a video tour for the sponsor, but other than that this area has been closed."

"Did the video tour for the sponsor include this room?"

Fia chewed her lip. "I was told the sponsor wanted to see everything. We were early in the negotiation stage and he or she wasn't sure which areas they wanted filmed. I didn't see the harm in it. Are you saying the sponsor is the killer?"

"It's my job to ask loads of questions," Siobhán said. "Be careful not to read into any of them."

Fia swallowed. "I sent the footage to the solicitor who passed it onto the sponsor. And I wouldn't be surprised if they sent it to Ruth and Charlie."

"That's good to know," Siobhán said. "Now please put it out of your mind." Fia wiped her brow, and continued to nibble on her bottom lip. Siobhán had the feeling that Fia wanted to be anywhere but down here. Was it a guilty conscience or the shock that someone had used her father's old rat poison to murder someone on the grounds? Or was it because that "someone" was her?

Fia pointed to the empty shaft. "A bag would have sat right below the shelf to collect the flour. Back in the day this mill could generate 550 pounds of flour in a single day."

"That is impressive," Macdara said.

Fia beamed. "They used to be able to control how fine the wheat was ground by the distance between the stones." Fia pointed to a stairwell. "Shall I take you to the middle floor and show you the grinding stones?"

"Please," Siobhán said. The stairs were narrow, and they headed up single file. It opened into a medium-sized room. In the center, mounted on poles, were two large circular stones.

Fia pointed to the bottom wheel. "This one is called the bed stone. It's immobile. The top stone—called the runner stone—was the one that moved and thus did the grinding." She held up her hand. "We would test the flour with the 'rule of thumb.' Literally we would just sift it between our thumb and forefinger to test the consistency."

"Fascinating," Siobhán said. She and Macdara stared at their thumbs for a moment.

"Guess it's better than twiddling them," Macdara said. Fia laughed as Siobhán rolled her eyes at the joke. This was one of the job perks, the opportunity to tour places that were closed to the general public.

"It truly is fascinating," Fia agreed. "The wheels rotated approximately thirteen and a half times with each rotation of the water wheel at a speed of approximately eighty revolutions per minute." She stared at it wistfully. "I used to love watching them turn. You could adjust the size of the grain by how far apart the wheels were set—the farther apart, the coarser the grain."

"Have you looked into the cost of getting the wheel fixed?" Siobhán asked.

Fia sighed. "At this point it's more than just the wheel. We'd need to replace the entire machinery inside as well. And who knows what else inspectors would find if I wanted to throw this into production again. They always find something."

"I understand," Siobhán said.

"There isn't much to the upper floor," Fia said. "That's where the bag of grain would get tipped in."

"We appreciate the tour," Macdara said. "Have you shown any of the other contestants or judges around?"

"No, I don't give tours anymore," Fia said.

"And you always keep the door locked?"

"Always."

"Someone came down and took the poison," Siobhán said. "Do you have any clue who could have done it and how they managed to get in?"

"If I had any idea whatsoever I would have told you straightaway," Fia said. "There's a back door but it's been boarded shut for ages."

"A back door?" Siobhán said.

Fia blinked. "Yes."

"When we had the front entrance closed down I asked you if there was a back door."

"Right. There is. Off the event space."

"But you never mentioned another back door."

"I didn't realize you needed to know about every single door into the building."

"I see," Siobhán said, trying to control her temper. Had this been an innocent mistake as Fia was trying to make it seem, or had she purposely kept this other door from them?

"I'd like to see it," Macdara said.

Fia sighed. "Follow me."

She led them down a dark hall past the storage room where they'd found the poison. A few feet from their destination and everything became clear. At the end of the hall was a door with a person-shaped hole through the center.

Fia's reaction was immediate. "What?" she said, running toward it. "This is impossible." She stepped through the opening before they could say a word.

"She seemed genuinely surprised," Macdara said.

"I agree."

Fia stepped back in through the giant hole in the door, talking to herself. "How did I not hear someone beating down the door?"

Siobhán didn't answer her out loud, but she did have an answer. *Because of the protester and his bullhorn.* While he was busy screaming, the killer was busy hacking into the door. The killer knew about the storage room and the strychnine. The killer mixed the poison into Aoife's powder. And although the noise did cover up the sound of an axe, or whatever yoke was used to break down the door, there was a complication. The protester was so loud, he not only obscured the noise of the killer breaking into the door, he drew Aoife McBride's attention. And for some reason his shiny nose bothered her enough that she decided to be kind and powder it. It saved her life, but not for long. Had she realized something might be wrong with the powder after the protester died? If so, why didn't she confide in Siobhán? Was Aoife McBride caught up in something scandalous? Too afraid to come forward?

Scenario two—Aoife McBride intended on killing George O'Leary. She knew there was poison in her powder. But then who killed her? Siobhán knew that freak accidents happened, but she was more inclined to believe there was a single killer who had meant to target Aoife all along. Regardless, all theories had to be checked out.

"We need to find out if there's a link between George O'Leary and Aoife McBride," Siobhán said.

"Then let's go talk to this agent," Macdara said.

"What about my door?" Fia called.

"We'll get the guards to board it up and put crime tape around it," Macdara said. "It's safe to assume no one is going to be coming in or out of it for quite some time."

Chapter 17

Once back at the garda station, Siobhán and Macdara cozied into his office to make the video call. The talent agent soon appeared on screen, his face too close to the camera. He had pudgy cheeks with large eyes and a bulbous nose.

"Do you mind backing up a little?" Siobhán said.

"Pardon?" The man fussed with something and soon the image was upside-down. She was looking at his trousers and his shiny black shoes. "Is this better?"

"Much," Macdara said.

Siobhán punched him. "Sorry, luv, he's only messing. Now you're upside-down." There was another moment of fumbling with his phone and soon he was right-side up, and holding the camera at a decent angle. "You're grand, you're grand." Siobhán smiled, hoping to calm him down a bit. He offered a shy smile in return. She pegged him to be in his sixties, and it was obvious he wasn't a fan of technology. Siobhán and Macdara introduced themselves.

"Pleased to meet you," the man said. "I'm Brendan Connor."

"And you represent theatrical talent?" Macdara asked.

Brendan nodded. "I was just notified about George O'Leary's passing," he said. "Terrible, terrible tragedy."

"Between us, it may be more than accidental," Siobhán said.

The agent's brow shot up. "Oh?"

"Foul play," Macdara said.

Brendan slapped his hand over his mouth. "Who did it?"

"That's what we're trying to find out. Who contacted you about hiring George for the baking show?"

"A solicitor," Brendan said without hesitation. "He represented Aoife McBride."

"What was this solicitor's name?" Siobhán asked.

"William Bains." Once again he answered without hesitation.

"Did you ever meet Mr. Bains in person?" Siobhán asked.

The agent frowned. "No. I simply took his requests over the phone."

Requests. "Was there more than one actor you hired for the baking show?" Siobhán asked.

"Yes. I sent George O'Leary and Elizabeth Wynne." Siobhán and Macdara exchanged a look. Brendan picked up on it and his expression morphed to one of alarm. "Please tell me Elizabeth is alright."

"We don't have any reason to believe she isn't," Siobhán said. "But we need to speak with her."

"Elizabeth is a good soul. I'm sure she wouldn't hesitate to speak with you."

"What can you tell us about her?" Macdara asked.

Some people would have balked at such an open-ended question but Brendan Connor dove right in. "She started out behind the scenes, and then caught the bug." He grinned.

"The bug?" Siobhán asked.

"The acting bug."

"Ah, right," she and Macdara said in stereo.

"Jinx," Macdara said. "You owe me a Guinness."

"You said she started out behind the scenes," Siobhán said. "As in a cameraman?"

"Heavens, no. She was a makeup artist."

"Makeup artist?" Siobhán felt a ripple of apprehension move through her. A makeup artist might know how to mix a poison into a face powder. Was Elizabeth Wynne their killer? Had she come in the hacked-up door on the ground floor, snuck upstairs, replaced Aoife McBride's face powder, then disappeared? Maybe later she mixed in with the crowd, just to taunt them.

"Did you not ask why George O'Leary was hired to play a protester?" Macdara asked.

The agent frowned. "It's one of those competition shows, is it not?"

"It is," Macdara acknowledged.

The agent shrugged. He moved away from the camera and Siobhán could see that he was seated in a leather office chair. He had relaxed into the call and was now leaning back, his hands folded across his belly. He was probably the type who put his feet up on the desk and hollered at his secretary through multiple rooms, demanding to know where his cup of tea was when it was sitting right next to him. "I figured it was a cross between *Survivor* and *The Great British Baking Show*."

Macdara glanced at Siobhán. "Is he speaking English?" Siobhán laughed. Other than hurling and football matches, Macdara wasn't one to watch telly.

"Do you watch those reality shows?" the agent asked, as if reading Siobhán's mind. Macdara shook his head. "I do," the agent continued. "They're outrageous. And if you're making a new one and you want to stand out, you need conflict. And what better way to start conflict than with a protester?" He pumped his fist. "Sugar kills," he recited with a grin.

"I see," Macdara said.

"What part was Elizabeth Wynne hired to play?" Siobhán asked.

A bead of sweat broke out on the agent's forehead and trailed down the side of his cheek. He dropped his hands and once again smooshed his face too close to the camera. "She was hired for multiple roles. An extra in the crowd, a stand-in . . . I'd have to look at the job description again, but I do remember they were using her as a catch-all. Would you like me to send you her CV and headshot?"

Multiple roles . . . "We would," Siobhán said.

"We need it now," Macdara added.

"I'll send it straightaway, however it's going to take me a few minutes to get back to the office."

"You're in the office," Siobhán said.

"I'm in the office because I was told the guards wanted to talk to me. My secretary is at lunch, and I was on my way to Grafton Street for fish and chips." He grinned. "It's all you can eat day at the chipper."

"Every day is all-you-can-eat day if you pay for it," Macdara said.

Siobhán figured the real reason the talent agent was stalling was because his secretary was the only one who knew how to fax, or scan, or email. *Typical.* "We need this before you go to lunch Mr. Connor."

"Please," he croaked, staring at the computer screen as if it might bite him. "Call me Brendan." He licked his lips. "My secretary is always changing the password. Let me just give her a bell."

"We're also going to need a phone number for Elizabeth Wynne," Macdara said.

Brendan nodded so vigorously he reminded Siobhán of a Bobble-head doll. "I'll scroll through my contacts and send you her portfolio—you'll have more pictures of her than you ever wanted to see." He laughed at his own joke.

"Please don't give her a heads-up," Siobhán said. "We'd like to be the first to speak to her about this matter."

"No worries there, I assure you. She's a lovely woman, and lucky to get parts for her age, and her build. but she's very flighty. She hasn't even checked in with me, once she started this assignment. Actors!"

For her age and her build... "Wait," Siobhán said. "You mentioned she hadn't checked in with you. Was she *supposed* to?"

He nodded. "It's not a requirement but a standard courtesy. I certainly expected to hear from her after poor George O'Leary died. But not a word. I tell ye, actors!" The call was severed and the screen disconnected.

Siobhán and Macdara looked at each other. "If he doesn't get us her photo in a few minutes, I'm calling the headquarters in Dublin to storm his office," Macdara said.

"Elizabeth Wynne," Siobhán said, trying out her name, wondering if it was the name of their killer. It took fifteen minutes but soon Macdara's phone dinged. He logged into his email and clicked around. Soon, he emitted a low whistle.

"Show me." He turned the screen toward Siobhán and she found herself staring at a woman that was the same age and same build as Aoife McBride.

Macdara raised an eyebrow. "What do you think?"

"I think," Siobhán said, "she played a much bigger part in this than we realized."

"Are you saying what I think you're saying?" Macdara asked.

"Do you think I'm saying what I think you think I'm saying?"

Macdara laughed. "I thought I did. Now I'm not so sure."

Siobhán nodded. "Let me mull on it some more."

"A woman of mystery," Macdara said with a wink. He stood. "Come on. We're due at the bookshop. Do you think you can walk and mull at the same time?"

Siobhán punched his arm. "I can definitely punch and mull at the same time so I don't see why not."

Turn the Page bookshop was located on the other side of the town square from the garda station. Given they had an hour or so to kill before hearing back from the agent, or the agent's secretary to be exact, they decided to pop into the shop and see if the owners had had any contact with either their missing actors, the solicitor, or any of the contestants. The bookshop had just celebrated their one-year anniversary. Deflated balloons and a banner remained, sagging from the windows. The bell dinged as they entered, and Siobhán immediately felt a sense of calm. The shop was filled with comforting mahogany woodwork, and shelves of neatly stacked books. Classical music played overhead. Both owners were present. Padraig was hunched over a book at the counter while Oran fussed with an Aoife McBride display in the front of the shop. "Did you do the blue stickers yet?" Padraig called across the shop to Oran.

Oran groaned. "Why do you insist on discounting everything?"

"It's good for business."

Oran rolled his eyes at Siobhán as they passed. He strode to the counter and picked up a package of blue stickers as Siobhán gravitated to the display. Glossy covers of desserts adorned Aoife's many cookbooks. They were more colorful than the plain versions her mam had owned; these were the revised editions. No doubt after this baking show they would print more with a label that screamed: *Now Streaming!* Would sales also skyrocket now that she was gone? Aoife McBride's husband was deceased and they did not have children. Who was the beneficiary of her will? They needed to find this out. She removed her trusty notebook from her pocket and jotted a reminder down. Siobhán said her hellos to the owners and picked up one of the revised books. Macdara lingered behind her.

Oran was now a few shelves over, grudgingly applying blue stickers to the corners of books. Siobhán caught his eye and gestured to the display. "I have my mam's original collection."

"There's nothing wrong with that," Oran said. "Nothing at all. However . . ." He glanced up as if to see if Padraig was watching, then put his discount-stickers down and meandered over. He picked up a book and thumbed through it carefully. "These have a new forward from Aoife McBride, and digitally enhanced color photos." He turned the book to show her a close-up shot of strawberry shortcake. Macdara groaned next to her.

"Gorgeous," she said. "I'm tempted to lick the page."

"If you promise to do that, I'll buy you the set," Macdara said.

"Right?" Oran laughed, which was a rare sound coming from him. Even Padraig lifted his head from his book, and then his eyebrow. "If you must know, she's improved on some of the recipes," Oran continued. He waited to see if Siobhán was going to take the bait. "It might be fun to have a brand-new set and compare notes?"

Siobhán did like the shiny new covers and digitally enhanced photos. They would make a brilliant gift for Eoin's new restaurant. Even if he didn't use any of the recipes, they would be lovely on display. If there was a wait for tables, the guests could flip through them as well. And if Eoin wasn't as thrilled about them as she was, then she could use the new set to begin her own baking habit, thus preserving her mam's older set, which was quite frankly getting a bit delicate. These pages she could get smudges on and not have to worry. But she couldn't get smudges on Eoin's set. Maybe she should buy two sets.

"Are you alright there, guards?" Padraig called over.

"I'm right here if they need me," Oran said.

"Did you ask them if they'd like a cup of tea?" Padraig shouted. "Or a delicious treat from the bakery?"

"Bakery?" Macdara called back. "Treats?" Padraig gestured to the counter, where indeed tantalizing white boxes sat. Macdara headed over. "Might as well have a look at them."

"Please, help yourself," Oran called after him. "Aoife McBride brought us those treats the day she arrived in town as a thank-you for our lovely display."

Siobhán held still. Macdara, nose-deep in the boxes of pastries, did not seem to grasp what Oran had just said.

"What about you, Siobhán?" Padraig asked. "Cup of tea?"

"That would be lovely." Siobhán headed over to the counter. Padraig had the tea kettle set up nearby, so she used the opportunity to chat with him while he prepared them each a cup.

"Did you get a chance to chat with her when she dropped them off?"

"I'd love to say that I did. She was in a hurry. And even then she was conscious about recycling! Now there's a great human being for ye." He stopped and when he turned he had tears in his eyes. "I can't believe she's gone."

Siobhán nodded and took a moment so that he would see she was paying her respects while also respecting she had a job to do. "Recycling?"

"Yes." He pointed to the small round pastry boxes that were currently occupying all of Macdara's attention. "She wanted to set up a display for us of the pastries, but when I went to toss the empty boxes she insisted on taking them.

She said bakers could always use them." He handed Siobhán her tea.

"Thank you."

"Maybe that's not exactly recycling, or even up-cycling, unless she did something fancy with them, but I assume she's just reusing them. Which is the same, is it not?" Padraig smiled, and waited for Siobhán's reaction.

"It's a fair point."

She took her tea and wandered over to the boxes that Elizabeth had left. "How many pastry boxes did she take?"

"Heavens," Padraig said. "She brought loads. She carried them in, stacked so high I could barely see her face. The boxes are small, and you know what this town is like, the samples were nearly gone before noon. The only reason Macdara is able to enjoy the offerings is that I held some of the boxes back. I knew they would be scooped up as soon as they were set down!"

He hadn't exactly answered the question, but Siobhán wasn't even sure why she was asking. There couldn't be anything to it, and she had to remind herself not everything was a clue. But if Aoife planned on reusing them, where were they? Siobhán hadn't seen any pastry boxes like them lying around the bakery. These were pink and round—they could fit a small pie, cake, or several cookies. Given no one had been harmed with a pastry box, unless of course you counted the fact that sugar was a form of poison, then she was just chasing after sweet nothings. Perhaps Elizabeth thought taking the pastry boxes was something that "Aoife" would do and she was getting into her role. Either the real Aoife McBride was alive and the evil mastermind behind this entire charade, or something awful had happened to her. Siobhán was having trouble figuring out whether she would eventually love her or hate her, feel for her, or feel for those she'd hurt with this madness. She hoped the Donegal Gardaí were ramping up their search, although once word got out who they were searching for, it wouldn't be long before it trickled into Kilbane. Maybe it was time to break the news to everyone at the bakery. Macdara finally stopped imbibing sweets and was happily sipping his tea.

"I've done it," Oran said. "I've put blue stickers on way too many books."

"Good man. Well done." Padraig grinned. Oran shrugged. The pair were chalk and cheese, but the affection between the husbands was obvious to anyone who walked in. Oran looked like a human sheep, with curly black hair, big brown eyes, and a pasty complexion. Padraig was younger, and handsome, and usually at the counter with his nose in a book. Yet somehow he still saw and heard everything, even from across the room.

"I'm debating whether to get one set or two," Siobhán said, gravitating back to the Aoife McBride books. Oran followed her.

"If you buy two sets, I can give you a discount," Oran said. "How does ten percent sound?"

"Not as good as twenty-five," Macdara answered from across the room.

"Give her twenty-five off," Padraig said.

Oran bowed his head. "How generous of us."

Siobhán nosed through one of the books. The author photo was that of a much younger Aoife McBride sporting strawberry-blonde hair and a pixie nose. "I was hoping for a more recent photo," Siobhán said out loud.

Oran crossed himself. "We're so lucky she updated her collection before she passed."

Siobhán grinned. "I'll take two sets," she announced. Macdara groaned. There were ten books to a set.

"I'm going to need a box," Oran called to Padraig.

"And not one of those measly don't-worry-we'll-find-a-way-to-upcycle-them pastry ones." Padraig lifted his head and beamed.

Macdara carried her box out of the bookshop, grumbling a bit under the weight. "Why on earth did you need two sets?"

"There's a set for me so I can start a baking hobby without ruining me mam's set, and a new set for Eoin's restaurant."

"Baking hobby," Macdara said, pulling her in for a quick kiss. "In that case, are you sure you bought enough books?" Before she could answer, a buzz sounded from Macdara's trousers, making him jump.

"Me phone."

Siobhán laughed and reached into his pocket.

"I should carry books for you more often," he joked. She removed his mobile, and held it up to his ear.

"DS Flannery speaking. Already? Brilliant." He nodded and Siobhán turned the phone off. He picked up his pace, heading across the square to the station. "Just got the judge's warrant. We can search Aoife McBride's room at the Twins' Inn."

Emma and Eileen, the identical twins who owned the inn, were late meeting Siobhán and Macdara. They lingered restlessly at the door to Aoife's room. Macdara glanced at his watch. "You told them we were coming?"

"I did." Their gaze swiveled toward the cottage next to the inn as if it was a teakettle and they were watching it boil. When no twins emerged, Siobhán turned and studied the inn. The rooms were arranged in a U-shape in front of the car park. Both the cottage and inn were painted a cheerful yellow with bright blue window trim. Finally, the door to the cottage opened and one of the twins poked her head out. Her face was white, not the pasty white of most of the Irish in town, but actual white. She was covered in flour. "Be right there," she called.

A few minutes later, both twins exited and hurried over to them. They were sporting matching pink aprons that read: BAKE SOMEONE HAPPY. Splotches of flour blotted their pretty faces and petite bodies. Thirty-something, the twins were identical. They leaned into it, even wearing their curly golden locks in the same shoulder-length cut, with feathered fringes. "We were just doing a little baking," Eileen said. Siobhán assumed it was Eileen, for her name was printed under the message. For all Siobhán knew they had switched aprons just to mess with people. That's probably what she would have done if she was a twin.

"What are you baking?" Macdara asked.

"Aoife's famous shortbread," Emma said. "She gave us a secret recipe!" They grinned in stereo.

"May she rest in peace," Macdara reminded them.

Their smiles evaporated. "I keep forgetting," Emma said. "I just can't believe it."

"Electrocuted," Eileen said. "It's horrible."

"May she rest in peace," Siobhán echoed. If they were looking for gossip they weren't going to get it. Siobhán glanced at Aoife's door. They had given Aoife McBride the middle room, which Siobhán knew from past investigations was the largest one of all.

"You must have been rather friendly with her," Siobhán said.

"We adored her," Emma said. "Even if she was a bit grouchy."

"Grouchy?" Macdara asked, taking out his notebook and Biro.

"We probably annoyed her a tad," Eileen said. "Asking after the recipe. I feel bad now."

"At least her famous shortbread will live on through us," Emma said.

"How did it turn out?" Macdara asked.

"Settle there, cowboy," Siobhán said. "You've barely had time to digest whatever you ate at the bookshop."

"Apple tarts," he said wiggling his eyebrows. "But don't you worry, wifey. I saved room for shortbread."

"I'll give you something to worry about if you keep calling me wifey."

Emma thrust her hand in her apron pocket and lifted up a timer. "We'll know how the shortbread turned out in seven minutes."

"Plus at least five minutes to cool," Eileen added.

"I'd say longer," Emma said, not making eye contact with Macdara.

"If you need an impartial taster, I'd be happy to oblige," Macdara said.

"Do you have the warrant?" Emma asked.

"For the shortbread?" Macdara asked, sounding panicked. Siobhán laughed. She was normally the one sticking her foot in her mouth, but no longer. Thank heavens for husbands.

"For the room," Emma said, with a quick glance at Eileen. *He's a nutter.*

Siobhán nudged her cookie-obsessed husband out of the way and pulled out the warrant. "Her solicitor is probably going to have a fit, but a warrant is a warrant," Eileen said after glancing at it and unlocking the door.

"Solicitor?" Siobhán said. "Is he a short bald man who wears suits and black glasses?"

"That's the one," Emma said. "He warned us that folks

might try all kinds of crazy tricks to sneak into Aoife's room."

"When was this?" Siobhán asked. She tried to keep the desperation out of her voice, but from the startled looks on their faces, she knew she had failed.

"We really can't let the shortbread burn," Eileen said.

"No, you cannot," Macdara said.

Siobhán wasn't going to win this one. "We need to talk to you about the solicitor as soon as we're finished in here."

The twins saluted. Eileen stepped forward and opened the door. "You're going to put on your outfits, right?"

"Our gloves, booties, and suits," Siobhán said. "Yes, don't worry, we will."

Macdara and Siobhán waited until the twins had disappeared into their nearby cottage before suiting up. "How do I look in my outfit?" Macdara asked when they were all set, wiggling his eyebrows.

"Murderous," Siobhán said. He laughed and opened the door. From force of habit, Siobhán was usually prepared for anything, but she was taken aback when they laid eyes on the chaos that was Aoife McBride's room. Clothing was strewn everywhere. Piled on the bed, obscuring the tops of the dresser, hanging off the table and chairs near the window, and as they stepped further inside the room, there were even articles of clothing in the bathroom sink. The closet door was open and it too was stuffed with clothing.

"This is odd, right?" Macdara said, turning to Siobhán.

"I'm gobsmacked."

"Looking at this mess makes me realize that I love how little you care about your outfits."

Siobhán frowned, feeling as if his compliment had really been an insult. "I care about my outfits," she said. "At least once in a great while I do."

"You look good in everything," Macdara said. "Perhaps what I should have said is that I'm thrilled I've never come home to this." He stared into the room and shook his head.

"I never imagined Aoife McBride was a slob." Siobhán had a feeling that Aoife would never want the details of this untidy room leaked to the public.

Siobhán didn't know where to focus. An open suitcase sitting in the middle of the bed, and nearly engulfed by clothing, held a pile of wigs. *Interesting*. Siobhán moved toward them. "Look." She pointed them out to Macdara. They were all long and gray, just in slightly different styles.

"That doesn't seem normal either," Macdara said. "Was she losing her hair?"

"Women wear wigs for many reasons," Siobhán said.

"Someone would pay a fortune to have a wig made out of your hair," Macdara said.

"If you ever enter our bedroom with scissors I'm filing for divorce."

Macdara laughed. "I wouldn't dare."

"We'll have to ask Jeanie Brady if Aoife was wearing a wig when they brought her in."

Siobhán studied everything in the room again, her mind whirring. The mess reminded her of Gráinne's room. Given Gráinne was a personal stylist, growing up, her portion of her room had always been a heap of clothing and makeup, whereas Ann's side was much neater. Many artists were messy. Siobhán thought of George O'Leary. The talent agent. The actress Elizabeth Wynne. *She used to be a makeup artist*. This room looked like it belonged to an actress-slash-makeup-artist who was in an awful hurry to find just the right outfit. "Look for a handbag, or any papers, anything with her identification."

"Identification?" Macdara asked. "Wasn't Aoife McBride's identification found on her person?"

Siobhán nodded. "In her apron pocket, according to Doctor Brady. And I find that odd." Who kept their motor license in an apron pocket? What if the killer had slipped Aoife McBride's identification into her apron pocket after she was electrocuted? Siobhán began opening drawers, hoping for answers. One drawer was piled with makeup. A second held a flowered dress and a floppy hat. Siobhán lifted the hat. She turned to the nightstand and opened it. There, beneath the Bible, was a résumé.

Elizabeth Wynne
Actress

"What is that?" Macdara asked, coming up behind her.

"Elizabeth Wynne's CV," Siobhán said.

"Why would Aoife McBride have Elizabeth Wynne's CV?"

"That," Siobhán said, "is a most interesting question."

"I know that tone," Macdara said. "What are you thinking?"

"I'm thinking Aoife McBride never stayed in this room."

Macdara whistled. "You think this room belongs to Elizabeth Wynne?"

"I do," Siobhán said.

"I don't quite follow," Macdara said. "What exactly are you thinking?"

They were interrupted by a loud bang on the door. Macdara went and opened it. Emma and Eileen stood with a pan covered in little white biscuits.

"Something is terribly, terribly wrong," Emma said.

"Or Aoife McBride was taking the piss," Eileen added.

"These are horrible," Emma said, scrunching up her face. "The worst, chalky, bitter-with-an-aftertaste *awful*." She shoved the tray at Macdara. "Taste them."

Before Siobhán could scold them for asking her husband to taste something disgusting, he already had it in his mouth. To his credit, he swallowed, but the look on his face said it all.

"You're right," he said. "Does anyone have a mint?" When no one did, Macdara whirled around, and soon they heard running water in the sink. No doubt he had his head stuck under it.

"She hated us," Emma said. "Aoife McBride hated us."

"She didn't hate you, luv," Siobhán said. The last bit of her thought was case-related and so Siobhán was forced to cut it off. *Aoife McBride didn't hate you, luv, because Aoife McBride never even met you.*

Chapter 18

Siobhán stepped out to the garden in the back of the inn where there was a lovely gazebo with seating. The spring flowers were in full bloom. Yellow tulips, and bluebells, and orange poppies painted a cheery picture. Siobhán paced among them while she placed her call. Jeanie Brady answered straightaway. "What a relief to have our victim identified," she said before Siobhán could even speak.

"Pardon?" Siobhán stopped to watch a butterfly land on a nearby leaf, its wings flexing in the sun.

"George O'Leary."

"Right, so. That is a relief."

"I take it that's not why you're calling," Jeanie said.

"How did you confirm Aoife McBride's identity?" Siobhán asked.

She knew Jeanie Brady so well she could nearly feel that a frown had broken out on her face. "There wasn't any need. Her motor license was in her apron pocket, and when I was called to the scene I was told it was Aoife McBride." She hesitated. "Are you saying our female victim is not Aoife McBride?"

"I think the victim's name is Elizabeth Wynne. I think she was hired to be Aoife McBride's double."

"Tell me why."

Siobhán was prepared for this. Jeanie Brady was good at her job because she was methodical. "Elizabeth Wynne was an actress and a former makeup artist hired for the baking show as an extra of sorts. A *catchall* her agent called it. She was supposed to check in with him, but he hasn't heard from her since she took the assignment. Not even when George O'Leary was killed. But I think the killer had a much bigger role in mind for her. She's the same age and build as Aoife McBride—most likely the killer 'discovered' her at the Aoife McBride Fan Club Appreciation event in Donegal a few months ago. Elizabeth Wynne and our fake protester were hired from the same talent agency. Remember you found it odd that Aoife McBride's motor license was in her apron pocket?"

"Now. I did find that odd."

"Our killer made a mistake doing that," Siobhán said. *Overkill.* He or she wanted to make sure to convince the authorities that the victim was indeed Aoife McBride. But no one else had a motor license in his or her apron pocket, thus drawing unnecessary attention to that particular detail. This killer was cunning but not perfect. And imperfection was an investigator's best friend.

"Someone was trying too hard to convince us," Jeanie agreed.

"Furthermore, Aoife's room at the Twins' Inn was jammed with clothing, makeup, wigs, and Elizabeth Wynne's CV. I also found allergy meds in her room, and our judges informed us that they brought Aoife McBride flowers but later saw her storm past their window with them, as if insulted. I believe Elizabeth was rejecting them because she was allergic. And last but not least—Aoife supposedly gave the twins a shortbread recipe. They made it and it tasted like cardboard."

"Worse than cardboard," Macdara said, sneaking up on Siobhán and startling her. "I can still taste it."

"Are you saying Aoife McBride was never even here?" Jeanie asked.

"That's my theory," Siobhán said. "Our next call is going to be to the Donegal Gardaí to perform a wellness check. She lives in a cottage near Donegal Bay."

"Performing a wellness check on a woman you thought was dead," Jeanie said. "I can only imagine that phone call."

"I know. They're going to think we're crackpots."

"Do you know any next of kin for Elizabeth Wynne?" Jeanie asked.

"Not yet, but we'll ask her agent."

"I'll have to request dental records for both women," Jeanie said. "I'll send in the request."

"How long will that take?"

"It depends on whether or not Elizabeth Wynne or Aoife McBride had regular dental work and how quickly we can trace their dentists."

"Elizabeth and George's agent is out of Dublin," Siobhán said. "I'll ask for Elizabeth's address as well."

"George O'Leary was Dublin as well, but he did a lot of traveling," Jeanie remarked.

"An actor's life," Siobhán said.

For information on Aoife McBride's dental records they'd be dealing with the Donegal Garda Station once again. Distance meant time. Time they didn't have if they wanted to get to the bottom of this case quickly. "If I hadn't requested them, would you have checked Aoife's dental records against the victim?" Siobhán asked.

"No," Jeanie said. "We only do that when we do not

have a positive identification on the victim. I requested George O'Leary's records, but you provided his identification first. His records still haven't come in."

Siobhán let the statement sink in. Yet another instance where time was on the killer's side. If their female victim was Elizabeth Wynne and *not* Aoife McBride, then they had better find out if the real Aoife McBride was unharmed before the news of the mistaken identification leaked. But if Aoife McBride was still alive, why hadn't she come forward? The possible answers were troubling, but if their victim was indeed Elizabeth Wynne, then at least that gave them one more piece of the puzzle. The killer had counted on them *not* questioning her identity. But the killer had also made mistakes. Hiring more than one actor, if that's who their female victim turned out to be, was one of those mistakes. Had George O'Leary not been on the scene, they may have chalked up "Aoife's" death to a terrible accident and no one would have ever suspected murder.

"Looks like I'm going to be in town a while," Jeanie said.

"Why don't you come to our house for supper," Siobhán said. "If we're going to spring a new victim identity on you, the least we can do is feed you."

A small group converged onto Siobhán and Macdara's farmhouse to discuss the case. Garda Aretta Dabiri and Doctor Jeanie Brady sat at the small table in the kitchen. Siobhán, who had been itching to do it since the baking show started, was making brown bread as they talked. Keeping her hands busy was essential to helping her think. She spoke aloud as she lined up the baking tins. She had already sorted out all the necessary ingredients: stone-ground Irish whole wheat flour, all-purpose flour, rolled oats, salt, baking soda, buttermilk, treacle, and a can of Guinness, of which she would use just a little to taste. She whisked it with the buttermilk and molasses. There would be most of the Guinness left, and after this case, she'd be happy-out drinking it. She could make brown bread in her sleep and kept an easy rhythm while chatting. They were waiting on word from the Donegal Gardaí. Was it possible Aoife McBride was still alive? What if she was behind this? She wouldn't be the first person to fake her own death, but she may very well be the first to hire and then kill off a double in order to do it. If that was her plan, part of it was quite brilliant. The event was being streamed to thousands of viewers, all who believed the woman was Aoife McBride.

"At least two actors were hired. Two actors murdered. One solicitor—if he even is a solicitor—in the wind," Siobhán said as she preheated the cooker and combined the dry ingredients into a large bowl.

"I hope no harm has come to her," Jeanie Brady said.

"Could Aoife McBride herself be doing this?" Aretta asked. "Faking her own death?" Aretta's voice squeaked. Siobhán knew why. It was just so hard to fathom. Yet not out of the range of possibility.

"I was just thinking about that," Siobhán said. Macdara's eyes were glued to the smaller bowl where Siobhán whisked up the buttermilk, treacle, and Guinness. "It's a possibility."

"Imagine," Jeanie said. "If our victim turns out to be our killer." She shook her head. "That would be one for the books."

"Does anyone else want a Guinness?" Macdara asked. All hands around the table raised and Macdara sorted them out. Siobhán mixed the smaller bowl in with the larger one, then covered her hands with flour as she began to knead the dough in the bowl, forming it into a ball. Finally she made crosses on top of each loaf and arranged them into the tins.

"Perhaps she was afraid of someone," Macdara said. "And she's gone into hiding."

"Perhaps," Siobhán said as she slid the tins into the cooker. She liked to bake them longer at a lower heat. They would take an hour, but they would be soft in the middle and crisp on top. If only the baking contest were all about brown bread, Siobhán O'Sullivan would be the champion.

"What on earth are you going to tell the other contestants?" Doctor Brady asked. "Won't this terrify them?"

"That's another reason we're here," Siobhán said. "To discuss what happens with the baking show."

Jeanie crossed her arms and stared at the cooker. "I thought we were here so you could torture me with your brown bread." Jeanie Brady had recently sworn off all breads. Siobhán couldn't imagine such a thing.

"If you think this is tempting, try working at that bakery every day with all those amazing, delicious scents," Siobhán said. "It's only been a few days and I feel like I've gained ten stone."

"I don't think we need to tell anyone just yet," Macdara said.

"About my weight gain?" Siobhán asked.

"That Aoife McBride may not be our victim," Macdara said. He laughed to himself and shook his head. "If you gain weight there's just more of you to love."

"Do you think it's ethical to keep the true identity of our female victim a secret?" Aretta asked.

Siobhán turned to Macdara. "What you were supposed to say, and you're going to want to remember this for the future—was—'Darling, you actually look like you *lost* ten stone.'"

Macdara nearly choked on his Guinness. "Right." He tapped his forehead with his index finger. "It's locked in now."

Siobhán smiled and turned to Aretta. "I'm sorry, pet. What did you say?"

"I was wondering about the ethics of allowing the rest of our players to go on assuming that Aoife McBride is dead."

"It may not be ethical," Siobhán said. "But it may be what's needed to catch a killer."

"They're all such big Aoife McBride fans," Aretta continued. "Or enemies . . . What if they find out through another channel? They won't have any trust in us at all."

"I hear your point," Siobhán said. "And right now we do not know whether or not Aoife McBride is alive or dead. But this killer needs Aoife to be dead—for whatever reason—and so far he or she thinks his plan is working."

"Think of the panic this revelation could cause," Macdara added. "Whatever decision we make we have to think it through very carefully."

"In the meantime we can continue to dig into George O'Leary." Siobhán pointed to her fridge, where she had posted his sketch. "If he was hired by the killer, maybe someone spotted them together, or has information pertinent to the case."

Jeanie gazed at the sketch. "I imagined the pair of ye hanging children's artwork on the fridge," she said. "Not murder victims."

"To be fair, it's a big fridge," Siobhán said.

"I want to find this solicitor," Macdara said. "He could even be our killer."

Jeanie Brady's phone rang, startling them all. "I'll be right back," Jeanie said, taking the call outside. Siobhán offered everyone tea in lieu of pacing. Moments later

Jeanie Brady entered, and Siobhán knew from her face what she was going to say, even before the words came out of her mouth.

"One small blessing, depending on how you look at it. Elizabeth Wynne has had a lot of dental work. And she is indeed our victim."

Chapter 19

"Bakers, bakers, bakers," Ronan began. He stood in the large back room of the mill, facing the new kitchen stations. A camera was once again rolling, but this time, all the reporters had been relocated to the streaming locations, and the only live filming was being done by Charlie Holiday. Ruth stood beside him, a finger over her mouth, as if willing herself not to speak. The event was being streamed to O'Rourke's Pub, Turn the Page bookshop, and the café formerly known as Naomi's Bistro. It was now called Pat's Café, but Siobhán could not yet bring herself to call it by a new name. Pat hadn't even officially opened but the cafe permitted a soft opening for the streaming. He would serve tea and coffee and they would order pastries from the bakery. It was strange imagining another café in their former family-run bistro, but life was constant change, and Siobhán was thrilled for their new direction as a family. Not to mention she had a murderer to catch. Aretta Dabiri had a bit of paperwork to catch up on at the office and would meet them at the bakery when she was finished. "Welcome to your second chance!" Ronan boomed.

Philomena pointed a long fingernail, today painted a soft pink, directly at Sophia. "We mostly mean you," she said. "This is your second chance."

"Thank you," Sophia said, clasping her hands and giving a little bow. "I'm ever so grateful."

"Don't thank us yet," Ronan said. "For today we're about to turn your worlds upside down." He reached behind him, and when he thrust his hand up again, there was a large pineapple resting in his palm.

"Pineapple upside-down cake!" Phil shouted, beating Ronan to the punch. Siobhán and Macdara waited as they explained the challenge. "You will have two hours to make as many pineapple upside-down cakes as you are able, and then you are to present your best one to the judges." Ronan strode over to the ingredients tables and stared down at them. "Where are the pineapples?" Panic rang from his voice as he looked to Fia O'Farrell and then his fellow judge.

"Don't look at me," Phil said.

"I didn't receive any pineapples," Fia said.

Heads turned as the contestants all exchanged glances. "Don't tell me there's going to be another delay," Sophia said. "If I don't start again me nerves are going to take me down!"

"Let's just move on to the next challenge," Phil said. "These ingredients are all for . . ." She beckoned to Ronan with her index finger. "C'mere to me."

He sighed but obeyed. She whispered in his ear. "You're right, you're right," he said. "Someone messed up the order of the bakes!"

"We're live if you haven't forgotten," Ruth said. "Just skip to the next bake."

Ronan whipped a pocket square out of his suit and used

it to wipe his brow. "It's a different *script* for the next bake, so you'll at least have to give me ten minutes to prepare."

"Ten minutes," Ruth boomed. "Ten minutes and we start with or without you." Fia O'Farrell zoomed into the shot.

"Good folks of Kilbane, listening to our live streaming event from town. Now is your chance to order more pastries! Get them by the dozen. Cookies, tarts, pies, donuts, soda bread . . ."

As she rattled on, Siobhán took a moment to walk around the perimeter of the room as she formulated her thoughts. Last night, as the task of baking brown bread had helped her think through the case, Siobhán realized there was a much better approach to their official interviews. Instead of taking the bakers away from their precious baking time and forcing them to sit at a table, where they were most likely distracted with the baking task ahead of them, they could ask the players questions *while* they baked.

It might even work to their advantage. The subjects would be in their comfort zone, which would help them relax. But no doubt they would still have half of their mind on their bakes. When one was so concentrated on a task, it made it difficult to keep track of one's lies. And the purpose of Siobhán's questions had now shifted in her mind. Often, the question was—who benefitted the most from the victim's death? In this case the true victim was Elizabeth Wynne. Only the killer knew that. What else did the killer know? Did the killer know his or her victim was actually Elizabeth Wynne or did he or she believe he or she had murdered Aoife McBride? If this was the case, and the killer realized his or her mistake, the Donegal Guards needed to locate Aoife before she too was dead. But there was another possibility, the one that Siobhán had been obsessing over. Elizabeth Wynne was an actress for hire. The question: Why was she hired and then killed? There was a troubling possible answer. She knew too much. What if someone had already killed Aoife McBride, and this someone needed the world to realize Aoife McBride was dead? If Aoife McBride was "killed" in front of a live audience, wouldn't that be a perfect way to never be suspected of her murder? Aoife had supposedly been staying out of the spotlight lately. Could this be why? She had reported trouble to the guards after the Fan Club Appreciation Day event. What if she'd been in more trouble than anyone had realized?

On the other hand, what if Aoife McBride herself was behind this? The Donegal Gardaí had spoken with Macdara early this morning. A late-night wellness check had yielded no results. Her cottage was neat as a pin and locked tight with no one home. Because of the nature of the inquiry, the gardaí had gained entrance to the cottage, but there were no signs of a struggle, but there were also no signs of the woman.

A thought struck Siobhán. If Elizabeth was not a great baker and she was about to impersonate the *best*—was it possible Elizabeth Wynne was purposefully killed before someone realized she couldn't bake? In this case, what had Elizabeth been told about this assignment? She must have realized it wouldn't be possible to emulate Aoife's baking—then again perhaps she was delusional about her baking skills, and it was possible she had Aoife McBride's recipes to work with. The killer had put the strychnine in the face powder first. She was meant to die *before* the baking show began. The first challenge instructed each contestant to make their signature dish. Aoife McBride's was a cherry pie. Even the twins had commented on the terrible shortbread, it wasn't a stretch that the killer became worried that someone else would call out the discrepancy. After all, Barry Ryan had a photographic taste-memory. Would he have realized the woman was an imposter?

Ronan strode back into the room. "I'm ready," he said.

"Finally," Phil said. "I've been ready."

Ronan flicked her an irritated look but when he turned to the camera he was all smiles. "As many of you may know, Aoife McBride was going to use this baking show to present the world with a new take on her famous chocolate cake."

Siobhán snapped to attention. She had not known that.

Ronan cleared his throat and glanced at a sheet of paper in front of him. Phil nudged him. "Go on."

"I'm wondering if we shouldn't change the title," Ronan said, glancing nervously at the recipe once more.

"I think these good folks have had enough change for one week," Phil said. She snatched the script out of his hand. "Today's challenge is called 'Death by Chocolate.'" There were a few gasps and a few cheers.

Ronan nudged Phil out of the spotlight and took over once more. "We want you to make Aoife McBride's signature chocolate cake. We have the recipe right here—but it will be up to your imagination to add Aoife's new secret ingredient. On this table we have a selection of items. There might be up to three different ingredients she used to enhance her Death by Chocolate cake. Who knows? Perhaps there is just one. Perhaps two."

"We get it," Phil said. "It can be any combination—or not—of three ingredients on the table."

"It has to be at least one," Ronan said.

"Don't scream at me!" Philomena said. Arguably, she said it whilst screaming. What was with those two this morning? They were like carts rolling downhill with their wheels coming off.

Ronan dabbed his forehead again, took a deep breath, and straightened his spine. "Whosoever gets the closest in taste to Aoife's Death by Chocolate cake wins. For while you are all baking your creations, Ronan and Philomena—that's us—are going to bake Aoife's chocolate cake with the secret ingredient or ingredients."

"How is it that you have Aoife McBride's secret recipe?" Siobhán asked.

"It was provided for us because of this challenge," Ronan said. "This was all planned before poor Ms. McBride face-planted into her pie."

Martin Murphy turned to Sophia. "Did you know this was coming?"

"Me?" she said. "Why would I?"

"Is it just a coincidence that you asked me to make Pie Pie Love out of chocolate?"

Sophia asked Martin to make that sculpture? Siobhán didn't know if that was relevant but it was new information, so she nudged closer to listen.

Sophia cocked her head. "What else would it be?"

"Sabotage!" Martin said, thrusting his finger in the air.

Sophia placed her hands on her hips. "How on earth was I sabotaging you?"

"Maybe you knew this challenge was coming up."

"Don't be ridiculous. And what does it even matter?"

Martin banged a pan on his counter. "I'm sick of chocolate now. How am I supposed to make a chocolate cake when I can't even look at chocolate? And am I going to have to guard my sugar this time?"

"I thought I'd been forgiven," Sophia said. "But in case you didn't hear it the first hundred times I said it—I'm sorry. Alright? I am so, so sorry."

Martin folded his arms across his chest. His muscles flexed and bulged.

"If your little tantrum is over, can we get on with the games?" Ronan asked.

Martin gave a shrug and a nod. Philomena passed out the Death by Chocolate recipes. They spoke the last line in unison. "On your mark, get set, die."

All noise immediately halted as every head snapped to Philomena and Ronan. The camera moved in closer.

"What?" Philomena said, flashing a Cheshire grin. "What did we say?"

Siobhán and Macdara hovered over Martin's station, giving him just enough time to get his station organized before peppering him with questions. Martin's little outburst had shown that he was emotionally off-kilter and Siobhán wanted to keep him that way. He was unwrapping large chocolate bars that he dropped into a saucepan with butter to melt.

"What's your secret ingredient?" Macdara asked.

Martin frowned and glanced at a nearby towel that was draped over a mysterious lump. "I don't think you can ask me that," he said.

Siobhán nudged in. "Did you have any interaction with Aoife McBride on your night off, or really any interaction at any time with Aoife McBride since you arrived?"

Martin stirred a large bowl of cake batter. "She did make a bit of a pass at me," he said. "I wouldn't have believed it if I hadn't experienced it meself."

"What happened?" Siobhán asked. Macdara was staring at the batter. Siobhán suspected Macdara was waiting for Martin to turn his back so that he could dip a spoon into it. She hoped he wasn't going to embarrass her.

"It was the night we all went to that little pub," Martin said. "She was staring at me from across the room. You know the look," he said. "We all know the look."

"The 'come hither' look?" Macdara asked.

"Exactly," Martin said.

"What look am I giving you now?" Siobhán said as she turned to her husband and laid one on him.

"That's your 'shut your gob' look," Macdara said without hesitation.

Siobhán shrugged and turned back to Martin with an impressed nod. "Is there any chance she was looking at someone else?"

Martin cocked his head. "You find it surprising that she would be checking me out?"

"You're quite a bit younger."

"Exactly," Martin said. "She wanted my youth, and my muscles." His gaze shifted momentarily to Sophia Hughes, who after a moment locked eyes with him. Her face flushed as red as her hair.

"Did this flirtation go any further?" Macdara asked in a tone that suggested he was tired of Martin crowing about his youth and his muscles.

"She asked me if I wanted to dance," Martin said. "I had just crossed the room to talk to someone when she intercepted me."

"Did you dance?" Macdara asked.

"One dance," Martin said. "How could I have refused?"

"Had you ever met Aoife McBride in person before this?" Siobhán asked. She kept her voice light, hoping the question wouldn't set off any alarm bells. Then again, if it did, perhaps it was because Martin Murphy knew the woman he danced with wasn't Aoife McBride.

"Only through her work," Martin said. "This was the first time I'd ever met her in person."

Siobhán nodded. "Who were you crossing the room to meet?"

Martin frowned. "It was that funny little man who delivered our red envelopes."

Siobhán felt Macdara straighten up beside her. "He was beckoning you from across the room?" Macdara asked.

"He was," Martin said. "Waving his arms at me like he was bringing in an airplane. I finally had to see what he wanted."

"But you never made it all the way across the room," Siobhán said.

"That's when Aoife McBride swooped in." He shook his head. "She was mad to dance with me."

Interesting. Siobhán had no idea what this was all about, but she couldn't help but feel it was something.

"Did she say anything to you during this dance?" Macdara asked.

Martin cracked an egg and stirred it into the batter. "She said she couldn't wait until this baking show was over." Martin stirred his concoction some more, then poured the batter into a cake pan.

"Anything else?" Macdara asked.

"No," Martin said. "That was the last time I talked to her."

"What about William Bains?" Siobhán asked.

"Who?"

"The funny little man who was waving to you across the room," Macdara prodded.

"Right," Martin said. "After the dance, Aoife wanted another one. I tried to pull away." He shook his head.

"She had a strong grip. By the time the second dance was over, I never saw Mr. Bains again." He sighed, and looked down at his oven mitts. "Thank goodness I said yes to the dance. Imagine how I'd feel now if I hadn't? The last dance partner of her life. At least it was with a youthful and strong man, am I right?" Martin flashed a grin at Macdara. "Perhaps I'll write my own memoir one day. *Aoife McBride's Last Dance*. It could be something, don't ye think?"

"You're certainly something," Macdara said.

"I'm sure it was a lovely last dance," Siobhán said. She was thinking now of memoirs and how Aoife not only had one in the works, but she'd just released a new cookbook set as well. She sent a text to Helen at the station, asking if they'd had any luck in tracking down Aoife McBride's literary agent yet. Had Martin Murphy killed Aoife McBride just to write a tell-all memoir of his own?

As soon as they ended their discussion with Martin Murphy, Macdara pulled Siobhán to the back of the room. Although Siobhán was getting somewhat used to the damp nature of the old flour mill, since they'd moved to the new space she was constantly distracted by the sound of water dripping and echoing. "What do you think?" Macdara asked. "Is Muscles Martin a truth-teller or a liar?"

"Let us assume for a moment that Martin Murphy is not our killer."

Macdara nodded. "Right."

"I think William Bains was waving at someone else from across the room."

"Why do you think that?"

"I think Elizabeth Wynne was instructed to intercept Martin and prevent him from realizing that William Bains had been waving to someone else. I think that someone else is our killer. And then, after the first dance ended, our killer was still engaged with William Bains, which is why Elizabeth had to keep Martin occupied through a *second* dance."

"Meaning at this point Elizabeth Wynne is still going along with whatever these acting duties of hers were?"

"Correct." Siobhán nodded. "At that stage it had not been confirmed that George O'Leary had met with foul play. But after his death Elizabeth Wynne had to have been suspicious and on edge. In fact, I interrogated her afterward. She was taken aback that he died, but at first there was no recognition that her actions may have contributed to it in anyway. I saw her stress increase as we spoke." Siobhán took a moment to take a deep breath.

"It's not your fault," Macdara said.

"Technically, I know that. But at some point she realized she was in trouble. Maybe she would have come to us if I hadn't been so harsh."

"No," Macdara said. "If that was the case she could have just walked into the Kilbane Garda Station. She didn't come to the guards because she was afraid of her culpability in whatever this mess is."

Siobhán nodded. He was right. "Maybe she was afraid of angering our killer, trying to prove her loyalty."

Before they could discuss the development any further, Fia O'Farrell barreled toward them, her face a portrait of shock. Chris Holiday quickly moved in with the camera.

"What's going on?" Siobhán asked.

"Can we take that entrance again from the top?" Ruth asked, stepping out of the shadows. "Maybe this time, Fia, you could vocalize something?"

Fia froze. "What?" She glanced at the camera like it was a wild animal.

"Run in again. And yell something. Like 'Help! Help!' "

"No," Siobhán said. She turned to Fia. "What's the story?"

"You told me to tell you if anything else odd happened," Fia said. Her gaze flicked toward the east wall and then back to Siobhán. "Remember?"

"Of course," Siobhán said. "What is it?" From the look on Fia's face it was something astonishing.

"The waterwheel," Fia said. "It's turning."

Chapter 20

Excitement thrummed through the group as they rushed to the side of the mill. Aretta had just arrived and joined them in time to witness the drama. The giant cast-iron wheel was churning the water with gusto. It had a lovely meditative effect on Siobhán and for a moment she forgot about everything but the waterwheel turning, losing herself in the noise and motion as it continuously sprayed.

"I don't understand," Siobhán said. "How did this happen?"

"Someone fixed it," Charlie said. He pumped his fist in the air while still holding the recorder. "Well played, whoever you are. Well played!"

"Are you saying someone fixed the wheel and you have no idea who?" Macdara asked.

Fia looked around. "I'm making sure Father Kearney isn't in earshot." Once satisfied the local priest wasn't hiding behind a bush to listen to her sins, she began. "Although I attend mass a bit more regularly than most in this town . . ." She gave Siobhán and Macdara a pointed look. "That notwithstanding, I'm not one to believe in miracles. Even that time when me own mother insisted she saw the

Virgin Mary in our biscuits, I'm the one who faced the family wrath by eating it."

"Noted," Siobhán said. "The waterwheel did not miraculously start churning."

Fia visibly relaxed, then crossed herself. "Amen."

"Have you spoken with any contractors about getting it fixed?" Aretta asked.

"It seems the producers of the baking show would have inquired about the waterwheel," Siobhán added.

"Do you think this was meant to be a surprise for hosting the baking show?" Fia asked.

"No, I wasn't thinking that exactly—" Siobhán started.

"You know what? I don't care who did it." Fia threw her arms open. "This *is* a miracle of sorts. If we get the wheel fixed I'll be one step closer to grinding flour again. We can eventually open for tours. This might be the answer to all my misery!"

"Why don't you give us a quick tutorial explaining how this waterwheel works," Siobhán said. She hated to break up a good surprise, but she had a sinking feeling that whoever fixed this old wheel had something more in mind than magnanimity.

"In order to fix that wheel, not only would someone need all the missing parts, and even I couldn't tell you what they are, someone needed access to the ground floor of the mill," Fia said. "As I mentioned when you toured it, that area is closed to the public."

"And the door to the ground floor is the one that was previously hacked into but we sealed it off recently, is that correct?" Siobhán asked.

"That door is the only entrance and exit other than the inside door on the east wall at the far end of the event space," Fia said.

"And you keep that door locked?" Siobhán asked.

"Of course." Fia nibbled on her bottom lip.

"But?"

"But it's been so chaotic lately, everyone moving into the event space and then you asked for the tour. I'm pretty sure I locked the door after, but I'm only human! I guess it's possible I left the key lying around somewhere."

"We'll check the outer door first," Macdara said. "Aretta, will you check the inner door? Note whether or not it is locked, see if it's been disturbed in any way, and also mark it with crime scene tape?"

"Straightaway," Aretta said.

"I'm going to call in for extra guards," Macdara said.

"I'm grateful for whoever fixed this," Fia remarked. "Does it really alarm you so much?"

"Can you identify any part of the wheel that wasn't working?" Macdara asked.

Fia scrunched her face. "I believe at one point we had a problem with the sluice gate. You open and close it to start and stop the water. Water builds up in the slots in the wheel and that's what makes it turn. But I never paid proper attention. Even now I don't know that I would trust the flour—there could be rust or other contaminants in this old machinery."

"Don't you use bags of flour for this baking show?" Siobhán asked.

"Of course." Fia frowned. "Obviously I source the flour locally since I can't produce my own."

Siobhán's mind was churning along with the water-wheel. Was someone planning on replacing the store-bought flour with milled flour that might be contaminated? What if they weren't done killing? "We need guards watching the flour that the contestants use," Siobhán said.

Macdara was in step with her as he held up his mobile phone. "I'll give that order now."

Siobhán turned to Fia. "Can you show me the sluice gate?"

"I wish I could have enjoyed this moment a little more," Fia said sullenly, as she led them down the river.

"Sure, lookit." Siobhán gave her best *What can you do?* face.

"I'm going to check the inside of the mill," Macdara said. "I want to see if someone was not only operating the wheel but grinding bags of flour."

"Grand," Siobhán said. "Divide and conquer."

Aretta joined Macdara while Siobhán continued to follow Fia along the river. Soon Ruth and Charlie were on their heels, chattering away. "Whatever you were discussing, can you start from the top and project your voices?" Ruth asked.

"Should I get in front of them?" Charlie said. "Otherwise we'll just see their backs as they talk."

Fia stopped and turned to wait for Ruth and Charlie to catch up. Siobhán felt her patience slipping, but reminded herself of how much was on the line for Fia. This baking show needed to be a success or her bakery was finished. And objectively, it was off to a rocky, not to mention deadly, start.

"Charlie, look at it go," Ruth said, pointing to the wheel. "Are you filming that?" Charlie turned the camera to the wheel. If he was tired of her commands, he was outwardly being a good sport. The wheel did look glorious, happily thrashing the water as it turned.

"It makes sense now why they call it a babbling creek," Siobhán said.

"It's a river," Ruth said. "Do rivers babble?"

"I would say it's more of a burble, or a gurgle," Charlie said. "Although right now this baby is roiling!"

"Can we grind our own flour now?" The voice was male, and he came up from behind. Everyone turned. Ethan Brown stood behind them, grinning as if he was a magician and had just materialized through a haze of smoke.

"No," Fia said. "We do not have the time nor resources to test the flour coming out of this mill. It's four hundred years old and it hasn't been running since I was a child."

"And that was *so very long ago*," Ruth said. Ethan and Charlie laughed and Fia shot them a death glare.

"I'd be willing to test it," Ethan said. "I'd be willing to grind some flour, make a nice pound cake, and test it myself."

"We cannot allow that," Siobhán said.

Ethan Brown's eyes flicked over her for a second. "Pity."

"While you're here," Siobhán said, "do you mind answering a few questions?"

Ethan held her gaze. "Not at all. But is it possible to answer questions and go into town?"

"Town?"

"We're on a two-hour break," Ethan said. "I was hoping for a change of scenery."

"I thought everyone was practicing their Death by Chocolate cake," Ruth said.

"Our time was cut short when everyone ran out to see the wheel," Ethan explained. "If we continue now it won't be long until it is time for a lunch break. Everyone agreed to take a break now, then return and run a little later into the evening."

The other reason was that the guards needed time to replace all the bags of flour just to make sure they hadn't been tampered with, but they weren't going to get the contestants all riled up by telling them that.

"Well, then," Siobhán said. "I'd be happy to chat with you while you go about town."

Ethan grinned. "I've been wanting to have a gander around Kilbane." He flashed a hopeful expression.

Siobhán lifted her gaze and caught Macdara staring at

them. He motioned for Siobhán to join him for a private conversation. They wandered away from the crowd.

"What's the story?" Siobhán asked.

Macdara lowered his voice. "If he's a killer, I don't like you alone with him."

"I've been alone with killers before. I'll be grand."

"I have no doubt," Macdara said. "But that won't stop me from worrying."

"Tell me about it," Siobhán said, leaning in to ruffle his messy hair and give him a quick kiss. "The entire time I'm away I'll be imagining you pinned underneath a giant cast-iron wheel, crying for your wifey."

Chapter 21

Siobhán and Ethan Brown stood on Sarsfield Street in front of O'Rourke's Pub. She pointed out their old bistro, with a sign announcing: PAT'S CAFÉ COMING SOON. Inside, she could see the crowd gathered for the streaming event. Even though the baking show was taking a lunch break, the crowd was still gathered. No doubt Pat was thrilled for the early business. "I used to live there with my siblings," Siobhán explained. "It was Naomi's Bistro. We lived above. Three of my siblings still live above it, but the owner of the building decided he wanted to open his own café." Although Siobhán was thrilled with their new home and new restaurant-to-be, she couldn't help for a bit of nostalgia to creep into her. It was hard to let go of the past.

"It's for the best," Ethan said confidently, striding away from it. "If I were you I wouldn't go near nor next to the place."

His fervor surprised her. She had to jog to catch up. "Why is that?"

"The past," he said. "Never look back, that's my motto."

Was there something in his past he didn't want to face? Perhaps a murder or two . . . "It's going to be alright,"

Siobhán said. "My brother is opening a farm-to-table restaurant on our new property."

"A dream come true," Ethan said. "Does he have a pastry chef?" There was a twinkle in Ethan's eye. He was a charmer.

"We're only in the early stages of the build," Siobhán said. "But I'm sure you can leave your CV for him." *Once we've determined you're not a killer . . .*

"I love smaller Irish villages," Ethan said. "Because of my work I'm usually at castles and five-star resorts." He made it sound like she should take pity on him.

"A resort or a castle," she said with a sigh. "Heaven."

He laughed. "It does have its perks. But I still love the charm of a village."

They lingered in front of O'Rourke's but Ethan had yet to step in. For a moment she wondered if he was a smoker who wanted to light up before going inside, but his hands were jammed in the pockets of his trousers. Was he stalling? Had something happened in there the last time he was here? Ethan had definitely rolled in the next morning looking as if he'd partied hard. Perhaps he was embarrassed. Or had something specific happened that he was ashamed of?

Siobhán needed to speak with Declan about CCTV tapes from the night the bakers and judges went to O'Rourke's; perhaps they would be able to spot William Bains in a video and with a little luck see if they could figure out who he had been trying to wave to from across the room. *Like he was bringing in an airplane*, Martin Murphy had said. It sounded urgent. But Siobhán couldn't speak to Declan with Ethan tagging along. Right now Ethan was talkative and friendly, and she wanted to keep it that way. "Do you want to have lunch at O'Rourke's?"

"If you are hungry we certainly can eat there," Ethan said. "But I never have an appetite when I'm in a competition, and to tell you the truth I was hoping to walk around town with a local and see what there is to see."

"Brilliant," Siobhán said. "The more calories I burn, the more pastries I can eat."

Ethan laughed. "You look fantastic to me."

The flattery gave Siobhán pause. On the one hand, it wasn't appropriate given she was a guard, and he could show a bit of respect. On the other hand, he didn't come off as lecherous, and he was still talkative. Either way she couldn't wait to drop it into conversation with Macdara later. "Aw, thanks," she said. "My husband thinks so too." She cringed a little for saying it, but wasn't that what married couples were supposed to do? It wasn't that one would never be attracted to anyone else, it was that one would never cross a line. Or lead someone else on. But as a guard, the comment taught her something. Ethan was trying to mold their relationship into a friendship. He'd asked her to join him away from the bakery, he was chatty and attentive, and now he was flattering her. But this was not a date, and the only explanation for his approach was that Ethan Brown was either very nervous about something, or very worried.

"Could you tell me about the night everyone went to the pub?" Siobhán asked.

Ethan's friendly demeanor vanished. "I know you've spoken to Sophia Hughes," he said. His tone was bitter.

Siobhán waited to hear if he would elaborate. He did not. "We certainly did." Siobhán made her tone sound as if Sophia had told her something shocking, while searching her memory to see if Sophia had mentioned Ethan Brown at all.

Ethan frowned and pawed the ground with the tip of his shoe. "She was very eager to be interviewed first, wasn't she?"

"I cannot divulge what another witness has said," Siob-

hán said. "But you and I both know what she told us."
Siobhán had come up blank. Sophia hadn't said a single
thing about Ethan. "I just figured there were two sides to
the story."

"She's a master manipulator, that one," Ethan said.
"How she was even chosen for this competition is mind-
boggling."

"Why do you say that?"

Ethan shook his head. "She's a disaster. I've watched
her. I'm telling you, she's not qualified."

Was she another actress? Or was Ethan being too
harsh? It wasn't her fault her first bake had burned, it was
Martin's for turning up her cooker, but Siobhán hadn't
shared that with the larger group.

They had walked nearly to the end of Sarsfield Street.
To the right was their gorgeous ruined abbey, and up
ahead was King John's Castle and the town square. Siobhán loved her medieval walled town. They paused for a
moment as Ethan took it all in. He pointed across the
street to Gordon's Comics.

"Can we walk down the other way? I wanted to look in
the comic shop."

"Not a bother." They continued along. "Take me through
what happened," Siobhán said. "I really want to hear
your side."

"I was only letting off some steam, having a few pints, a
bit of the craic," Ethan began. It was a misty day, the skies
were spitting on them, and Saint Mary's Cathedral was
barely visible in the distance. "Baking is serious business,
so when I get a chance to let loose, I don't hold back, ya
know what I mean?"

"Every fixture needs a release valve," Siobhán said.

Ethan grinned. "I like your style."

"Now. There you were, throwing back a few pints, letting off some steam—and then what?"

"I didn't mean to watch them. I was just taken aback, and froze on the spot, you know?"

I have no idea. Absolutely none. Now she was forced to be an actress and it wasn't a comfortable position to be in. "I do know. But I also need you to go through it as if I'm a right eejit who doesn't have the first clue." For a moment she thought she had laid it on too thick, but soon he threw his head back and laughed.

"Right," he said. "I was taking me pint out to the patio to have a smoke. I was looking at me phone so when I stepped out, I didn't know anyone else was on the patio until I heard the noises." He shook his head. "I bet she didn't tell you how loud they were, did she?"

"I'll never tell."

"You'd be good at poker, your face doesn't give a thing away."

"Comes with the job."

"So I see them, and of course I'm just in a bit of shock, as you can imagine."

"I can imagine." This was grueling. Whatever it was, why didn't he just come out with it?

"By the time they noticed me, I suppose it looked like I was creeping on them. Especially since I had my phone in me hand. She actually accused me of *filming* their dirty business." He stopped and shook his finger. "I am not a peeper, or some kind of creep. If she said anything of the sort, she's a mad cow, so she is." The more he spoke, the angrier he became. "I was only stepping out to have a smoke, which is allowed on the patio. I don't believe knocking boots is condoned, so why am I the one being treated like some kind of Peeping Tom?"

"Why indeed." *Who was Sophia knocking boots with?* "And to be clear, you saw Sophia Hughes with whom?"

He stopped. "Do you think it's illegal? To hook up with a fellow contestant?"

Siobhán quickly ran through the possibilities. Barry "The Sponge" didn't seem like a candidate. It wasn't Ethan, and he would have phrased it differently if Sophia had been with another woman. That left only one. *Martin Murphy.* "I don't know what the rules of the game are," Siobhán said. "I got the impression Martin wasn't that fond of Ms. Hughes. After all, she had sabotaged his rendition of Pie Pie Love."

"Unless they're trying to get a bun in the oven together, it seems they could have held their lust back until this was all over," Ethan said, shaking his head with disgust.

If something of that nature had occurred at O'Rourke's Pub, Siobhán was surprised Maria or Declan himself hadn't given her a bell. Even without a murder inquiry, gossip like that was too good to ignore. And Declan O'Rourke never missed a trick. If Sophia Hughes and Martin Murphy were up to no good on his patio surely he would have known about it. Unless the crowd was simply too much and his usual keen eye had slipped. This ratcheted up her need to stop in to see both Declan and Maria. She also needed to speak to the local chemist to see if Elizabeth had purchased the infamous face powder there, and if she could learn anything more about the mysterious Ms. Wynne. "What about Aoife McBride?" Siobhán said casually. "Did you see or speak to her that evening?"

"Right?" he said. "What a mess, isn't it?"

"Indeed. But once again I need you to tell me what happened."

"Sophia noticed me standing there and screamed as if I was the one in the wrong, and Martin was effin and blinding and that's when I darted back inside and ran into the Queen herself. *Literally.*" He bowed his head. "I found out," he said, leaning in. "Her secret."

Siobhán came to a halt. "What secret?"

"Do we have to do this?" Ethan asked. "Do you have to pretend you're hearing all of this for the first time?"

Siobhán sighed. "I'm afraid that's the law, pet. And you never know when a witness will add something to the story, so it's best to tell everything from the beginning."

"Cancer," he said. "I know she had cancer."

"Cancer?" Siobhán couldn't hold back her surprise.

He shook his head. "I wondered for a moment, if she hadn't . . . you know, taken her own life."

"Taken her own life?"

"The mixer," he said. "How did she not notice water leaking from the fridge?"

Sophia had been telling the truth. They all knew. Siobhán thought they had been so smart, keeping everything from them. She should have known better. One saving grace was that none of them seemed to know that their victim was not Aoife McBride. "Can we go back to running into Aoife McBride in the pub?"

Ethan's legs bounced; he was finding it challenging to stand still. "Right."

"Are you saying she told you she had cancer?"

"No, no, nothing like that. I'm making an assumption," he said.

"It's got to be based on something."

"When we collided, it knocked her wig sideways." He paused. "She was also thinner than the last time I saw her."

"The last time you saw her? When was that?"

"We attended the same cooking show in Dublin a few years ago."

"I see." Siobhán willed herself to breathe normally. Maybe she'd been mistaken. *Did* he know the woman wasn't Aoife McBride? Was he sussing out *her* reaction? Or did he really believe she had cancer? "There are many reasons a person might choose to wear a wig."

"I suppose." He didn't sound as if he agreed.

"Did she say anything to you? Was she upset you noticed she had a wig?" *Terrified that her cover had been blown?*

"Upset?" he said. "She was downright weird."

"Weird how?"

"She grabbed me, leaned in, and said: 'You mustn't say a word to anyone. It's not safe.' " They had arrived at Gordon's Comic Shop.

"What do you think she meant?" Siobhán asked, hoping to keep Ethan focused for a little while longer. "What do you think she meant by 'It's not safe'?"

"Batman!" Ethan said so loudly that Siobhán jumped.

Batman? She'd nearly forgotten they were standing in front of a comic shop. Chris Gordon must have purchased new Batman paraphernalia, for the windows were covered in posters. "Right," she said, trying to drum up some enthusiasm.

"I'd like to go in," he said. His cheeks flushed and he looked at his watch. "Do you have more questions?"

Many, many more, she thought. "That will do for now," she said. "But we'll need to do a formal sit-down later. Ethan nodded and zipped into the shop. Siobhán was heading for the garda station when a Batman quote in the window caught her eye: *I wear a mask. And that mask is not to hide who I am but create what I am.*

Interesting. Just like their killer? Had the killer seen this quote and then devised their wicked plan? Was it Ethan Brown? Was he so bold as to show her it was him by bringing her right to this quote? He had acted as if he had never walked about town before, but perhaps it had all been a lie. She already knew the killer was quite bold. And, Siobhán had to grudgingly admit, quite skilled. Everything had been done right under her nose. Had he drawn her right to this shop, this quote, because he was so confident she would never figure it out?

Otherwise, this meant their killer could be a local. Fia O'Farrell. She would have seen this sign as well. Even though the bakery was outside of town, Fia came to town to do her messages and could have seen the Batman poster and quote. Maybe it was the spark that created this grand plan. And the mill was underwater, Fia was in desperate need of money and a baking show starring Aoife McBride would bring attention. Her very public death would ensure that the attention was magnified and would last a very long time. But that wasn't plausible. People struggled with money issues all the time and if there was a financial benefit to Fia for killing Aoife McBride—Siobhán couldn't see it. Did Fia have any history or quarrels with Elizabeth Wynne or George O'Leary? It was only because Siobhán was working through all these permutations that she was still lingering in front of the comic shop. A movement caught her eye and she looked up just in time to see Ethan Brown, the "Batman lover," escaping out the back door of the shop without so much as cracking open a single comic.

Chapter 22

"Death by Chocolate, take two," Ruth called out. The lunch break was over and the filming had resumed. There was a bit of excitement in the air, no doubt everyone was buoyed by the waterwheel churning.

"Sounds like resurrection by chocolate," Barry Ryan quipped.

Trisha Mayweather threw her head back and laughed loudly. "Oh, Barry," she said, reaching across the stations to place her hand on his arm. Barry beamed. Nearly everyone else rolled their eyes.

"Leave the jokes to us," Philomena pouted.

Siobhán spotted Aretta and Macdara in the corner of the room. They noticed her and waved her over.

"Ethan returned before you," Macdara said. "Did something happen?"

Siobhán glanced over to Ethan's station. He was immersed in his project. She filled him in on the experience.

"Interesting," Macdara said. "That will have to wait." His gaze shifted to the door to the working part of the mill.

Siobhán knew that look. "You found something?"

"Follow us." He glanced at the curtains that separated the interview area from the contestants. He didn't want to kick up a fuss. Siobhán, Macdara, and Aretta scurried to the door, and slipped in.

The smell of damp, and flour, filled the air. Macdara flicked on a torch, which meant he'd been waiting to show Siobhán whatever he discovered. They descended to the ground floor. Macdara maneuvered behind the shaft, and first pointed out a flour bag sitting beneath the chute.

"That wasn't there when Fia gave us the tour," Siobhán said. "Was someone trying to grind their own flour?"

"Personally I think someone was just trying to entertain themselves," Macdara said. He headed for the stairway that led to the middle floor. Siobhán took in the stones used to grind the flour, the bed stone and the runner stone. She could not see anything out of the ordinary.

"Remember that Fia never took us up to the top floor."

Siobhán had a sinking feeling. "Right."

"We should have insisted."

He aimed the torch at another set of stairs, much narrower than the previous two. "It's a tight fit, and there are a few rickety steps, just take it easy."

Macdara led the way and Siobhán followed. "I'll wait down here," Aretta called up.

At the top, Macdara quickly moved to the side. "Here's the pulley Fia spoke of," he said. "The grain is poured through this chute." He illuminated first the chain that was used to hoist bags of flour from the ground gloor, then showed her the chute. "Bag tips into the chute and the grain flows down to the stones, the stones do their thing, then it flows down to the bag waiting at the ground floor."

"Lovely," Siobhán said. "But unless you're trying to tell

me you want a career change, what are we really doing up
here?"

He swung the light of the torch to the back corner. A
sleeping bag lay in the corner. Next to it was an empty box
of pastries, a mineral can, a bottle of water, a pair of eyeglasses, and a book.

"Someone was hiding up here," Siobhán said. She patted her pockets. "Do you have gloves?"

Macdara handed her a pair. Some husbands might fetch
their wives slippers or a cup of tea, but she was thrilled
how well hers knew her. She donned the gloves and Macdara held the light as she approached the mini-campsite.
First, she looked at the book. *Waterwheel Repair.*

"Whoever bought this purchased it from Turn the
Page," Siobhán said.

"How do you know that?" Macdara asked, a hint of
disbelief in his voice.

Siobhán pointed out the corner of the book where a
blue dot was prominent. "Remember Oran was placing
blue discount stickers on books while we were there?"

"He was?"

Siobhán punched his arm. "You were too busy working
yourself into a sugar coma."

"It was worth it." Macdara stared at the sleeping bag.
"Thanks to your fabulous memory and observation skills,
we might be able to get a bead on our stowaway."

"I'll give the bookshop a bell," Aretta said from down
below. "But I'll need to go back to the event space to get
reception on me phone."

"Call from outside," Macdara said. "I don't want anyone to hear the conversation."

"Not a bother," Aretta said. They could hear her footsteps hurrying down the steps to the ground floor.

"Shine the light on the drinks, and glasses." Macdara illuminated the area. Siobhán stepped closer. She lifted the spectacles. "These look familiar." Her mind flashed to William Bains wheeling in his trolly. "It's our funny little man," she said.

"Just as I was thinking." Macdara sounded slightly disappointed that he didn't get to drop the mic.

"Let's recap what we have here," Siobhán said.

"Story time," Macdara said. "Proceed."

"First, have we verified that William Bains was indeed a genuine solicitor?"

"We did," Macdara said. "The station got back to me while you were out with Ethan. And get this—he was out of Donegal."

"All roads lead to Donegal," Siobhán said. "We might need to make a trip."

"A romantic one or a business one?"

She gave him a look.

"Right. Business first."

"William Bains is hired to partake in this televised baking show, no doubt because he had admiration for Aoife McBride and lived in Donegal."

"Sorry to interrupt, but are you thinking he believed Elizabeth Wynne was actually Aoife McBride, or was he in on the switcheroo?"

"I'm not sure. Let's just stick to what we do know for a minute. William Bains, solicitor out of Donegal, is hired for Aoife McBride's baking show."

"Right."

"He's given last-minute instructions to roll in the trolley and secret weapons."

"How do we know that?"

"We cannot be absolute, but it's my theory that the killer intended for the powder to kill Elizabeth. The mastermind behind this performance did not want her partaking in any of the actual bakes, because someone—or all of them—would have quickly realized she wasn't Aoife McBride."

"But when the powder killed our protester instead, the killer had to come up with a new plan," Macdara said.

Siobhán nodded. "That's why it's so important we find William Bains. Last-minute plans mean mistakes. And once Elizabeth was killed, I think he grew worried. Just before she was killed it seems Elizabeth Wynne grew worried as well—unfortunately she did not take her suspicions to the guards. What if William Bains knows who our killer is and that's why he disappeared?"

Macdara pointed to the sleeping bag. "You call this disappearing?"

"It worked, didn't it?"

"Why here?"

"Martin Murphy told us that he thought William Bains was waving him over at O'Rourke's the night they all went to the pub. 'Like he was bringing in an airplane.' I believe that Aoife—who we now know was Elizabeth—was sent in to dance with him and distract him. She made a comment too—something about it not being safe. Both William and Elizabeth were starting to suspect something was going on after the protester died. I don't think William was waving at Ethan. I think it was someone else."

"Our killer?"

"Possibly. And my guess is the killer is part of this baking show and that's why William Bains hid in the flour mill. Perhaps the killer was looking for him everywhere but here. It was smart, I'll give him that. But it would have been much smarter had he come to us instead."

"Not only much smarter but this makes him look guilty, if you ask me."

"Had we not verified that he was indeed a solicitor I would agree with you. I think he is worried he has some culpability, otherwise he would have sought us out. But I don't think he's our killer. He's simply another bug trapped in the killer's web."

Macdara rubbed his chin. "Where does this leave us?"

"William must have fixed the wheel in order to create a big enough distraction to escape from his hiding place. And that means that our killer was in the mill when we all ran out to see the wheel."

"One of our contestants, judges, or Fia O'Farrell."

"Correct. I suppose we have to lump in the director and cameraman, but something tells me it's someone in the inner circle of baking."

"We need to find that funny little man."

"We do. But we should probably stop calling him 'that funny little man.'"

"We can still call him that to each other, can we not?"

"As much as you'd like." Siobhán leaned in and gave her husband a little kiss.

Macdara put a pair of gloves on and leafed through the book. "He's underlined passages about the sluice gate. Must have been what needed fixing."

"Fair play to him. Too bad he wasn't able to stick around to take credit for it. Fia O'Farrell is over the moon. Now maybe she can start making her own flour again, she can give tours again, and save the bakery."

"Something good came out of something wicked."

Siobhán smiled. "May I see the book?"

Macdara handed it to her. Siobhán began to leaf through it. She skimmed past the underlined passages about sluice gates and how to repair them. She continued to flip through the book. When she was nearly at the end, a napkin fell out. O'ROURKE'S was printed across it in black lettering. Blue ink was scrawled across it. *I was such an admirer of hers, but this has gone too far . . .*

"A note!" Siobhán handed it to Macdara.

Macdara read it silently. "This seems to suggest he believed Elizabeth Wynne was Aoife McBride."

"Or someone. We can't be sure who wrote this note," Siobhán said.

"It's a good assumption it was William."

"I agree."

Macdara grinned. "Be still my heart."

Siobhán gently shoved him. "In that case . . . was he writing it to himself or someone else?"

Macdara groaned and rested his head on her shoulder for a moment. "I just wanted to eat pastries with me wife and watch a few professional bakers compete."

Siobhán rubbed his back. "As did I, husband. As did I."

"Welcome back," Ronan said. "After the sad and tragic passing of Aoife McBride, we are back in this ancient flour mill, with a constant dripping sound and slight draft—"

Philomena elbowed Ronan in the side. He'd been whining nonstop since they'd relocated. Siobhán glanced at Ethan Brown. She had already filled Macdara and Aretta in on her afternoon with him, the Batman quote, and how he'd run out the back door. Ethan was either very concentrated on his chocolate cake or he was intentionally avoiding eye contact with Siobhán. Where had he gone after he'd slipped out the back door of Gordon's? She hadn't spoken to Chris Gordon in a while, but he would have contacted her if anything stranger than that had occurred. Ethan had obviously been hoping to slip away from Siobhán. *Why?*

"Does anyone here play golf?" Philomena asked.

"Wrong crowd, darling," Ronan said.

"Do you know what a mulligan is?" she continued cheerfully.

"Can you eat it?" Ronan asked, making a face at the camera.

"It's a do-over."

"Do-over!" Ronan said. "A fresh tart." He slapped his hand over his mouth. "I meant start."

"We are starting from scratch, and so are our bakers. Shall we reintroduce them?"

A groan rose from one of the contestants, the loudest coming from Trisha Mayweather.

"Is there something the matter?" Ronan asked her.

She brandished a whisk. "How many times have we started over? This is madness. Between the guards, and now the judges questioning us, I don't see how any of us can concentrate." She slammed the whisk down on her counter.

"You're a pro, are you not?" Ronan asked.

Trisha's face turned bright red. She clamped her lips shut.

"As I thought."

"We'll keep it short," Philomena said. She turned to Ronan. "There's no need to be rude."

"Apologies," Ronan said. "But this group is trying my patience!"

"You're right, you're right," Trisha said. "Sugar crash, folks! Forgive me!"

Philomena pointed to Ethan. "In station one we have Ethan Brown. Parisian trained. Accountant by day." Ethan waved. "In station two, Trisha Mayweather. Her mother was once good friends with Aoife."

"Best friends," Trisha said. "For a time." She lowered her head.

Philomena crossed herself. "May she rest in peace. I bet the angels are thrilled to have such an esteemed baker among them."

"They already have one," Trisha said. "My mother."

"Well, well, well," Ronan said. "Are you saying your mother was a better baker than Aoife McBride?"

"That's exactly what I'm saying." Trisha crossed herself, leaving little dabs of flour on her forehead and chest.

"Perhaps there's room enough for both of them." Ronan gestured upward. "I wonder if they're lying on a cloud eating angel food cake."

Trisha made a face but if she had a retort she kept it to herself.

Philomena made the universal gesture for sleeping by palming her hands and pretending to rest her pretty head on them. "Sounds heavenly."

"In station three we have The Sponge, aka Barry Ryan," Ronan continued. "A local tow truck operator by day, and baker at night."

Barry held up his sponge and squeezed it. "Other way around," he said. "I bake in daylight and repossess cars at night."

"Correction noted," Ronan said. "Bakes by day, steals cars at night."

"Repossess," Barry said. "That's what happens when you don't pay your bills."

Philomena laughed and pointed at Ronan. "You've been schooled!"

Ronan smirked. "In station four we have Martin Murphy. Known as the baking-builder, we've already seen his grand replication of this bakery, made of chocolate."

"And what a pity it was ruined by his neighbor," Philomena said. Martin raised his hand. Philomena frowned as if Martin was going off script. When he continued to keep his hand raised she finally nodded.

"I think the salt someone added to my structure was a happy accident. It reminded me that a touch of sea salt in chocolate is a wondrous thing." He flicked a glance at Sophia, who smiled and blushed. Siobhán watched them, trying to see if their demeanor fit with Ethan Brown's story of the two of them knocking boots on the patio of O'Rourke's. At the least there was definitely a flirtation going on.

"That wasn't sea salt, that was table salt," Barry said. "Your chocolate bakery was ruined."

"She thought it was part of the game," Martin said. "I forgive her."

"I bet you do," Ethan said.

Interesting . . .

Sophia let out a little squeak.

"In station five, we seem to have a little mouse," Ronan said. "Otherwise known as Sophia Hughes."

Sophia laughed and squeaked again. "Thank you for giving me a second chance," she said. "I'm a big believer in second chances."

"And now for a big surprise," Ronan said, barely containing a grin. "We have a new contestant for station six." A gasp rose from nearly everyone in the room.

"Did you know about this?" Macdara asked.

"I don't even know what this is," Siobhán said, her adrenaline churning.

"Philomena Lemon, our esteemed and gorgeous judge, is going to take Aoife McBride's place in the baking show!"

Chapter 23

After making his surprise announcement, Ronan beamed, waiting, it seemed, for cheers and applause. Philomena Lemon grinned. She seemed to be waiting for a wave of adoration as well.

"Philomena is going to take Aoife's place?" Sophia said. "How is that fair?" Her lips formed a perfect little pout.

"It seems Sophia is only a fan of second chances if it applies to her," Ronan said with a smirk.

"She was never a contestant, so how is that a second chance?" Sophia shot back.

"Aoife McBride was the reason all of you were on your toes," Ronan said. "We need a sufficient replacement to ensure we have a real competition here."

"You're saying we're not good enough to compete with each other?" Trisha Mayweather's outrage surpassed Sophia's.

"Are you alright?" Barry Ryan leaned in and asked her in a comforting tone.

Trisha's face softened. "I'm fine. Just a bit flustered. Given this was going to be on telly, I suppose I expected it to be a bit more *professional*." She directed the last word at their judges.

"Are you afraid of the competition?" Philomena asked, placing a hand on her hip.

"None of us are afraid of competition," Barry said. "But this has been a clown show from the very beginning."

"And that's coming from Sponge Barry Round Pants," Martin said.

"Hilarious," Barry said. "I may not have your muscles, but you definitely don't have my taste buds." He grinned.

"Maybe we should just cancel the event," Ethan said. "I'm losing confidence in it every day."

"We still want to get paid for the entire duration," Ruth said. "Charlie and I get paid even if it cancels."

Charlie popped his head out from behind the camera. "What she said."

"People, please," Tia said. "I need this. We all need this."

Ronan and Philomena took it all in with gusto. If they were going for shock value, they'd succeeded. And once again the guards were not being kept in the loop. On one hand keeping the guards out of the loop on major changes to the production was grounds to halt the entire show. On the other, this could mean the killer was still among them, flicking everyone like marbles, trying to control the narrative and stir the pot. If they shut everything down now, the killer would go free. What if that was exactly what the killer intended? Siobhán was glued to the development, not for the drama, but she felt as if she was chasing after a car, and a large truck had just pulled in front of her, blocking her view. Had something like this been the plan all along? Had Philomena eliminated Aoife McBride so she could take her spot?

As everyone watched, Philomena strode over to Aoife's empty station and stood behind it, waving like a princess to the peasants. Siobhán tried to run through a scenario in which Philomena Lemon was coldhearted enough to murder Aoife McBride just to get her twenty thousand euro and fifteen minutes of fame. It seemed ludicrous. But every scenario seemed ludicrous. No one should die in a baking competition. Did any of them truly need twenty thousand euro so badly they would kill for it? Background checks were being done on the contestants but nothing major had come to light as of yet. And even if some of them were in financial straits, unless one of them was a beneficiary in Elizabeth Wynne or Aoife McBride's will Siobhán just couldn't see it as a motive for murder. Something else was going on here. Something bigger.

"Stop thinking," Macdara said. "It's distracting."

Siobhán shook her head. "Maybe you should *start* thinking."

"Your thoughts are so loud they're chasing all the quiet ones right out of me poor head," Macdara said.

"Philomena," Barry "The Sponge" said. "Whereas I'm not afraid to take you on, it does seem a bit unfair that as a judge you're privy to the way Ronan thinks and how he will be judging."

"So?" Phil asked.

"I call that an unfair advantage," Barry said.

A few heads nodded. "Maybe we should vote," Ethan said.

"This is a game," Ronan said. "There's no voting in games."

"The judging standards are transparent," Phil said, crossing her arms underneath her ample bosom. "Taste and presentation."

"She is correct," Ronan said. "I am a man enthralled with taste and presentation."

"We'll only have one judge?" Martin asked. "That seems a bit unfair to me as well."

"That's our second announcement," Ronan said. "The esteemed owner of this bakery, Fia O'Farrell, will become the second judge."

Fia popped up and waved. "I'm so honored," she said. "You have no idea."

"I can agree with that," Siobhán said to Macdara. "Something is going on here. But whatever it is, I have no idea."

The contestants, including Philomena Lemon, were in place. "You've all had time to practice our first do-over challenge," Ronan said. "Death by Chocolate."

"Yes," Macdara said, a little too loudly, garnering laughs from the crowd, and no doubt from the places where it was streaming.

Behind Ronan, tables had been laid out in a row, covered with a tablecloth. He gestured to it. "Just like with the practice, all the ingredients you need can be found on this table. When we sound the bell, everyone will have a chance to come up and grab what they think they need." He gave a little sly smile and turned to Fia. "There may be a little extra," he said.

Fia nodded, enthusiastically stepping into her new role. "And there may not be enough of everything."

The contestants all looked alarmed. "Or we're big fat liars," Ronan said.

"Should we stop this?" Siobhán leaned over and asked Macdara.

"I've had all the items carefully checked," Macdara said. "We should be good to go."

The bell rang and the contestants flew up to the table, grabbing ingredients, ferrying between the table and their stations as quickly as possible. It wasn't long before Trisha Mayweather and Barry Ryan collided somewhere in the middle. A crack was heard, then a gasp, then a scream as eggs hit the floor, smashing and sending rivers of yellow goo between their legs.

"Five second rule!" Barry yelled as he looked around in a wild panic, his hands still full of ingredients. "Someone get the eggs! Help! Take pity on us!"

To Siobhán's surprise, Garda Aretta Dabiri ran up and began scooping up the broken eggs using a little tea cup. One of the large television screens mounted around the room erupted in cheers. Siobhán looked up to see townsfolk crammed into O'Rourke's, cheering on Aretta for being a good sport. Soon the mess was cleared, and Trisha and Barry hurried back to their stations as Aretta strolled back to Siobhán and Macdara, who treated her to another round of cheers and pats on the back. "Well played," Macdara said. Aretta grinned.

"As they're baking their chocolate cakes," Ronan said, "Fia and I will be going station to station and talking to each contestant about their process."

"Why don't we start with our newest contestant," Fia said.

Charlie Holiday quickly followed Ruth over to station six, where Philomena was in her element. She hummed as she whipped batter in a bowl, seemingly confident about the assignment.

"I love a good chocolate cake," Phil purred. "And I snagged the only can of Guinness on the table."

"A chocolate Guinness cake," Ronan said. "Brilliant."

"The trick is making a frothy head," Phil shot back.

"Isn't it just!" Ronan said.

"You two," Fia said. "You just can't help yourselves."

"Everyone will be helping themselves to a second slice when I'm done," Philomena said. "Even the handsome cameraman and our esteemed director."

Charlie put down his camera for a second and beamed. Ruth rolled her eyes. "Next!" she said, moving over to station five, where Sophia was measuring out baking soda. The teaspoon looked enormous in her tiny hand. And that tiny hand was shaking.

"My, my, someone has a case of nerves," Ronan said. "You poor pet."

"Don't worry, chicken," Fia said. "Ignore us and concentrate."

"I'm grand!" Sophia said way too loudly. "I'm not going to mess this up."

"And did you choose any secret ingredients from the table?" Ronan asked.

Sophia struck a pose and batted her eyelashes. "Do I have to tell?"

"We've got a feisty one!" Ronan said. "I suppose you can keep your secrets, but if you won't tell us your secret ingredient, you'll have to tell us another secret. Something juicy."

"What?" Sophia stammered. She stared at the camera lens as if it was a firing squad.

"Where in Ireland do you live?" Fia said. "What is your occupation?"

"I'm from Roscommon," Sophia said. "I was a primary school teacher but I took this last year off to do some traveling."

"A wanderer," Ronan said. "I don't suppose you had much chance to bake on your travels."

"Maybe that's why I'm rusty," Sophia said.

"Where did you go?" Fia asked.

"France," Sophia said.

"France!" Ethan Brown bellowed all the way from station one. "And you never came to see little old me?"

"I'd never heard a thing about ya," Sophia said.

"Amateur," Ethan remarked. Siobhán was starting to wonder if Ethan actually had a little crush on Sophia Hughes.

"Well, that was exciting," Fia said sarcastically. "Moving on to Martin Murphy."

"And you can keep moving," Martin said. "I don't bake and chat."

"You don't have a choice," Ronan said.

"If you want to stand and have a gawp at me, be my guest. But I'm concentrating."

"Are you making another sculpture?" Fia asked as if he hadn't spoken.

"It's Death by Chocolate," Ronan said. "Are you going to build a bridge big enough for a final jump?"

"I'm making Excalibur," Martin said.

Ronan gasped and clasped his hands. "A chocolate sword! How original!"

"I'd take a stab at that," Fia said.

"Any secret ingredient?" Ronan asked.

"Absolutely," Martin said. "But trying to get it out of me would be like trying to remove a magic sword from a stone."

Ronan threw his head back and laughed. "He's a gas."

Fia moved on to Barry Ryan before Ronan could annoy Martin Murphy any further. "Have you ever made a Death by Chocolate cake before?" she asked.

"Chocolate cakes aren't my usual thing," Barry said.

"But I've tasted one or two in me life. And that's all I need to recreate anything. Just one little taste." He flashed a superior grin. No doubt the betting shops were going mad, taking bets from the locals on who was going to win this competition.

"How long ago did you taste a chocolate cake?" Ruth asked. Fia and Ronan shot her dirty looks but she either didn't see them or she didn't care.

"Less than a year ago, in Donegal," Barry said. He pointed to the camera and curled his finger, beckoning it to come closer. Charlie Holiday took a few steps forward and zoomed in on Barry's face. "It was Aoife McBride's new recipe."

All noise in the room suddenly stilled as the contestants turned their heads to Barry. "How is that possible?" Sophia asked. "She was only going to reveal it after this television event. You couldn't have tasted it."

"I tasted it, alright," Barry said. "That's all I can say."

"It was before she made changes then," Sophia said.

"Maybe," Barry said with a wink. "And maybe after I complimented her on the cake, she turned to me and said: 'Next time I'm thinking of adding a little *something-something* to it.'"

Sophia put her hands on her hips again. "Are you saying she actually named the something-something, or did she literally say something-something?"

"Maybe," Ronan said, "he's talking a whole lot of nothing."

"Or he's lying," Ethan said. "Just to rattle us."

"All is fair in love and baking," Ronan said.

"My creation will be in honor of Aoife McBride," Barry said.

"I love that," Fia said. "What a wonderful tribute." The rest of the contestants groaned.

They moved on to Trisha Mayweather. She was concentrating hard, her tongue poked out from the corner of her mouth. "How do you feel about this challenge?" Ronan asked. "Are you up to it?"

"My mam used to make the best chocolate cake," Trisha said. "I watched her like a hawk. She never let me help. But I believe she's watching over me now." Trisha stared into her bowl. "She's not lying on some cloud shooting the breeze with Aoife McBride, I'm telling ye that."

They moved on to Ethan Brown. He was rolling his mixture into little balls. "What do we have here?" Ronan asked.

"Chocolate bombs," Ethan said.

"How clever," Fia said.

"With a deadly surprise in the middle." Ethan grinned. "Tick tick, tick . . ."

"Have you used this technique before?" Ronan asked.

"I have not," Ethan said. "But how hard could it be?"

"That's what *she* said," Fia said.

Ronan threw his head back and roared with laughter. "She's giving you a run for your money, Phil!" he yelled down to her station.

Fia pumped her fist. Down the lane Martin Murphy furiously whisked something in a bowl. "I think people make sordid jokes when they don't have anything intelligent to say." He cracked two eggs into the bowl, splashed in some vanilla, and resumed whisking. "Can we be finished with these sexual innuendos?" He slammed down his whisk, sending bits of cream flying. "So juvenile!"

His outburst fascinated Siobhán. Juvenile as the judges might be, his reaction seemed out of place for a man who had been knocking boots with a fellow contestant on the patio in a public space. Was he a do-as-I say-not-as-I-do type person? Or did his personality change after a few drinks?

Siobhán turned to Macdara. "I need to make a call." Macdara, transfixed by all the chocolate in bowls, nodded. Siobhán moved out of the room and out to the exit. The skies were starting to spit so she stayed underneath the small awning in front of the door as she rang O'Rourke's Pub. Relief settled over her when Maria barked into the phone, "O'Rourke's, what do you want?"

"Heya, it's Siobhán."

"I nearly took your head off. Some lad's been calling nonstop asking if the bakers have come back in."

"They're a bit too busy here."

"I won't lie, I'll be happy-out when this show is done and dusted."

"Amen." They laughed. It was always a comfort to be on the same wavelength.

"What's the story?"

"I think I've gained three stone just smelling all the pastries," Siobhán said.

"You poor thing. We're jammers here with everyone gathered to watch it."

"I'm sorry to bother you when you're so busy, but does Declan still have CCTV cameras on the patio?"

"Are you joking me? Of course he does. Otherwise all sorts of shenanigans go on out there."

Just as she thought. "Can you go through the footage from the night all the contestants first came in?" Siobhán paused. "Scratch that. Can you check all the footage from inside and out, the night the contestants came in?"

"I can do it after me shift," Maria said. Despite Siobhán's adding extra work onto her friend, Maria didn't even hesitate.

"Thanks a million. I'll be there as soon as I can."

I'll make popcorn," Maria said. "What am I looking for?"

"Anything out of the ordinary," Siobhán said. "I'm sorry, I know it's a lot of extra work."

"I hope I find something good," Maria said. "I'm running out of shows on Netflix."

Chapter 24

The minute Siobhán and Macdara entered the chemist, an antiseptic smell greeted them. The front of the shop sold greeting cards and the back wall housed a small selection of makeup, including face powders. Today the section was empty, as earlier requested by the guards. Luckily, aside from Elizabeth's powder, the samples had all come back clean, but the shop was no doubt waiting for replacements to restock. The antiseptic smell grew stronger as they drew closer to the empty makeup shelves. The chemist had gone a bit mad with the Windex. Perhaps just the thought of poison being in one of the packages had sent her around the bend. Ann Kelly was at the back counter today. A no-nonsense woman in her thirties, she was pleasant but efficient with most of the customers. The sight of two uniformed gardaí in the shop made her eyes widen slightly as she finished tending to the customer in front of her, sending him off with a little bag of unknown medications.

"May I help you?" She looked around, then leaned over the high counter. "I was told the makeup did not contain any contaminants. I hope that was correct." She held up a bottle of Windex as if it were a deadly weapon and she was prepared for battle.

"That's correct," Macdara said. "But had there been, you know that wouldn't have done a thing." He pointed to the Windex.

Ann's shoulders relaxed slightly, but she was still on guard. She let the Windex drop. "How can I help you?"

"Were you here when one of the contestants purchased the face powder?" Siobhán asked. According to the report it was indeed Ann Kelly, but the question had to be asked.

Her eyes flicked to the front of the shop. "Yes, I was here."

"What can you tell us about the person who purchased it?" Siobhán asked, purposely switching out the word *woman* for *person*. The less one filled in the answers, the better.

"She was pleasant. A bit distracted."

"Did you recognize her?" Macdara asked.

"Recognize her? She wasn't a local."

Either she was not dressed as Aoife McBride or Ann Kelly wouldn't recognize Aoife McBride if she was standing in front of her. "A lot of people do recognize her," Siobhán said. "If you're a fan of baking."

"I am not." Ann Kelly did not offer any more. So much for chin-wagging. Perhaps her silence was the result of being a chemist, and dealing with all the ailments humans suffered from. Or perhaps, like Doctor Jeanie Brady, she was off the carbs.

Macdara stepped in. "What can you tell us about the transaction? Anything at all, no matter how insignificant it may seem."

Ann looked up and slightly to the left. "Right. She was a tall and lumpy woman. Her hair pulled back from her face so tightly I was surprised she didn't purchase head-ache tablets."

She hadn't donned her wigs yet. This was a small town. Elizabeth either didn't realize how small, or she had no idea the sinister reason she'd been hired to impersonate Aoife McBride. If the killer knew she was seen about town without her disguise on, no doubt he or she would have been alarmed. This told Siobhán that at the time she purchased the powders, Elizabeth Wynne had no idea she was in danger.

"Brilliant," Siobhán said. "Anything else?"

"She purchased one powder, and then I let her know that we were having a two-for-one sale."

"Right," Siobhán said. This explained why she didn't mind using one of her powders on George O'Leary. He was a fellow actor also hired for the gig, and she just happened to have a spare.

Ann Kelly fidgeted and eyed the Windex again. "If our powder was clean, I don't understand why you're asking these questions."

"We have to cover all the bases," Macdara said.

Ann Kelly sighed and glanced at the line that had now formed behind them and, no doubt, everyone was straining for any scrap of news they could get.

"How was her demeanor?" Siobhán asked.

"She was friendly. Excited about the baking show."

"Thank you," Siobhán said when it became clear that's all the woman had to say.

Ann Kelly nodded, then turned to greet the next person in line as Siobhán and Macdara moved out to the footpath.

"Well?" Macdara asked.

"On the one hand, Elizabeth was not trying to hide her identity. On the other, she also did not reveal that she would be impersonating Aoife McBride. It tells me that she knew it was a secret—but more like a surprise than something sinister. She also had not planned on purchasing two compacts of powder, there just happened to be a sale, and who's going to say no to a free item?"

"A two-for-one sale that killed poor George O'Leary," Macdara said.

"I believe that to be the case," Siobhán said. "Our killer didn't realize that Elizabeth bought two compacts. Perhaps the killer went through Elizabeth's handbag, or spotted the compact among her things. The killer added the poison, and thought the deed would be done before the show had begun." They took a moment to breathe. People were out and about, doing their messages. A steady stream of cars drove by, many of them exchanging waves and words with people on the footpaths.

"But why? This entire thing is more of a performance than a murder. Why did a killer go to such great lengths?"

"I have a theory."

"I was hoping you did," Macdara said.

Siobhán caught sight of folks streaming out of Pat's Café, all within earshot.

Macdara took her hand. "Shall we have a walkabout?"

Siobhán checked the time. Maria had said she'd be ready for them in a few hours. "To the abbey?"

"You read my mind."

Siobhán and Macdara stood in front of Kilbane's ruined abbey, the Dominican priory with its fifteenth-century bell tower and five-light windows. They had loved this place their entire lives, but given they held their wedding reception here, they now held it even closer to their hearts. They took a moment to enjoy a break from the rain, breathe in the fresh air, take in the green field and the river. Every time Siobhán gazed at it she imagined the monks who used to brew beer and live in the abbey, how awe-inspiring it was that one piece of land held so much history, so many stories. She was part of her village and it was part of her. Macdara snuck in a kiss, and then they were back to business.

"Your theory?"

"Our killer has gone to an enormous amount of trouble to 'kill' Aoife McBride in a very public way."

"Right. You don't get much more public than on telly."

"And when he or she failed once, the killer wasted no time in finding another way for her to die." Siobhán began to pace. "We know George O'Leary was never the intended victim, and poor Elizabeth Wynne was a pawn from the beginning. Our killer isn't just ruthless, he or she was desperate." Siobhán paused. "Desperate to get away with murder."

"Two murders," Macdara corrected.

Siobhán shook her head. "Three."

"Three? Who am I missing?"

"Aoife McBride," Siobhán said. "I think our killer staged all of this because he or she already murdered Aoife McBride."

Macdara let out a low whistle. "You think Aoife McBride was here in Kilbane after all?"

"No. I think Aoife McBride was killed in Donegal."

"Say more."

"Aoife hasn't been seen in public since that look-alike event. Sophia Hughes was at the event. She said Aoife wouldn't even sign autographs. After the event Aoife filed a report with the Donegal gardaí claiming someone was stalking her. And then, she stopped appearing in public."

"And everyone thought she was hiding out because of this so-called stalker."

"But maybe she wasn't hiding out at all," Siobhán said. "Maybe she was dead."

"I was briefed on her report by the Donegal guards," Macdara said.

"What did they say?"

"They didn't take it very seriously. She told them she didn't have any idea who it was, she just said she had a feeling she was being watched." He crossed his arms and took a deep breath. "I'm afraid they chalked it up to the look-alike event. Told her that seeing that many folks dressed up as her would have made anyone paranoid."

There was probably some truth to that. Siobhán couldn't imagine seeing anyone dressed up as her, even if they supposedly adored her. She'd have nightmares for ages. "Imagine for a moment that Aoife McBride was being stalked by a fan. Let's even assume she wasn't murdered in cold blood. Perhaps there was some kind of run-in. Something that escalated into a shove, or a fall. Aoife dies. And now the fan is left in a pickle. Turn herself in for killing the revered baker, or . . . kill her off in a very different way so that she is never a suspect in her murder."

"Are we narrowing this down to a female killer?" Macdara asked.

"I think it's most likely," Siobhán said. "However . . . men could have also attended the look-alike event. I just can't help thinking she would have been more specific about who was following her if it had been a man."

Macdara held up his hand. "I have a bone to pick with your theory. May I?"

"Pick away."

"Someone who accidentally kills another person may want to flee the scene, but I would argue that murdering two innocent actors to achieve his or her goal does indeed portray a cold-blooded killer."

"You're absolutely right," Siobhán said. This was why saying every thought about the case out loud was so critical.

"But I do think you're spot-on. There's zero chance the Donegal Gardaí would have been searching for a body if they thought Aoife McBride was killed in a flour mill in Kilbane."

"It suggests the killer is very confident the body won't be found," Siobhán said. Given Aoife's cottage abutted the Donegal Bay, Siobhán knew chances were good a body could hide in its depths forever.

"Most submerged bodies eventually surface," Macdara said. "But sometimes much too late to catch the killer." He frowned. "If you think she was confident about the body never being found—why would she go to all this trouble to stage her death?"

"My guess?" Siobhán said. "If everyone thinks Aoife McBride died of a freak accident then no one is going to start looking for her. It probably wouldn't have been long before someone insists that Aoife McBride isn't merely laying low. Especially since she has a memoir being released soon."

They stopped to listen to the river babble, taking comfort in the sound. "Want to hear the good news?" Siobhán asked.

"Do I ever."

"I think we can rule out Charlie Holiday. I don't think the Yank had anything to do with it."

"Why do you say that?"

"I had a brief chat with the lad the other day. I asked him if he'd ever been to Donegal and he said, 'I've never visited *any* insurance company.'"

Maria greeted them the minute they entered O'Rourke's, then insisted they have ham and cheese toasties and crisps before watching the CCTV footage. There was still a nice crowd and she ushered them quickly into the back room.

"I think your man was lying to you," Maria said. "There were no shenanigans on the patio." They all sat in folding chairs in front of the security images on a computer. "I have still shots of all the contestants. These photos cover the entire time your suspects were here."

"Well done, you," Siobhán said. Maria grinned.

They studied each frame. In the fifth one, Martin was seen standing on the back patio sipping a pint with Barry Ryan, but Sophia Hughes was nowhere in sight.

"He lied straight to me face and then he gave me the slip," Siobhán said. Maria's face was a portrait of confusion and Siobhán filled her in on how Ethan pretended he wanted to have a nose around Gordon's Comics, only to dash out the back door.

"Did you say anything right before?" Maria said.

Siobhán shook her head. "No. But he was jittery and I believe he received a text."

"Why didn't you mention that before?" Macdara asked.

"Honestly, I just remembered. He glanced at his mobile but then shoved it back in his pocket. If it was that text that alarmed him, I'd advise ye never to play poker with him."

"Is there anything unusual on these tapes from that evening?" Macdara asked.

"Someone's in a hurry," Maria observed.

Siobhán gave Maria a look. "He wants to get back to the bakery just as their chocolate cakes are coming out of the cooker."

"That's the best moment," Macdara said dreamily. "That just-out-of-the-cooker moment."

"Lucky for youse I've done all the work for ye." Maria switched to another set of stills. "I saw nothing out of the ordinary, but I did capture all the shots of Aoife McBride and the little solicitor."

Siobhán shook her head at Macdara. "What?" he said. "I told her you didn't want us to call him 'the funny little man.' "

"I tried," Maria said to Macdara with a shrug and a wink.

"His name is William Bains. Whether or not he's odd is none of our immediate concern, and I would hardly like it if someone called me that tall female garda."

"They do, like," Maria said. "That tall female garda with the hair on fire." Off Siobhán's next look, Maria cackled. "The missing solicitor, is that what you want me to call him?"

"Why don't we just stick with William Bains," Siobhán said. "I swear it's a bad idea getting the two of you in the same room together."

This time Maria and Macdara chuckled in stereo. Truthfully, she loved that her husband and best mate got along like a house on fire. But they would be impossible to deal with if they knew that.

The screen switched to multiple stills of Elizabeth Wynne, dressed as Aoife McBride, huddled with William Bains.

"I bet he knew who she really was," Siobhán said. "They're sticking together." Maria, of course, knew the twist by now, that Elizabeth Wynne was their victim and not Aoife McBride, but Siobhán trusted her with her life. Not only did publicans never speak out of school, that went double for best friends.

"There is one odd thing," Maria said. From her tone, she'd been saving the best for last. She scrolled to another shot. The bar was packed, a trad band was playing in the corner. William Bains was visibly waving his arms above his head. "Like bringing in an airplane," Siobhán said. In this one, Elizabeth Wynne was crossing the room toward Martin Murphy. "It checks out."

"But wait," Maria said. "There's more." She pointed to another screen. "This is the opposite view—but you'll see from the time stamp it's the same time." She pointed to a woman with long gray hair. Tall and bulky, just like Elizabeth Wynne, and Aoife McBride. "If that's Elizabeth Wynne," she said, pointing to Elizabeth in the middle of the floor, "then who is that?"

"Can we zoom in on it?" Macdara asked.

"That's already zoomed in," Maria said. "It's blurry and I know you can't see her face. But on their shape and hair alone—they look like they could be twins."

Siobhán felt like a cement block had lodged in her chest. It couldn't be. Was Aoife McBride still alive? Was that her in the camera shot? And if so . . . was Aoife McBride their killer?

Chapter 25

When they walked back into the old mill, the scent of chocolate wrapped around them. The cakes were all cooling, and the contestants were on a short break. Soon, the first round of judging would begin. They needed to question Ethan Brown pronto. Something, or someone, had texted him with a message alarming enough that he gave Siobhán the slip. Was it a text from Aoife McBride? Siobhán had begged Macdara not to share the footage with the Donegal Gardaí. If they thought there was a chance their victim was still alive, they would never spend money or manpower looking for her, and all possibilities needed to be thoroughly sussed out. Macdara had been treating Siobhán with kid gloves, which could only mean he was convinced the woman on CCTV was most likely Aoife McBride. Siobhán, on the other hand, was not.

"D. B. Cooper," Macdara said. "He was never found."

Siobhán wanted to grab Ethan by the collar and question him now, but she agreed it would be best to let the first round come to an end; there had already been way too many disruptions. She stood in the bakery staring at the portrait on the wall of Fia's grandfather. Once again his intense eyes seemed to be following her everywhere she went. "Who on earth is D. B. Cooper?"

"An American man who hijacked an airplane in 1971. Demanded a huge cash ransom, then parachuted from the plane with the money. He was never seen again." Macdara sounded excited at the prospect.

"What is the equivalence here?"

"People disappear all the time. Fake their own deaths."

Siobhán nodded, then held up a finger. "However, we've seen no evidence that Aoife McBride needed the world to think she was dead."

Macdara rubbed his chin, his go-to gesture whenever he was mulling something over. "What about this new book she had coming out?"

"What about it?"

"Maybe she thought sales would skyrocket if she was dead."

"And how on earth would she collect the money?"

Macdara held his hand in front of her eyes. "Stop staring at that portrait. He's watching me now."

They turned their backs to the painting. "Maybe William Bains is partnering with Aoife McBride," Macdara said. "He was in fact waving his little arms at someone. *Sorry.* He was waving his smaller-than-the-average-man's arms at the woman who looked like Aoife McBride. Which means he knows a lot about what's going on. They could be in on it together."

"Then why was he hiding in the mill?"

"Maybe she turned on him. Maybe she decided her partner was a liability."

It was possible. "I just bought two sets of her new edition cookbooks," Siobhán said. "If she's still alive, I'm going to live to regret that."

"Let's take a breath, have a cup of tea and see who wins the Death by Chocolate challenge. Then we'll get the truth out of Ethan McBride if we have to whisk and batter him."

Siobhán rolled her eyes, laughed, then punched her husband on the shoulder. He chuckled and threw an arm around her. "Don't worry. We're going to turn up the heat on this killer, and roll him or her into a little ball."

Siobhán sighed. "You have more, don't you?"

"So much more," Macdara agreed. "So much more."

Ronan and Fia stood in front of the bakers. A new table had been set up in front of the kitchen station and one by one the bakers placed their Death by Chocolate creations in front of their station numbers. Ethan's chocolate bombs came with a chocolate tank, with red and orange icing inside the cannon to represent fire. Even though she was browned off with him, Siobhán couldn't help but be impressed. Trisha Mayweather presented a traditional-looking chocolate cake fringed with white icing in delicate patterns and topped with a white dove, no doubt a nod to her late mam. Barry Ryan's chocolate cake also looked traditional, but his was covered in little red envelopes, along with a pair of lips and a finger shushing them. It gave Siobhán the creeps. Why do that when those secret messages had been followed by a fellow contestant's death? Was he the killer and flaunting it?

Next, instead of a chocolate sword, Martin Murphy had constructed a bridge made of chocolate, with a figure going over the edge, but another clinging to him up top as if saving his or her life. It was becoming apparent that the murder had gotten into all of their psyches. Perhaps they should have canceled the baking show after all. Siobhán was starting to worry that they had made a mistake keeping the true victim's identity from them. Then again, they were already coming unglued. How would they react if they knew Aoife

McBride was not only *not* one of the victims, but she may very well be the murderer? The longer they waited to tell them, the worse the revelation could be. But what choice did they have? It was one advantage they had over this killer. The killer had yet to strike again, because he or she believed he or she was getting away with it. *Maddening.*

Sophia was next to place her bake on the table, and she balanced a large sheet cake, tottering on heels way too high for her. She set it down on the table with a clank and looked hopefully at the judges. The cake had a lovely buttercream icing, but no other adornments.

"Well," Ronan said. "She didn't burn it."

"Aw, chicken," Fia O'Farrell said. "Can you tell us why you decided to bake something so plain?"

"The surprise comes when you cut into it," Sophia said with a satisfied grin. "You'll see."

Fia shook her head. "Unless you've got doves flying out of it, pet, I think you've missed the mark."

"Look at our new judge with her plain talk," Ronan said.

"At this stage of the competition we expect more," Fia said.

"At this stage?" Sophia said. "It's our first official bake, like."

"That can't be true," Fia said. "This feels like it's gone on for ages."

"Power through," Ronan said, placing his hand on Fia's shoulder. "We've only just begun."

Philomena was last. Her cake was shaped like a giant pint glass topped with icing to replicate the foam atop a well-poured Guinness. Oohs and aahs erupted from the television screens. Philomena grinned and gave them her signature wave.

"Cheers," Ronan said. "It looks good enough to drink."

"Let's taste, shall we?" Ronan announced, brandishing

an enormous gold fork. Siobhán could nearly feel her husband vibrating beside her as the pair headed for Ethan's chocolate bombs.

Sounds of pleasure erupted from the judges as they tasted Ethan's concoction. "Now that's the bomb," Ronan said. "Smooth dark chocolate, with a surprise caramel and sea salt hit in the middle, and I do believe your secret ingredient is raspberry."

"It is indeed," Ethan said, beaming.

"I want to sell these in my shop," Fia said.

"I'll be opening a shop of me own soon," Ethan said. "With the prize money. I'm afraid this is the closest you're ever going to get to my chocolate bombs."

Macdara leaned into Siobhán. "Do you think we could have a taste before confronting him with his lies and accusing him of murder?"

"I would have said no," Siobhán said. "But a caramel center with sea salt and a hit of raspberry is giving me pause."

"I knew I married the right woman," Macdara said, sneaking an arm around her waist.

"Although I could stand here and nosh on them all, we must move on," Ronan said, sidling over to Trisha Mayweather's station.

Trisha's chocolate cake was round and tall, disguising an untold number of layers. "Although it's definitely big, I was hoping for more huzzah," Ronan said.

"It's plain on the outside, but a celebration on the inside," Trisha said, with a confident smile. "Although not as plain as Sophia's."

Sophia's eyes narrowed into little slits and her hands flew to her hips. Ronan handed the knife to Fia O'Farrell. It gleamed under the spotlight. She cut into it. A rainbow of color revealed itself.

"My, my, my," Ronan said. "It's a rainbow."

Trisha applauded herself. "What's an Irish chocolate cake without a rainbow?"

"How did you get these layers so precise?" Fia asked. "Remarkable."

"Each layer has a different flavor as well," Trisha said. "But I think you'll find they blend brilliantly together."

The judges sank their forks into the cake and then into their gobs. "Brilliant," Ronan said. "Lemon, mint, chocolate. I don't know how you did it, but I can taste the individual layers, and yet it does all blend seamlessly."

"Well done, you," Fia said. "You made your mother proud."

"Don't judge a cake by its cover," Trisha said with a laugh.

Ronan nodded, his eyes glued to the cake. "I do wish we had time for more than just a bite of each."

"Was that his way of asking for volunteer tasters?" Macdara asked.

"No," Ronan answered without turning around.

As the judges moved on to Martin Murphy, Ethan Brown slipped away from his station and headed for the exit. Siobhán nudged Macdara.

"Follow him," Macdara said. "I'll keep me eye on this lot."

Siobhán gave it a moment and then slipped out after Ethan. He was nearly across the field, having broken out into a run.

"Wait," Siobhán called after him. "Stop." Ethan did not stop. The ground was soft and wet from the on-and-off rain, making it difficult to give chase. He either had not heard her calling him, or he was deliberately trying to lose her again. Should she scream at him once more to stop, or should she follow him to see where he was going? Did he really think no one would notice him escaping?

He stopped abruptly and whirled around, ending her

dilemma. He waited until she caught up, a guilty expression on his face.

"Sorry," he said. "Family emergency. I was just stepping out to make a call."

"This is more than 'stepping out,'" Siobhán pointed out, wishing she wasn't so out of breath. "You sprinted halfway across the field."

"It sounds ridiculous, but I needed to be as far away from the bakery as possible. When I'm in there I feel like I'm being watched."

"That is indeed how a television show works," Siobhán said.

Ethan laughed, then quickly stopped and cleared his throat. "It's more than that. Just a feeling of eyes and ears everywhere."

"Given what's occurred in the bakery, I would think eyes and ears everywhere is a comfort," Siobhán said.

"I didn't mean the guards, if that's what you're implying."

"Are you sure?"

"Of course."

"I suppose you'd never lie to a guard."

"Never."

"Or give one the slip."

"The slip?"

"Out the back door of Gordon's Comics."

Ethan's face contorted. "You saw me."

"Indeed." She crossed her arms. "I also had a look at the CCTV tapes from O'Rourke's the night you lot were all cozied up together. There are cameras on the patio."

"I see." He stared at the ground.

"What do you see?"

He finally made eye contact. "Perhaps I was mistaken about Sophia and Martin knocking boots, but I assure you they've formed an alliance."

"I'm going to need you to come into the Kilbane Garda Station with me," Siobhán said.

"You're joking."

"I assure you, I am not."

Ethan glanced behind him before turning back. "It's not what you think."

"I'm not going to conduct an official inquiry standing in a field while the skies are spitting on us. You've lied to me, you've run from me, and now you look as if you're ready to bolt again. I assure you, that will not end well for you in the long run." In the short run, Siobhán knew he was capable of outrunning her, but there were only so many places he could go. And just as she had the thought, she turned to see Macdara and Aretta hurrying across the field. Backup had arrived. Ethan hung his head.

"Perhaps it's for the best," he said. "I'm a baker, not a spy. And I'm in way over me head."

Chapter 26

Back at the Kilbane Garda Station they set Ethan Brown up in interview-station one. The rest of the group were told that Ethan had a family emergency. Given the Death by Chocolate contest was ending, the competition would be over for the rest of the day, and if cleared, Ethan could rejoin them tomorrow. Otherwise, if Ethan was their killer, the guards could return tomorrow and announce that they solved the case. Ethan traced the tabletop with his index finger, and like a musician playing air guitar, would once in a while appear to be cracking an invisible egg, or whisking something unseen. He was nervous. Siobhán found herself hoping he wasn't guilty—a talented young man with his entire career ahead of him. His dream of opening his own bakery was well within reach. And he was personable. But that did not mean he was not a killer. They already knew their killer was comfortable committing his or her crimes while working closely with the suspects, and television cameras and guards. Theirs was not a shy killer. Ethan waltzed in looking confident, but the minute he saw Macdara's stern face across the table, he adjusted his attitude and folded his hands in front of him on the table.

"William Bains," he said before any of them could say a word.

Macdara frowned, then held up his finger. "I must give you the caution first."

Ethan nodded. "Caution away."

Macdara stared him down until Ethan looked at the table. "You are not obliged to say anything unless you wish to do so, but anything you say will be taken down in writing and may be given in evidence."

Ethan eyed their notebooks and Biros, and recording device. "Understood."

"Are you here today to give voluntary information?" Macdara asked.

"Indeed."

"When this interview is completed your statement will be read back to you and you will be required to sign it." Macdara held up the paperwork.

"Finally," Ethan said with a grin. "I've been waiting for someone to ask me for me autograph."

His eager and cheeky attitude had Siobhán on guard. He had already lied to them once, and he would soon realize his boyish charm would only get him in hot water. Would the pressure of an official interview straighten him out, or was he about to spill more tall tales? "Please make your intent clear for the record," Siobhán said.

"I am here today, *voluntarily*, to give my true account of why I gave Garda Siobhán O'Sullivan the slip and how they can catch William Bains."

Macdara nodded at Siobhán to begin. "Let's go back to the day I was supposed to give you a tour around Kilbane," Siobhán said.

Ethan swallowed. "I found the town charming, what I saw of it."

"This is not a social call," Macdara said. "I advise you to stop treating it as such."

Ethan's smile evaporated. "Yes, Detective Sergeant."

Siobhán inwardly cheered; she loved when Macdara laid down the law.

"The first incident I would like to cover is the lie," Macdara said. Ethan swallowed, glanced at Siobhán, and then nodded.

"Why did you tell me you saw Sophia Hughes and Martin Murphy engaged in sexual activity on the patio of O'Rourke's Pub?" Siobhán glanced at her notes and read the date and time of the gathering at the pub.

"I was expecting a text and knew that the minute it came in I would have to bolt. I hoped if I gave you something juicy, you would end the interview and focus on someone else."

"Who were you expecting this text from?" Macdara asked.

"William Bains."

"Do you know where William Bains is at this very moment?" Siobhán knew Ethan could hear the urgency in her voice, there was no sense hiding it.

"I do not. He's moving around. He texts me."

"Would you be willing to submit your mobile phone to the gardaí for examination?"

"How long would it be until I get it back?" Ethan fumbled in his pocket and brought out his phone. "You're welcome to have someone look through it while we chat and take down whatever information you need. But I am a working chef. And unless you're arresting me for stretching the truth to a guard, I do not voluntarily submit my mobile phone into evidence for longer than the duration of this interview."

Macdara accepted the mobile phone, then walked out with it. Ethan stared at Siobhán while he was gone, until her steady gaze finally made him drop his. "I'm sorry," he said to the tabletop. "I only lied because I was afraid."

Siobhán waited for Macdara to return before she spoke. "Please repeat what you just said."

Ethan sighed. "I apologized to Garda O'Sullivan and explained that I only lied because I am frightened for my life."

"How long have you been in touch with William Bains?" Macdara asked.

"Since I discovered one of his spy cameras in the flour mill," Ethan answered.

Spy cameras in the mill? Siobhán wanted to jump on it, but she could see Macdara was boiling, and she was going to let him at it.

Macdara put down his Biro. "It sounds like you have a lot to tell us. Why don't we let you do that? In your own words, tell us everything you think we'd like to know and we'll take it from there."

Ethan nodded. "After Aoife McBride was killed, I could see the way the guards were reacting. Despite keeping us in the dark, it was obvious you didn't think her death was an accident. And that meant—the protester's death was not an accident, and of course someone changed the sign to ZERO DAYS SINCE THE LAST ACCIDENT. It made me reflect on how every time I was in the bakery I felt as if someone was watching me."

"That portrait," Siobhán couldn't help but interject. "It must be some kind of optical illusion."

"That's where you're wrong," Ethan said. "With all due respect."

Siobhán straightened up. "What do you mean?"

"Those eyes *are* watching us. One of the spy cameras is in the portrait."

"Is?" Macdara said. "It's still there?"

Ethan nodded. "Yes. You'll be able to verify my statement when you look behind the portrait."

Macdara jotted down a note. "Who mounted this camera to the portrait?"

"I thought it was William Bains. But he insists it's the killer. And given I've never seen him with a laptop since he went into hiding, I'm inclined to agree." He leaned in. "I might have lied about Sophia Hughes and Martin Murphy's activities on the patio. But they have formed an alliance. That's the important bit. Maybe they're working together."

Siobhán sifted through that conjecture and reeled her mind back to the investigation. If Ethan was correct and there were spy cameras in the mill, that means the killer had been following their entire investigation. Was there audio or only visuals?

"How did you become aware of the camera behind the portrait?" Macdara asked.

"William Bains was hiding in the flour mill for the first few days after Aoife McBride's death. He saw me staring at it. I think he trusted me. After all, why would the killer stand in front of the portrait examining it suspiciously if he or she knew there was a camera inside?" He looked at Siobhán and Macdara as if expecting them to immediately pronounce him an innocent man.

"Go on," Siobhán said. "Continue from that moment."

Ethan nodded. "I think he watched me for a little while longer after that. He was hiding on the top floor of the mill." He waited to see if they would confirm this. They did not. "He even figured out how to fix the waterwheel so that he could make his escape."

"I feel you're skipping ahead," Macdara said. "Please return to the chronological events. When did William Bains first make contact with you?"

"I believe it was the day after I started staring at that portrait, I received a text." Distress played out on his face and sweat formed on his brow. "Listen. I know I lied. I'm sorry. I'm truly sorry. What I'm about to say is going to sound crazy, and listen—for all I know, William Bains is crazy. Or a murderer. Maybe he's just pretending to be afraid because he's the killer. Don't think that hasn't crossed me mind, because I assure you it has. Brace yourself." He took a deep breath. "William Bains claims that—"

"A woman named Elizabeth Wynne is our victim, not Aoife McBride," Siobhán finished.

Ethan's mouth dropped open, then disappointment fell across his face. He leaned back and crossed his arms. "It's true then?"

"You're still not giving us what we need," Macdara said. "A play-by-play of your interaction with William Bains."

"If he's telling the truth about that . . ." Ethan trailed off for a moment before leaning forward. "What does this mean? Is Aoife McBride still alive?"

"We don't know," Siobhán said honestly. "The investigation is ongoing."

"I thought she looked different. Does this mean she doesn't have cancer?"

"We do not believe Elizabeth Wynne had cancer," Siobhán said. "The wig was part of her disguise."

Ethan slammed his hand on the table, making them jump. "Wow. Just. Wow. I take it the other bakers don't know that it wasn't Aoife McBride who was killed?"

Ethan Brown was no fool. He was now making it clear that he had information he could leak to the others. He was scrambling for some control. Macdara waited, allowing silence to build up, increasing the tension. "We have not divulged that information yet to the others, that is correct."

Ethan nodded rapidly. "I can see why. Tell me. Why are we still having a baking show?" Now his tone was accusatory.

"Because one of you is a killer and the only way of catching him or her is to not let the killer run away before we figure it out," Siobhán said.

"We've had an extra guard presence on set and believe me, the baking show is the safest place you can be. We're checking every piece of equipment and the ingredients," Macdara added.

"William Bains knows who the killer is," Ethan said. "But he wouldn't tell me."

"Why wouldn't he tell you?" Siobhán said.

"Why wouldn't he tell *us*?" Macdara said.

Siobhán nodded. "Fair play to ya, that's the real question."

Ethan squirmed in his seat. "He's a very paranoid man. He thinks the killer has more security cameras mounted and . . . he has an insurance policy."

"What on earth does that mean?" Siobhán asked.

"He said he has something the killer wants. And as long as he has it—he thinks he's safe."

Macdara screeched back in his chair and loomed over Ethan. "Where is he?"

"I honestly have no idea. He texts me."

"Why did he text you that afternoon we were having our little chat?" Siobhán said. "What was so urgent?"

"I'd like to know the same thing," Ethan said. "He told me to meet him at the ruined abbey. He said he was ready to tell me everything, and he wanted my help in convincing the guards he was innocent. The killer told him he was too involved, that he would be blamed for the murder. I think he saw us chatting and thought I could help convince you that he's a victim. I went straightaway. He never showed up. I haven't heard from him since."

The door opened and a guard returned with Ethan's phone. "We took down all the messages—"

"All of them?" Ethan asked. "Or just the ones from William Bains?"

"Something the matter?" Macdara asked him.

"I do have a private life. A few online flirtations. I didn't think you'd be snooping into *everything*."

Macdara slid the phone across to Ethan. "Text him," he said. "Tell him it's urgent and you have to meet."

"I have been texting him. I haven't heard from him since that day. I swear."

"Maybe that's not the way to go about it," Siobhán said. "Maybe he needs someone else to text him."

"He doesn't want to talk to the guards until he has more proof," Ethan said.

"I wasn't talking about the guards," Siobhán said. "I think Mr. Bains needs to hear from our killer."

Chapter 27

Siobhán and Macdara stood outside the garda station, looking out at the square. Aretta was on her way to the bakery with several other guards to sweep the mill for the security cameras before everyone was back from the break. They would immediately return to the station. Would the footage reveal anything about their killer? The sun was making an appearance, and since the baking show was on a break, people were out and about. To their right was King John's Castle and across the way Oran stood outside of Turn the Page, catching a bit of sun. "Did Aretta say who won the chocolate competition?" Macdara asked.

"Dunno, let me text Aretta." She did and seconds later a reply came. "Still deliberating," Siobhán said.

"I bet they pick Philomena's Guinness cake," Macdara said. He rocked back on his heels and people-watched for a moment before turning to Siobhán. "How's the thinking going?" They had been mulling over the wording of the text they wanted to send to William Bains. He was smart, and obviously spooked. They had to be careful not to give themselves away. The killer had probably not been texting

William Bains with his or her personal phone, although it was a possibility. Getting a warrant for all their mobile phone records would take precious time. It was also possible that the killer had used a burner phone. And if not, they could probably convince William that they had switched to a burner phone as a caution. And if the killer had been using a burner phone, it was also reasonable that the killer would occasionally swap it out for a new one.

"How about—'Give me what I want and you can go free'?" Siobhán said.

"He is free," Macdara said. "That is, if he's still alive."

Siobhán gasped. "You think there's a chance he's not?"

"If Ethan is to be believed, he hasn't heard from William Bains since your outing with him."

"True. But it wasn't that long ago."

Siobhán tried out a few texts: **Clever. Fixing the wheel. Now why don't you tell me what you want so you can give me what's mine** . . . She showed it to Macdara. "This clocks with what Ethan said—how Bains has something the killer wanted."

"It does indeed," Macdara said with a nod. "But what if William Bains has already set his terms for the item?"

"True." She tried again. **Using a new phone. Guess who? The guards found the cameras. Ethan was interrogated. We need to meet. Ruined Abbey. 10 PM.** It was now half four.

"Close," Macdara said. "But it needs to be threatening enough to get his attention."

Siobhán nodded. **You think you're so clever, fixing the wheel. Ethan Brown was taken into custody. The mill had a spy camera. Wonder what he said about you? Help me and I help you. Otherwise I will make sure you burn. Ruined Abbey. 10 PM. Don't be late.**

"Perfect," Macdara said. "It's vague enough that it could either be from the killer or someone else who's figured out

what's going on. William Bains shouldn't be able to resist."
Macdara's phone buzzed. "It's Aretta." He turned the screen
toward Siobhán so she could read the text:

**Cut wires found behind the oil painting of Donal O'Farrell.
Camera gone.**

Siobhán clenched her fist. "This killer is always several
steps ahead of us."

Macdara nodded. "I'll tell them to sweep for more cameras, although I doubt we'll get that lucky. Let's hope we
get some answers tonight."

Siobhán glanced at the clock tower in the square. It was
going on 5:00 p.m. Would William Bains be at the ruined
abbey at ten? "Five hours to kill," Siobhán said, immediately wincing at her choice of words.

"Only one thing to do," Macdara said. "Are those dinner bells I hear?"

Siobhan stood by the kitchen window looking out at
their land, and enjoying the sounds and smells of a house
full of people cooking a feast. It was much needed, and her
siblings had done all the cooking: bacon and cabbage, and
a hearty salad that Eoin wanted to try out in the restaurant, and parsnips and potatoes, and fresh-baked rolls. It
was a feast for the eyes, all laid out on the table they had
moved into the sitting room for such occasions. Siobhán
wanted to put murder out of her mind, but given the upcoming meeting at the abbey, she was on edge. William
Bains had not responded to the text. Would he show?
Guards dressed as landscape maintenance folks were currently canvassing the area around the abbey for hiding
spaces that either the killer or William Bains might use.
Macdara would dress in all-black to pretend to be the
killer, but given they didn't know the height of the perpe-
trator, they agreed he could sit in the corner of the abbey,

hunched over in a dark robe. Like the monks from days of yore . . .

"Are you just going to stand there all night staring out the window?" The comment came from Gráinne, who was trying to maneuver behind Siobhán with a heavy pot. Gráinne nudged Siobhán out of the way with her hip and let the pot drop into the sink with a thud.

"Whoa," Ciarán said from the sitting room. "It's like Christmas in May."

It was an enormous amount of food. Eoin grabbed an additional two chairs from the kitchen. "What are you doing?" Siobhán asked. There were already seven chairs set up around the dining table.

"He didn't tell you, did he?" Eoin said with a wink.

Siobhán glanced at Macdara who, now that Eoin mentioned something, seemed to be standing by the front door as if waiting for someone.

"Ronan O'Keefe is coming to dinner," Ann said. "And Fia O'Farrell."

This was indeed a surprise. Siobhán stared at Macdara until she remembered. *Lemon meringue pie.*

The door opened and James walked in. He was wearing his work clothes and covered in dirt, but a grin lit up his face. "The restaurant has electricity," he announced.

"Deadly," Eoin said. "We're sucking diesel now."

"When do you think you'll officially open?" Siobhán asked.

"Three months on, if we're lucky," Eoin said. "Depends on a few permits."

Siobhán was excited for Eoin, but she was focused on this evening's dinner. "Set the table for ten," she said. It would be a tight squeeze but they could make it work.

"Ten?" Macdara arched an eyebrow. "Who's the extra?"

Siobhán laughed. "Do you really think Philomena Lemon is going to let Ronan and Fia come to dinner without her?"

"Good call," Macdara said.

"You haven't mentioned the winner of the first challenge," Gráinne said. "Did you get to taste all the Death by Chocolate offerings?"

"No," Macdara said like a child who had lost his puppy.

"We had to go back to the station," Siobhán said. "Who won?"

Gráinne's eyes lit up. "I can't believe you didn't hear."

"Go on, so," Siobhán said.

"A massive upset!" Gráinne was clearly enjoying dragging it out.

"Who won?" Siobhán demanded. Macdara edged forward.

"Sophia Hughes," Ann cut in before Gráinne could torture them any further. Siobhán hadn't even noticed her sitting at the kitchen table, draped over homework.

"Sophia Hughes?" Macdara said. "With that plain cake?"

"It wasn't plain inside," Eoin piped in. "When they cut into it they discovered she had replicated every single contestant's signature dish!"

"Wow," Siobhán said. "Fair play to her."

"Every dish?" Macdara asked.

"She had to tweak some," James said. "She wasn't able to replicate Trisha Mayweather's seven-layer-cake, so she did Trisha's signature peach pie."

"A pie within a cake," Macdara said, mesmerized.

"And Aoife's cherry pie became cherry and chocolate, but it was a nod to every single one of them," Gráinne added.

"You should have seen all the shocked faces," Ciarán said. "Gobsmacked!"

A knock on the door startled all of them. "Looks like you'll have to console yourself with lemon meringue pie," Siobhán said to her husband. He didn't reply; he was too busy opening the door and ushering in Ronan and Fia, their arms loaded with pastry boxes. But the biggest surprise came when Macdara went to shut the door, then swiveled it open again. Ronan and Fia hadn't just brought pastries and Philomena Lemon. They'd also brought with them all of the contestants, a director, and a cameraman. It was a good thing they had made a feast.

The O'Sullivan Six and Macdara stood outside the farmhouse, debating on how to handle their surprise visitors. The dining table was barely large enough to fit eight people, let alone an additional nine tagalongs.

"The restaurant!" Eoin exclaimed, glancing over at the barn.

"You don't have everything sorted," Siobhán said.

"The meal is already cooked," Ethan said. "We just need a gathering place."

"And we now have electricity, and farm tables," James said.

Siobhán turned to Eoin. "Are you sure you want this lot traipsing around your new restaurant?"

"It's *our* restaurant," Eoin said.

"It's true that it's in the rough," Eoin said. "But all I need to do is move one of the tables and benches out from the back room, and then we'll have to move it back because we're waiting on the new flooring."

"You have electricity, but the chandeliers have yet to be installed," Gráinne said.

"We have lamps," Ann said. "One in my room and one in Ciarán's."

"And candles," Gráinne said. She held her finger up to Siobhán. "And before you say a word about fire—each candle has a glass cover."

"Yes," Ciarán said. "Someone hand me a lighter, I want to light them all."

"What could go wrong?" Macdara said with a flat delivery.

"We have a fire extinguisher too, Detective Sergeant, and Garda O'Sullivan," Eoin said.

Ciarán laughed. "I'm calling you both that from now on."

"What you don't have is permits," Macdara said.

"It's not like we're charging them," Ann pointed out. "Is there a law against having family and friends in for an early dinner?"

Family, friends, and murderers . . . From inside her house she heard the sound of something clanking. "Let's do it," she said. "Let's move everyone out to the barn. But under no circumstance is anyone handing Ciarán a lighter." He stuck his tongue out at her and she returned the gesture in kind.

For the first few hours of the bakers crashing their family supper, everyone had a brilliant time. They marveled at the O'Sullivan Six restaurant, complimenting it until Eoin's grin infected the rest of them. Then they sat at the farm table and everyone ate and chatted until they were fat and happy. Sophia was particularly jolly, no doubt still buzzing from her big win. Not only had Ronan followed through with his lemon meringue pie; each contestant had brought a dessert and Macdara was in hog heaven. After dinner and dessert, everyone helped put the leftovers away and clean up. Ruth Barnes was balancing a load in her hands, taking them to the house, when she nearly dropped a dish. Siobhán swooped in and before Ruth could protest, her siblings had taken nearly everything from her.

"I had it," Ruth said. She placed her hands behind her back. It was odd behavior. Siobhán reacted before she could think; she reached out and took Ruth's hands. Ruth tried to pull away. Siobhán was about to apologize, wondering what on earth had come over her, and worried that her usually killer instinct was going haywire, when she looked at the top of Ruth's right hand. There, on the back of her hand, was a nasty scar in the shape of a quarter moon. Even though it had long healed, there was no doubt the scar had come from a burn.

"You," Siobhán said. "You were the girl whose hand was burned at Pie Pie Love all those years ago." Siobhán let go and Ruth immediately used her good hand to cover the scarred one.

"Yes," she said, tracing the scar. "I guess my moon gave me away." She looked around. "You won't tell the others, will you?"

"We're going to need to bring you into the station for official questioning tomorrow," Siobhán said.

"What?" She shook her head. "My day is already jammers with the filming."

"Charlie Holiday seems capable of handling it on his own for a few hours."

"Don't be ridiculous. He needs my direction."

"You've withheld crucial information from us in the middle of a murder probe," Siobhán said. "You will come into the station tomorrow."

"Question me now. Here, there, anywhere. I don't care. Just get it over with."

"I'm afraid that's not possible." Not only did they have to see if William Bains or the killer would show up at the abbey at ten this evening, Siobhán was not going to let Ruth Barnes direct the garda inquiry like they were another production under her control.

"I swear to you, I harbor no anger against Fia O'Farrell. It was an accident."

"I am not officially listening to you right now," Siobhán said. "You will have to come into the station."

"It's not what you think!" Ruth was shouting now, growing red in the face.

"Ruth. Calm down." Macdara had been across the field but was suddenly by her side. He stood by Siobhán but did not interrupt.

"This scar has given me the life I have now. I didn't come to ruin Fia O'Farrell's livelihood. I came to *thank* her."

Chapter 28

"You came to thank Fia O'Farrell?" Siobhán parroted. "You've been hiding your hands under gloves this entire production. That's not the behavior of someone grateful." Despite her best intentions, Siobhán was being reeled into having a conversation. Ruth Barnes was indeed a slippery one.

"I don't believe in doing something just to bask in praise," Ruth said. "I wanted to remain anonymous."

"I'm not following."

"I'm the reason this baking show is being held at Pie Pie Love."

"I'm going to need to hear the story," Siobhán said. If Ruth wasn't the killer, the killer had to have known about her sordid past with the bakery. The connection could not be a coincidence.

"I filmed interviews for the Aoife McBride Fan Club Appreciation day," Ruth said. "When I heard there was a mysterious sponsor who wanted to host a baking show, I said I knew just the place for it."

Macdara approached from the barn and raised an eyebrow. Siobhán turned to him. "It turns out that Ruth

Barnes was once injured at the flour mill as a child. She was scarred for life and she sued Pie Pie Love."

"Hold up," Macdara said. He squared off with Ruth Barnes. "You once sued Pie Pie Love and yet told no one of this past affiliation?" Gráinne and Ann were passing by and flashed youthful smiles that filled Siobhán with joy. The sun was starting to set, painting the skies a dusty pink. Ironically, a quarter moon was visible, as if shining a spotlight on Ruth's scar.

"She brought the past incident up to Fia the first day of filming," Siobhán said. "Acted as if she was getting the scoop on someone else's old story, but never mentioned she was the girl in the story."

Ruth pursed her lips. "My *parents* sued the bakery, I was only a child."

"But now, as an adult, you brought the event up to Fia O'Farrell and acted as if it happened to a total stranger. And it didn't sound as if you were trying to *save* her bakery."

"I suppose it was my chance to find out what story about the incident *she'd* grown up with," Ruth said. "We all have our stories."

"You lied," Macdara said. "Once you knew we were investigating a murder you could have come to us and cleared the air." The implication was clear—they could not trust her. What else might she be lying about?

Ruth shook her head. "No good deed goes unpunished."

"We're not squabbling over the deed," Siobhán said. "We're addressing the *lie*."

"Why all the secrecy? Does Fia O'Farrell know who you are?" Macdara added.

Ruth shook her head violently. "I don't want her to know. I'm not trying to stir up old drama or get a pat on the back. I just wanted to help her. I'm grateful for this scar. I truly am."

Macdara took in the scar. "That must have been painful. Especially for a young one." Given Ruth was rigid and defensive, he was trying a softer approach.

"Yes, it hurt, and yes, I had to go through surgery and a skin graft, and yes, other children made fun of me for years." She clasped her hands together. "But then a teacher told me that having a quarter moon on my hand was a sign that great things were to come. That I would be a leader and shine my light on others."

"I'm afraid you are going to have to come into the station tomorrow and give an official statement," Macdara said.

Ruth sighed. "What will I tell the others?"

"Everyone knows we're conducting our inquiries," Siobhán said. "Tell them it's your turn in the hot seat."

"Nine tomorrow morning at the Kilbane Garda Station," Macdara said.

Ruth crossed her arms. "Fine."

"Don't forget," Macdara said. "We want copies of all the footage you've shot so far."

"The guards already confiscated that yesterday." From Ruth's tone she was none too happy about it.

"You left out the B-roll," Macdara said.

Ruth pursed her lips. "Fine. You'll have it all in the morning." Presumably, before they could ask anything else of her, Ruth strode away.

"B-roll," Siobhán said, clapping him on the back. "Look at you learning the lingo."

Macdara grinned. "And . . . scene."

Siobhán and Macdara arrived at the abbey at 9:00 p.m., although for all they knew, the mysterious person or persons they may or may not be meeting had arrived even earlier. But they did have one advantage; this was their village and they knew all the hiding spots. Asking gardaí to pose as landscape maintenance folks had paid off. William Bains was hiding out on top of the roof of the Kilbane Museum. It was housed in a small shop located on the street that dead-ended into the field laid out in front of the abbey. He was reportedly up there with binoculars pointed at the abbey, and a small black satchel. The gardaí had caught sight of him from the rooftop of Butler's Undertaker, Lounge, and Pub across the way. Bains gave no indication that he was aware of being spotted, and the guards were confident that they had been sly enough to evade notice. They were still posted on Butler's roof and would alert them as soon as William Bains made a move.

Macdara was dressed in a brown hooded robe. He stood at the highest level of the abbey, near the bell tower. Siobhán was situated in a small back courtyard. This way they had both entrances covered. She paced the small patch of field bordered by crumbling limestone walls, wondering what William Bains would do next. Three plucked weeds later she had her answer when a text came from the guards stationed on Butler's roof: **He's on the move.**

Showtime. As they had rehearsed, Macdara was now flashing a torch three times to signal William Bains. Siobhán sat on a half-stone wall, her heart pattering in her chest. Four other guards were stationed around the abbey. Luckily there were plenty of walls left to hide behind. They had to take these precautions. What if William Bains was the killer and had a weapon? Macdara knew to be on the lookout for the solicitor handing him *anything* that could be laced with poison, and under his robe he was wearing gloves. Siobhán was in her regular clothes, denims and a wooly sweater. Even though it was May, the evenings cooled down. It was a gorgeous evening for a stakeout, and a dome of stars shone above. She wished she were out here just to hold her husband's hand and gaze at all the twinkling stars. If only life were that simple. It was an excruciating ten minutes before another text came in: **He's headed for the back of the abbey with satchel.**

Shiv? Macdara texted. It wasn't often that he called her Shiv, but right now they needed to be brief.

Ready. She crossed the little courtyard and hid behind the nearest stone wall. There was one with a gap small enough to peek through. She knew without him texting that Macdara would be headed her way. Hopefully once William Bains saw them he would realize it was time to tell them everything. And hopefully by the time midnight came around, their murderer would be caught and they could finish the baking show in peace. Soon the light from a small torch bounced into the courtyard. William thought he was going to sneak up on whoever was waiting in the bell tower. She waited until the bounce of light had just passed her to jump out.

"Halt. It's Garda O'Sullivan."

William Bains let out a high-pitched scream and dropped the torch. He cursed as she shone her light on him. His face turned toward her, eyes squinting from the sudden glare. "I knew it," he said. "I knew it."

"Good evening," Macdara said, causing another scream to escape the man. William reached for his satchel. "Don't move," Macdara warned.

Siobhán angled her torch to shine as much light as possible on the area. "We've got guards stationed all around you."

William stood straight and thrust his hands up. Sweat made his pale face shine. "It's terrible weather we're having this month," William said, his voice shaking with nerves.

The weather. The topic everyone covered when there was nothing left to say.

"I think it's a grand evening," Siobhán said.

"Even better now, wouldn't you say?" Macdara added.

"Lights," Macdara said. Instantly the lights that guards had set up around the perimeter came to life. Siobhán switched off her torch.

"Quite the production," William Bains said. "For little old me?"

Macdara nodded to a nearby guard. "Remove the satchel and take this man into custody."

"You're arresting me?" William Bains said. "I'm a solicitor!"

"Then you must realize we're well within our rights to bring you into the station for questioning," Macdara said. He proceeded to give the caution. "You are not obliged to say anything unless you wish to do so, but anything you say will be taken down in writing and may be given in evidence."

William Bains wasn't talking. He'd been sitting in the interview room for over two hours. The only item in the satchel had been a handwritten recipe book. Gloves on, Siobhán thumbed through it. "They're all desserts," she said. "I know this handwriting." The pages were old and yellow. There was one page in the middle of the book that had been torn out. "Just as I thought," Siobhán said.

Macdara arched an eyebrow. "I'm lost."

"Aretta and I found a handwritten recipe at Trisha's station—her 'secret weapon.' We believe it was an old recipe of Aoife McBride's. It should still be in the evidence room, and dollars to donuts it fits our missing page." The book was thick and chock-full of very detailed instructions. "I bet this is the original copy of what became Aoife's cookbook empire."

"Do you think it's worth a fair amount?"

Siobhán nodded. "Even if she's still alive I bet it would fetch a high price at an auction. And if she turns out to be dead—"

"It could be worth a fortune," Macdara said.

"I would gander it might be worth killing over."

"Do you think this is the 'insurance policy' William Bains mentioned—the thing the killer wanted?"

"That's my guess."

"Let's go back in and question him again. You take the lead this time and I'll just sit with this book in front of me, glaring at him."

"Brilliant," Siobhán said. "You do have the most withering glare."

William Bains was a difficult cookie and stuck to grumbling about the weather, and continuously said, "By the book."

"Yes," Macdara finally said. "We know you're a solicitor, but we would be doing everything by the book, no matter what."

"We also know this cookbook belonged to Aoife McBride," Siobhán said. "We have the missing page with the initials A.M. in evidence. It was given out to one of the contestants as a secret weapon."

"Of course we're by the book," Macdara said, still fixated on William's earlier comment. "Are you suggesting we're not?"

William sighed. "I'm not saying anything further without a solicitor."

"Why are you protecting a killer?" Siobhán asked. She was genuinely curious.

"Maybe he's the killer," Macdara said. So much for simply glaring; Macdara was finding it challenging to keep his gob shut.

"How did you get ahold of this book?" Siobhán asked. The recipe book sat in front of them. "Did the killer steal it from Aoife McBride?"

"Is Aoife McBride alive or dead?" Macdara chimed in.

"Terrible weather we're having—"

Siobhán slammed the book on the table. She'd had quite enough. "We understand that you most likely represent the killer. And whereas a solicitor and a client do share rights to privacy, that is all null and void when your client decides to murder two—and maybe three—persons in cold blood."

William suddenly leaned forward. "You look. There are many layers to this. You do not understand." He shook his head. "I've given you many signs."

"Signs," she said. "Are you the one who changed the accident sign to zero days?"

"Yes," he said. "I was hoping it would put a fire under you."

"My wife—" Macdara started. He cleared his throat. "Garda O'Sullivan doesn't need the likes of you or anyone else putting a fire under her. She's self-propelled."

Siobhán gave a nod, then tried a softer approach with William Bains. He was frightened, or he was a killer, and either way he knew the law, making him a strong opponent. They had to give him a little power back. "Explain it to us so we do understand," she said.

He shifted in his chair before leaning forward. "If I were afraid not just for my safety, but the safety of everyone else in this competition—that you have kept in the dark, by the way—then you must understand why I am not making any statements, bold moves, or declarations."

Siobhán chewed on this. He was right. If the killer was among everyone else, this person could retaliate at any time. The guards had kept secrets from the contestants for too long. It was time to inform the players of what was really going on. They had taken too big of a risk. Time to tell the truth and cancel the event. Even if it meant the bakery could not be saved and a killer would get away.

"We can hold you for twenty-four hours," Macdara said.

"Listen to me." William Bains squirmed in his seat and wiped his brow with a handkerchief from his wrinkled suit jacket. "I tried to find evidence. I *tried*. Why do you think I hid out in the flour mill? It wasn't for sport. It wasn't because I couldn't run across the field and get meself back to Dublin. It was to find evidence. Without that, all I have are suspicions. Against a *client*."

"The mysterious sponsor of this event," Siobhán said.

"Yes," William said. "Of course, when this all went down I advised my client to go to the guards. But I could not force this client to heed my advice."

"And you believe this client is our killer?" Macdara asked.

William Bains pursed his lips as if trying to keep his words locked tight inside. "What I believe and what I can prove are two very different things."

"We understand that very well," Siobhán said. "If you would just point us in the right direction we can investigate him or her."

William Bains arched an eyebrow. "But you're doing that already, aren't you?"

He was maddening. But he was also correct. "Knowing who to focus on first would significantly speed up our investigation," Macdara said.

"Believe me, I am trying to help you." William Bains leaned back and folded his hands across his stomach. "We are talking about a person with money and power. If I was to accuse a client of *murder* based on mere suspicions—that's the end of my career, and quite frankly irresponsible." A knock sounded on the door and a guard poked her head in. "A solicitor is here for Mr. Bains." William Bains dropped his hands. "I'm afraid that's all the time I have for you today." He stood. "I do hope you have a long think about what I've had to say." He gave Siobhán a long look. "I hope one day very soon you'll understand everything completely."

Chapter 29

Siobhán and Macdara called all the participants to an early morning meeting at the bakery. Nerves and little sleep drove them to be outside the flour mill before everyone else. As it had been all through the night, the central topic of conversation was William Bains. "All he had to do was give us the name of the benefactor-slash-killer," Siobhán said. "Would that have been so hard? No one would have even known."

Macdara gazed out at the horizon. "Even if he did give us a name—could we trust him?"

Siobhán focused on the streaks of pink light painting the sky. "He is a slippery one." The sun was slowly inching up. "All his little quips and double-talk. He's definitely a game player. He could even be our killer."

"However . . . if he was the killer, wouldn't it make sense to give us a name, even if the person was innocent?"

"That's a good point." Siobhán sighed. Macdara took her hand and gave it a squeeze before releasing it.

"We're doing the right thing," he said. Last night they had decided it was best to cancel the baking show.

"Are we?" She knew he was right, but she also didn't want to experience everyone's disappointment. The town, the bakers, the judges, Fia O'Farrell. Siobhán felt as if they were poised to be the bad guys when it was really the killer to blame.

"We'd better get inside and see if Fia will give us free pastries," Macdara said. "Because once we cancel this baking show, we're likely to be booted from the premises for life." A garda car pulled up and parked in the lot. Siobhán and Macdara waited as Aretta Dabiri joined them.

"This is going to be fun," she said with a straight face.

"Thank you for meeting us so early," Macdara began. "We have some news and it's going to come as a shock." They had gathered everyone into the event space. The ingredient table behind the judges was noticeably empty. Ruth Barnes and Charlie Holiday were not present; they were being told separately that the filming had been called off, and the guards would collect all the footage they had shot so far. Maybe there would be something on those tapes that could help solve the murder. Fia O'Farrell had been notified privately before the rest of them, and she was in her office weeping. Once she burst into tears, Siobhán and Macdara lost all appetite for sweets.

"I'm not doing Death by Chocolate one more time," Martin Murphy said. Others chimed in their agreement.

"As you know, there was a postmortem performed on one of our contestants who passed away at the beginning of the competition," Macdara began.

"Aoife McBride," Barry said. "The Queen."

"We all believed that the victim was Aoife McBride," Macdara said. Heads began to tilt in confusion. "What we discovered through our investigation is that the deceased is actually an actress named Elizabeth Wynne."

Gasps rang out. "An actress?" Sophia Hughes said.

"Yes," Siobhán said. "We believe she was hired from the Aoife McBride fan club event you attended in Donegal."

"I didn't recognize her," Sophia said. "No wonder you kept asking me about the event. And here I was worried you suspected me!"

"Wait," Barry said. "Does that mean Aoife McBride is alive and well?"

"We also discovered," Macdara said, ignoring Barry's question, "that the protester who died before the event began was also an actor."

"An actor?" Ethan said. "Part of the competition?" He looked around to see if others were getting it. Heads shook in confusion.

"Not part of the baking competition," Siobhán said. "Part of a murderer's scheme."

Ronan put his hand on his heart. "I feel like we're being pranked. Are we being pranked?" He glanced around. "Where is that cameraman?"

"Elizabeth Wynne was electrocuted with her secret weapon—a kitchen mixer, and the fridge behind her was tampered with so that it would leak right underneath her outlet," Siobhán continued. They had decided if they were going to come clean, they were going to tell everything. Being silent hadn't worked to their advantage, so when in doubt, try the opposite.

"The protester was poisoned with strychnine added to face powder," Aretta said. "We believe the face powder was meant for Elizabeth, only she noticed her fellow actor on camera and thought she would help him out."

"I'm going to faint," Trisha Mayweather said. "Why didn't you provide chairs for this meeting?"

"Let's move into the greenroom," Macdara said. "Everyone can sit down."

The group shuffled toward the greenroom and once there, Trisha, Ronan, and Philomena sank into the long sofa, whereas Sophia and the remaining men all found walls to lean against.

"Is Aoife McBride alive or not?" Barry demanded.

"We do not know," Siobhán said. "The Donegal Gardaí performed a wellness check at her residence but no one was home."

"There were also no signs of foul play," Macdara said.

"Why are you just telling us this now?" The question came from Philomena.

"We had to wait until we concluded that portion of our investigation," Siobhán said. "And given there was another incident, we felt we could no longer hold anything back."

"Another incident?" Ronan said. "Who died now?"

"William Bains is in a coma at Cork University Hospital," Siobhán said.

"A coma?" Trisha Mayweather cried. "What happened?"

"He was hiding in the mill and took a tumble down the steps," Siobhan said.

The plan had been hatched early this morning, and William Bains, hoping the news would grant him a reprieve from a nervous killer, if it was indeed his client, wholeheartedly agreed. William was actually on his way back to Dublin, but he insisted he was going to lie low. And on the off chance their killer wanted him dead sooner, they were going to station guards at Cork University Hospital. If even one of their contestants paid a visit, they would bring him or her into the station for immediate questioning.

"Who is William Bains?" Ronan demanded. Was he faking the question, or did he really not remember? To be fair, there had been a lot going on at once.

"The solicitor who represents the mysterious benefactor," Macdara said.

"We believe this benefactor may be the mastermind behind these cases," Aretta said.

"I don't understand. Why would they hire an actor to

pretend to be a protester?" Ethan Brown said, as if he had been on pause and was just now putting the pieces together.

"We think the murderer wanted a distraction so they could break into the working portion of the mill in order to obtain the strychnine that was in the storage room," Macdara said.

"A local then?" Barry said. "Someone who knew there was poison in the mill?"

"Fia O'Farrell!" Martin said. "Is it just a coincidence that she isn't here?"

"Have you arrested her?" Trisha added.

"Fia O'Farrell is still here, and no, we are not arresting anyone," Macdara said. "Unfortunately, given there is a killer targeting this event, the baking show has been canceled."

"Targeting this event or just Aoife McBride?" Trisha said. "Because we've all been safe since the terrible incident."

"That funny little man is in a coma," Philomena said. "We are not safe."

"Why aren't you arresting Fia O'Farrell?" Ronan said. "If the poison was taken from the mill, then it has to be her."

"It was not!" Everyone turned to see Fia O'Farrell standing in the bakery. She advanced into the greenroom. "I've done nothing wrong. I assure you I'm innocent." They had long processed the crime scene, but all the old refrigerators and stations had yet to be removed. Siobhán would start emptying the fridges as soon as they were finished here so that they could call for the removal of the equipment.

"To be fair, that's exactly what a guilty person would say," Ethan grumbled.

"How would anyone else know about the poison in the mill?" Philomena asked, directing the question to Fia.

"All I know is that I wouldn't have had to break the back door down if I wanted to steal my own strychnine—and if that funny little man was squatting on the top floor, obviously he and the killer had been snooping around, and given a local wouldn't need to snoop around, it brings it right back to one of you!"

"Can we please just refer to the solicitor as William Bains?" Siobhán said.

"My head is spinning, this is too much to take in," Sophia said.

"Why would someone hire an actress to play Aoife McBride and then kill her?" Trisha asked.

"We cannot share our theory on that just yet," Macdara said.

"Unfortunately, we can no longer guarantee the safety of any of the particpants we must stop the show," Siobhán repeated.

"No!" Trisha Mayweather shot off the sofa. "We cannot let the killer take everything from us."

"I agree with Trisha," Martin Murphy said. "If the killer wanted us dead, we'd be dead already."

"What will happen to the twenty thousand euro if we cancel the baking show?" Ethan asked.

"It will return to the benefactor," Macdara said.

"Even if the benefactor is a killer?" Barry asked.

"We can't control the finances of a person who hasn't been charged," Siobhán said.

"The benefactor must come forward," Trisha said. She looked around in case someone was about to spring forth.

"Wait a minute," Sophia said, taking a few steps forward. "What if Aoife McBride staged her own death?"

Siobhán was hoping no one would consider that.

"Why would she do that?" Philomena asked.

"Because of her new cookbook release!" Ronan said. "I bet sales will skyrocket once the word gets out."

"That goes double for her memoir," Barry said. Heads nodded in agreement.

The cookbook reminded Siobhán of the book William Bains had in his possession, the one thing they were able to get from him. Siobhán still didn't know whether or not it belonged to Aoife McBride, but it was another thing on her to-do list today: clean the refrigerators, watch footage of the baking show, read the old cookbook. The mill had been swept for additional spy cameras, but the one behind the portrait had been removed and they did not find any others hidden about the place.

"We are politely requesting that you all remain in town until you've had a formal sit-down with us," Macdara said. Groans rippled through the group.

"Your rooms are paid for, and you had planned this time off anyway. I'm sure the townsfolk would be more than happy to get autographs."

"You want us to stay when one of us is a killer?" Barry Ryan sounded outraged.

Macdara held up his hand. "If you wish to leave town, please see me, and I can arrange to have you interviewed as soon as possible."

Loaded up with rubbish bins and gloved and suited-up, Siobhán and Aretta began the unpleasant task of cleaning out the refrigerators. The contestants had all evacuated the premises, and even Fia O'Farrell had taken the rest of the day off to process what this meant for her future. Siobhán took the refrigerator that had been set up behind Elizabeth Wynne's station. She began pouring out milk and tossing the containers into recycling bins, throwing out eggs, and flour—everything had to be considered contaminated. Given they were too large to fit in one refrigerator, three sections of Trisha Mayweather's layer cake had been placed in one fridge, and four sections in another.

Siobhán's fridge had the top three sections. Even though no one in his or her right mind would want to eat this cake now, it felt like such a waste tossing the sections into the bins and watching the cake crumble.

Aretta stood by her fridge, watching her do it. "I guess it's my turn," she said.

The front door opened and Macdara returned. "Stop what you're doing," he said. "We've just heard from the Donegal Gardaí. They've pulled a body from the Donegal Bay this morning and they believe it's Aoife McBride."

Chapter 30

The news spread quickly. The woman everyone thought had been electrocuted during a live baking show had been found dead in the Donegal Bay. Although they would have to wait for an official postmortem report, they believed the body had been in the water for over a month. She had been wrapped in a woolen rug that was then secured with both tape and gardening twine that the guards believe had been taken from Aoife's cottage. And although it wasn't official yet, the Donegal Gardaí informed MacDara that it appeared Aoife McBride had taken a blow to the back of her head. This time when the Donegal guards searched Aoife's cottage they detected that someone had cleaned up with bleach and given what they now knew, it raised a red flag. In addition, a rug was missing from the sitting room leading them to believe that Aoife McBride had most likely been killed in her own home. Their estimated time of her death coincided with the date of the fan club gathering, and the last anyone heard from Aoife McBride was when she called the guards to report a stalker. If only they had been able to stop this person sooner, although given the slick nature of this killer, Siobhán could hardly blame the Donegal Gardaí. Stalkers were difficult to catch in most cases, especially if a crime had yet to be committed. Macdara requested the full report. Did Aoife McBride give them any hint of who she believed was harassing her? The guards insisted that she kept talking about "an awful feeling." Intuition. The little voice whispering that something is not right. It happened all the time, yet was not concrete enough for the authorities to act on. Maddening.

Siobhán cleared out a small office and set up the equipment to watch all the footage of the baking show, even the B-roll from the very beginning. There had to be something they'd missed. She settled in to watch, with a notebook, Biro, pot of tea and biscuits. Just as she was about to push play, Aretta popped her head in. "We caught a cheater."

"What?"

"The guards who finished cleaning out the fridge discovered that Trisha Mayweather's layer cake wasn't all the way finished. She used pink bakery boxes to mimic the layers. There was nothing but icing on top of them."

"You're joking me." That explained what happened to those pink bakery boxes Elizabeth Wynne had taken away from the bookshop.

"Don't let them throw those boxes away. Mark them as evidence."

Aretta raised an eyebrow. "We're going to nail her for cheating? The baking show has been canceled."

Siobhán hated cheaters, but the feelings coursing through her were due to something else. That little feeling . . . "Who's interviewing first with Macdara?"

Aretta frowned. "Trisha Mayweather. She wants to go home."

"Tell him to stall her."

"You're on to something?"

"I might be. Whatever you do—do not let Trisha leave."

Something William Bains said came crashing over her. "Terrible weather we're having this month." Why not just terrible weather? Why this month?" Why mention the weather? It was the month of May. Mayweather.

She thought of the pastry boxes. Why would Trisha choose such an elaborate project in the first place? Wedding cakes were not her signature bake. Had she wanted them to think there was no way she had time to bake a seven-layer cake whilst sabotaging a refrigerator? Siobhán had noticed her lingering in front of the fridge, but she'd blamed it on menopause.

And the other comment made by Mr. Bains: *By the book*. Macdara had understood him to mean by the book, as if doing everything according to strict procedure. That wasn't what he meant. He meant—*buy* the book.

Aoife's cookbooks. And Siobhán had bought a copy of the books—she had all of them—and the originals. Was there another clue to be gleaned by comparing the books? Aretta was still waiting by the doorway. "I also need the handwritten cookbook we obtained from William Bains, from the evidence locker."

"On it," Aretta said.

Siobhán thought back to the opening of the baking show when the contestants were first introduced. Trisha Mayweather was pushed out looking all rumpled. Perhaps she had just broken into the working part of the mill to fetch strychnine. What if Trisha Mayweather had gone to Donegal during the fan club convention? Aoife McBride had been set to come out with a new memoir and they were reprinting all her old cookbooks. Trisha would have met Ruth at the event, and Ruth had suggested Pie Pie Love as the perfect venue. It wasn't a stretch to think old mills would have rodent poison in the working portions of the building. It was quite possible Trisha and her mother may have even toured Pie Pie Love in the past. The strychnine container, with a photo of a gopher and the word *poison* slashed across it, would have been impossible to forget. All Trisha needed was a little time to look for it. Elizabeth Wynne had arrived early, most likely with Trisha. While George O'Leary distracted them with his bullhorn, Trisha would have been breaking into the ground floor of the mill, stealing the poison, mixing it into the powder, and waiting for Elizabeth to powder her nose. When the protester dropped dead instead, Trisha had a new problem on her hands. She could not waste an opportunity to pull off a perfect murder. The televised baking show would not only bring in an audience, they were an audience who would most likely turn around and purchase her cookbooks. What was this old grudge between Mary Mayweather and Aoife McBride? Siobhán turned on the tapes.

Charlie Holiday was a good cameraman. He covered all the contestants evenly. The excitement in the opening footage was palpable but nothing explicitly pointed to a killer. She went back through the very first introductions with all their little conflicts. Ethan Brown apologizing for the disparaging remarks he made about Aoife McBride to a Parisian newspaper. Next up was Trisha, stumbling onto the red carpet looking unkempt. Siobhán carefully watched her introduction. The judges had played up the past conflict between Mary Mayweather and Aoife McBride. An insult Mary Mayweather had hurled at McBride over preservative-filled icing versus fresh cream. Siobhán watched Trisha's answer:

"It wasn't an insult! The fresh cream is much better." The camera whipped to the facial expressions of the other contestants. "There's only one reason Aoife McBride didn't use fresh cream and that's because—"

Trisha was interrupted by Ronan. Siobhán paused the

tape and stared at the screen. What had she been about to say?

Aretta popped in holding an evidence bag with Aoife McBride's book of handwritten recipes. "Macdara just excused himself from the interview—stating a serious development in the case."

Siobhán nodded. "Where is Trisha Mayweather?"

"Interview room one."

Siobhán reached for the old recipe book. "Give me a minute here." Siobhán leafed through the old cookbook. She needed to compare it to the recent ones. Given hers were all at the farm, but Turn the Page was right across the street, she headed out of the station and crossed the square. Padraig was outside on the phone and gave her a smile and wave as she blew past him. She went right to the display of Aoife's cookbooks. To her shock, a mob of people were standing in front of it. It wasn't until Siobhán pushed her way through to grab one that she realized the display was empty. Oran was at the counter, happily ringing up customers. The stampede to buy the McBride cookbooks had already begun. Siobhán scanned the crowd for someone with a copy of *Aoife McBride Takes the Cake*—the first in the series. She soon found it clutched in a nearby hand.

"I need this for one second," she said gently, trying to pry it away.

"Hey!" The woman tugged it back.

"Seriously, just one moment." Siobhán nudged it her way again. The woman yanked it back. "This is official garda business."

Padraig cleared his throat loudly, finally capturing the woman's attention. "I'm sure Garda O'Sullivan will be quick and I'll give ya ten percent off for your troubles."

The woman narrowed her eyes. "Make it fifteen."

"Ten," Siobhán said with a final yank. She took the

book to a nearby shelf, propped it up against the original in her hands, and began thumbing through the pages. At first glance, page after page, the recipes were identical. Siobhán slowed down to compare them, and she noticed there were indeed very small tweaks to each recipe. Trisha's comment on the tape came back into Siobhán's mind:

There's only one reason Aoife McBride didn't use fresh cream and that's because . . .

Because Aoife McBride had stolen all of Mary Mayweather's recipes and slightly tweaked them. Probably not illegal, but maddening. Especially since Aoife McBride shot to fame, leaving Mary Mayweather baking in obscurity. The original handwritten book Siobhán held did not belong to Aoife. The initials *A.M.* written on the secret weapon given to Trisha Mayweather had thrown Siobhán. Aoife had been putting her initials on the recipes as she modified them.

Mary Mayweather had recently passed away. And now Aoife McBride was coming out with a memoir. Siobhán had a feeling it was not meant to be a tell-all. Had Trisha Mayweather exacted revenge for the wrongs done to her late mam? Had she gone to Donegal to persuade Aoife McBride into giving her a cut? Admitting what she'd done in her memoir? Or was Trisha Mayweather the new beneficiary of the McBride estate? Siobhán texted Macdara. I **believe Trisha Mayweather stands to inherit Aoife McBride's entire estate. Have Donegal Gardaí look into it.** Siobhán was convinced, but even if there was proof that Trisha Mayweather was going to inherit Aoife's estate, that alone would not prove she murdered her. There was no time to gather enough evidence to charge Trisha Mayweather before she headed out of town. There was no chance, unless . . . unless she could get Trisha to make a full confession. And perhaps there was no way to do that unless . . . Siobhán looked around at the crowd fawning all over Aoife McBride's recipes. Even if Trisha had threatened Aoife McBride into changing her will, this was about ego. About her late mam never getting the credit she deserved. Perhaps if they wanted a confession, they needed to gather too many cooks in the kitchen and turn up the heat. She knew one particular large open space that had just installed a few commercial cookers. Now she just had to convince her siblings that it was a good idea to hold a pre–Grand Opening baking event at the O'Sullivan Six in order to catch a killer.

Everyone had gathered at the O'Sullivan Six, and Eoin was thrilled with the fact that there was a cameraman and director who would be giving him early publicity. What he didn't realize yet is that they were only pretending to stream the event. She hoped her brother would forgive her for not letting him in on the twist, but their best chance was if everyone behaved normally, and Eoin O'Sullivan did not have a poker face. Gráinne and Ann were over the moon, ferrying between the contestants with offerings of tea and fashion advice. Ciarán, well into puberty, seemed to always position himself where he could gaze upon Philomena Lemon, who was spending most of her free time chatting up the oldest O'Sullivan, James. *Happy days.*

"Thank you for coming," Siobhán said. "Given how disappointed everyone was that we were canceling the baking show, a discussion was held and we all agreed we would have one more baking assignment show and from this single event crown the winner."

Ethan raised his hand. Feeling like a schoolteacher, Siobhán called on him. "Does that include the twenty thousand euro prize money?"

"Yes, it does." Of course there was no longer any kind of communication with the sponsor, given they were all pretending William Bains was in a coma, but Fia O'Farrell had already been transferred the prize money, and she had agreed to release it to a winner today. That too was a ruse. They were currently trying to trace the money to see if they could connect it to Trisha Mayweather or Aoife McBride's accounts. They were also searching for an executor of Aoife McBride's estate. But all of those developments would come too late. Siobhán did not want to let a killer walk away. Not one who had messed with her town so profusely. Not one who had so boldly murdered three innocent people. Maybe she was going to have to take up poker after this, for it took all she had not to shiver in revulsion every time she looked at Trisha Mayweather. "In honor of Aoife McBride, every contestant is going to bake a recipe from her revised cookbooks."

A gasp was heard all throughout the restaurant and it came from none other than Trisha. Heads swiveled her way. "We don't have multiple ovens here," Trisha said. "I do not see how we're going to pull this off."

"There are two commercial cookers here, and one at my farmhouse," Siobhán said. "We'll be baking them in shifts."

"There's another little twist," Ronan said, stepping up to the plate. "We have found a precious copy of Aoife McBride's *handwritten* edition of her very first cookbook—*Aoife McBride Takes the Cake*." He held up Mary Mayweather's original cookbook. The corner of Trisha's mouth began to twitch, followed by her left eye.

Siobhán was hoping that would get her blood boiling. She had murdered to restore her late mam's legacy. No doubt Aoife McBride had been forced to make a little confession in her upcoming memoir before she was murdered. *I stole the recipes from Mary Mayweather. Forgive me. I leave my entire estate to her* daughter . . .

"Stop," Trisha said. "How do we know that book was written by Aoife McBride?"

"I looked at all the recipes," Siobhán said. "They're identical."

"That's impossible."

"Her initials are on a page—it was torn out—in fact, it was your secret weapon—but it's the same handwriting."

Trisha removed eyeglasses from her apron pocket and held out her hand. "I would like to see it."

Barry Ryan stepped forward. "I don't see a problem. I'll make any recipe you give me. It doesn't matter whose recipe it is."

"It certainly does matter," Trisha snapped. Philomena began passing out copies of recipes taken from Mary May-weather's book. Siobhán had titled them all: Aoife McBride's Original Recipes.

"This is my mam's handwriting," Trisha exclaimed. "These are my mam's recipes."

"These recipes are the exact ones used to write *Aoife McBride Takes the Cake*," Siobhán said. Charlie moved the camera in on Trisha. Sweat appeared on her brow.

"She stole them," Trisha said. "She stole every single recipe from my mam." More gasps were heard around the room, and this time they were genuine.

"When did you realize this?" Siobhán asked.

"We've always known," Trisha said. "We just never had the power to do anything about it."

Siobhán nodded. "And your mam passed away without any of the recognition she deserved."

"This is all terribly upsetting. I no longer wish to be part of this baking show." Trisha removed her apron and tossed it on the communal dining table. She grabbed her handbag and made a move toward Siobhán. "I need that back." She pointed to the book.

Siobhán wagged the book. "You're saying this belongs to you."

"That's exactly what I'm saying."

"The book we found in William Bains's possession."

Trisha stopped. She chewed on her lip. "He's the killer! Aoife McBride had this book in her possession. That must be why he came here. To kill her and get the original cookbook!" She looked around as if trying to suss out whether or not anyone was buying it.

"Why would William Bains have to stage her death when she was already dead and he had the book in his possession?" Siobhán asked.

"Already dead?" Fia O'Farrell said. Heads whipped in Siobhán's direction, mouths open in shock.

"Aoife McBride's body was just pulled from the Donegal Bay," Macdara announced. "The guards are processing evidence as we speak." Gasps were heard all around the room.

Trisha eyed the exit. Siobhán stepped in front of her. "Care to answer the question? Why would William Bains do such a thing if he knew Aoife McBride was already dead?"

"Because he didn't want to be accused of her murder! If people thought she was still alive and she died on telly in front of a live audience . . ." Trisha wiped sweat off her face with the back of her sleeve.

"You murdered Aoife McBride," Siobhán said. "To avenge your late mam and make sure that Aoife McBride's upcoming memoir included a full confession of her sins."

Trisha opened and closed her mouth. "William Bains did it," she croaked. "If only he were awake to admit it."

"William Bains was never in a coma," Siobhán said. "He's been talking to us this entire time." That wasn't exactly a lie. He had been talking to them, just not about the case.

All color drained from Trisha McBride's face. "Look out!" Aretta shouted from across the room. Trisha was reaching for something on the table. Siobhán's first thought was—*no bother, she's only reaching for eggs*—when suddenly one hit her square on the forehead. She felt and heard the crack and then suddenly thick yellow goo was running into her eyes.

"Hey," she heard Macdara yell. Siobhán stumbled to the table as she tried to wipe her eyes. "Put that down," she heard Macdara yell. It was too late, Siobhán took another egg to the forehead, this time even closer to her eyes. A third one hit in rapid succession. The fourth hit was something soft—she had no idea what it was but it clung to the egg, obscuring her vision even further. *Flour*. Siobhán pawed the table, trying to find a napkin. Instead she felt an egg and instinctively she grabbed it and threw it in the direction the attacks had come from. She heard a crack and a squeal.

"Hey!" The voice was Philomena's and she was browned-off. All chaos erupted. Shouting, and the sounds of shoes screeching on the floor, liquid sloshing, eggs cracking, and a lot more effing and blinding, more appropriate to sailors than bakers. Macdara yelled for order, but it was either too loud for anyone to hear, or the frenzy was so great that no one was listening. Something soft and heavy was shoved in Siobhán's hands—to her relief it was a wet towel. She managed to clear her eyes in time to blink and make out a few unrecognizable faces around her, covered in goo, and flour, and chocolate. Ronan stumbled toward her, and at first it appeared that a great pox had broken out on his face, but as Siobhán peered closer she could see they were walnuts. Flour was flying across the room, creating a mist above their heads. Ethan Brown slipped on a yellow stream of yolk, and fell with a cry and a thud. Someone lobbed a mixing bowl and it landed on top of Ronan O'Keefe's head. Where was Trisha Mayweather? Siobhán realized she was no longer holding the old cookbook. "Where's Trisha?" she yelled.

Sophia Hughes picked up a large carton of eggs. "I'll check outside!"

"I'll take those eggs and check the kitchen," Ethan said, as Barry Ryan helped him up. Martin Murphy grabbed the egg carton from Sophia before Ethan could get his hands on it. "I've got it!" Martin yelled. Siobhán found Aretta in the corner. She had an apron draped over her head. Next to her Macdara was wearing oven mitts and holding them up defensively. They had lost all control. Milk dripped from Siobhán's hair along with egg, and the flour made it clump.

"She did not leave the premises," Macdara said. "I've been watching the door the entire time."

Siobhán's head whipped around. Nearly everyone was unrecognizable—their faces covered in goo. Suddenly, she caught sight of Gráinne waving her arms wildly. Siobhán's memory flashed to the CCTV footage of William Bains waving to someone across the room. When Siobhán had watched the footage the figure appeared to be Aoife McBride. It dawned on her now that Trisha Mayweather had the same tall and bulky figure. Most likely she'd donned a wig hoping not to be spotted on camera. Siobhán forced herself back to the present. Gráinne was pointing underneath the communal table. Visible beneath the once-white tablecloth was a large arse. Trisha Mayweather was on all fours cowering underneath the table, once more trying to hide in plain sight. Siobhán signaled Macdara and Aretta and they approached.

"It's over," Siobhán said. "We see you."

Trisha finally crawled out from under the table but she remained on the floor. "Aoife McBride deserved it," she said. "She had it coming."

Siobhán knelt. "You confronted her at the fan club event in Donegal?"

Trisha nodded. "I just wanted her to make things right. Admit that she stole every single recipe my mam wrote. Write a little confession in her memoir."

"But she wouldn't?"

"That conniving thief was bitter and resistant until her very last moments." Trisha balled up her fist. "Someone had to do something."

"Did she change her will? Did you force her to do it?"

"It's my money. That recipe book belongs to my mam. It's my money." She pounded her chest, sending another cloud of flour into the air.

"I need to hear from you exactly what happened," Siobhán said.

Trisha's eyes filled with tears. "She spotted me straight-away at the event, even though I had one of those stupid wigs on."

The same wig she wore later to O'Rourke's . . . "Go on."

"She couldn't get out of the room fast enough once she saw me in the Donegal bakery. I chased after her." Trisha wiped a tear rolling down her cheek. "I followed her all the way back to her cottage. I did threaten her—enough that she agreed to rectify my losses in her will and write two letters—one saying that she had stolen all of my mam's recipes, and the other saying very clearly that she was leaving me the estate in her will. That was the only way people would believe her confession, mind you. If she truly felt bad, of course, she would leave me her estate."

Siobhán's hunch had been spot-on, but she did not feel any satisfaction. Three people were dead. "If she wrote those letters, why did you kill her?"

"She was just putting on an act! I was on my way out the door with those letters when I saw her reaching for her mobile phone. I heard her tell the guards she had a *stalker*." Trisha shook her head. "The rolling pin was lying on the counter. I just . . . reached for it." Trisha pulled her arm back and went through the motions of hitting someone over the head. "It happened so fast. The next thing I knew she was on the floor. It was too late."

"Did you clean up the crime scene by yourself?" Macdara asked.

Trisha nodded. "She was a neat woman, there were plenty of cleaning products. And she had a wool rug hanging outside to dry."

It also didn't hurt that Aoife McBride's cottage backed up to the Donegal Bay. "And so you had to kill her all over again, in a very public way," Siobhán said.

"I couldn't have the entire country searching high and low for the great Aoife McBride," Trisha said. "She needed to die all over again, accidentally."

"And so you killed two more people to cover up your cowardly act." Siobhán could no longer hide her disgust.

Trisha's eyes flashed with anger. "I met Elizabeth Wynne at the so-called fan event. She told me what a miserable life she had—how she'd never found happiness—how she couldn't get jobs anymore. I was doing her a favor!"

"You murdered two more people in cold blood," Siobhán said. "I'd hardly call that a favor."

"I didn't mean for George O'Leary to die," Trisha said. "He was just supposed to be a distraction while I broke into the back of the mill. How was I to know Elizabeth was going to powder his fecking nose? His death wasn't my fault."

"You put poison in face powder," Siobhán said. "It certainly is your fault."

"Speaking of poison . . . how did you know about the strychnine stored on the ground floor?" This question came from Fia O'Farrell.

"You made a video of the mill for me, remember?"

Fia looked crestfallen. "I thought I was making it for a legitimate sponsor."

"I toured the mill years ago and noticed the poison. Your video showed me that everything was exactly the same as I remembered."

Fia sighed. "I should have known it was odd that the sponsor wanted to see *everything*. I just assumed it was part of being a producer."

"It's not your fault," Siobhán said. "It's no one's fault but Trisha's."

"Fia doesn't deserve any pats on the back," Trisha said. "Back when I toured the mill she wasn't giving tours of the working part of the mill, which made me want to see it even more. I snuck away from the group and had a nose around. Those bottles with *gopher bait* and *poison* written all over them. I could tell from the layers and layers of dust that they'd been down there for ages. It's not my fault she didn't have the sense to clear them out."

"And you figured out how to make the refrigerator leak?" Aretta asked.

"It's not difficult. I watched YouTube and created a clog."

"And where did you get the money for all this?" Siobhán asked. "The production, the prize money—you wouldn't have had access to Aoife's estate yet—so where did it come from?"

Trisha stared at her. "I may have swiped one or two of

her credit cards to finance some of it, and I took out a loan for the rest. I knew I'd pay it back soon enough."

"You were determined," Siobhán said. "Determined to get away with murder."

"It would have worked too. If not for that stupid woman powdering someone else's nose. Who does that?" Trisha shook her head with disgust.

Across the room a timer dinged. "Practice is over, people!" Ronan said, picking pieces of walnut off his face and flicking them at random contestants. "On your mark, get set, bake!"

Chapter 31

"I'll never take this for granted again." Siobhán, her husband, and her siblings all stood on the grounds of the old flour mill watching the wheel churn through the river.

"It's just a wheel," Ciarán said. "Going around and around like wheels are supposed to do."

Siobhán put her arms around Ciarán's shoulders until he winced and pushed her away. "It's a marvelous old mechanism brought back to life, that's going to reinvigorate our town bakery."

"Which means more sweets for us," Gráinne said, bumping him with her hip. They were all gathered at the bakery for the first official tour since they had reopened. And today, for a special VIP tour group, they would watch the mill grind its first bag of flour in ages, and even get to take home samples.

"I'm buying all the flour for the restaurant from this mill," Eoin said. He gave her the side-eye. "Or should I say *you're* buying all the flour from this mill?"

Siobhán laughed. "Even after I hired a cleaning crew?"

Eoin shook his head. "I'm still finding bits of cracked eggs everywhere I look. It's doing me head in."

"What if I bake you a chocolate Guinness cake?" Siobhán said. "Will that do?"

"No," Eoin said.

"Yes," Macdara said.

Trisha Mayweather was arrested after writing a full confession. After Aoife was killed with the rolling pin and wrapped in her own wool rug, Trisha only had to drag the body the length of Aoife's back field until she reached the Donegal Bay. It was while cleaning Aoife's cottage with bleach that she hatched her plan. The baking show. She was familiar with Pie Pie Love, she and her mother had once toured it together. She vividly remembered seeing the gopher bait-slash-poison—rows and rows of it in a small back room—and she just knew there would be some still lingering on the shelves. Her evil plan was born. Kill off the diva again, this time in front of a live television audience. And she almost got away with it too. Now that she was in custody, William Bains was giving them everything he had on her. He hadn't realized he was being used as a pawn in a murderous game until after Elizabeth Wynne had been murdered. Given he had no proof, William had been hesitant to tell Siobhán what he suspected, so he gave it to her in code, praying she'd figure it out.

At least justice had prevailed. The agent representing Aoife McBride's book was going to allow Ronan O'Keefe and Philomena Lemon to write a forward to the memoir with as much of the truth that they would be able to piece out from Mary Mayweather's original cookbook. Proceeds would go to charities. And in a few months the remaining contestants would return to Pie Pie Love for a do-over so that the twenty thousand euro could be appropriately awarded and a winner announced. By then, the O'Sullivan Six farm-to-table restaurant would be open for business and no food fights allowed.

"Welcome to Pie Pie Love," Fia O'Farrell said as she strode across the field. "Are you ready for the tour?"

"Will there be samples?" Macdara asked. "I heard there were going to be samples."

CHOCOLATE GUINNESS CAKE

Recipe by Nigella Lawson in the Cooking section of
The New York Times.

https://cooking.nytimes.com/recipes/1875-chocolate-guinness-cake

CAKE INGREDIENTS:

Butter (for the pan)
1 cup Guinness stout
10 tablespoons (1 stick & 2 tablespoons) unsalted
   Kerrygold Irish butter (or any butter, but of course we
   recommend Kerrygold)
¾ cup unsweetened cocoa
2 cups superfine sugar
¾ cup sour cream
2 large eggs
1 tablespoon vanilla extract
2 cups all-purpose flour
2½ teaspoons baking soda

TOPPING INGREDIENTS:

1¼ cups confectioners sugar
8 ounces cream cheese (room temperature)
½ cup heavy cream

PREPARATION:

Cake: Preheat cooker (oven) to 350 degrees. Butter a 9-inch springform pan and line with parchment paper. In a large saucepan, combine Guinness and butter. Place over medium-low heat. When butter melts remove from heat. Add cocoa and superfine sugar, then whisk.

In a small bowl, combine: sour cream, eggs, and vanilla. Mix well. Add to the Guinness mixture. Now the flour and baking soda. Whisk until smooth. Into the buttered pan she goes, and bake until risen and firm, 45 minutes to one hour. Place pan on a wire rack and cool completely in pan.

Topping: In a food processor or by hand, combine confectioners sugar (break up lumps) and cream cheese and blend until smooth. Add heavy cream, mix until spreadable.

Remove cake from pan. Place on a platter or cake stand. Ice top of cake, make it look like a nice pint of Guinness with a frothy head.

TWEAK

Add some Baileys Irish Cream in the frosting—to taste